PRAISE FOR

Palmetto Moon

"The richness of the locale, the uniqueness of the characters, and the slow-moving but engrossing rhythm of the story make *Palmetto Moon* a fairy tale to be savored . . . Pick up *Palmetto Moon* and let her take you on a delightful journey to the Lowcountry. It is a magical place where fairy tales are a part of real-life adventures."

—*The Huffington Post*

"Boykin does a marvelous job of depicting life in postwar America. The details of cars, clothing, dusty country roads, and small-town life are evocative of the late 1940s, and the people are drawn with depth and insight. Readers will fall in love with Frank, be charmed by Vada, and cheer for Claire and her boys. An extra bonus in this excellent novel is the inclusion of recipes for the mouthwatering Lowcountry food described throughout."

—*BookPage*

"This book had me from the very beginning. The cover caught my eye but the story drew me in and kept me captivated . . . This read is like a breath of fresh air."

—*A Southern Girl's Bookshelf*

"A book that blends innocence, determination, friendship, and romance into the perfect book."

—*Open Book Society*

"Beautifully descriptive writing . . . Distinct characters, a sweet romance, and a strong theme of independence are the highlights of this thought-provoking, nostalgic, and tender story. Every word Boykin writes will captivate readers."

—*RT Book Reviews*

continued . . .

"A beautiful novel . . . Kim Boykin's ability to set the scene is incredible . . . A beautifully authentic and inspiring story."

—*A Novel Thought*

"*Palmetto Moon* is superbly written and does a great job of bringing you along in the story . . . The characters are all well written . . . Overall, I really enjoyed this book and I can't wait to read her others."

—*Southeast by Midwest*

"If you're after a sweet Southern romance, then *Palmetto Moon* could well be for you."

—*Have Book Will Read*

PRAISE FOR

The Wisdom of Hair

"In Kim Boykin's novel, hair is not only wise, it's witty and eloquent. As we've long suspected, our hair can define us. It can also teach us things about ourselves that will surprise and change us. *The Wisdom of Hair* is a lovely, engaging novel. Zora Adams is a heroine to root for!"

—Wendy Wax, *USA Today* bestselling author of
The House on Mermaid Point

"*The Wisdom of Hair* has a big, beating heart, and I couldn't put it down. What I loved best about the book was the pervasive kindness; page after page, good people try their best, sometimes succeeding and sometimes failing. It's hard to write an engaging novel about (mostly) nice people, but Kim Boykin has pulled it off."

—Ann Napolitano, author of *A Good Hard Look*

"Well-drawn characters and depth lie beneath the beauty treatments in this affecting debut."

—*Kirkus Reviews*

"Boykin is a new voice in Southern women's fiction, and her strong, flawed female characters should appeal to fans of Dorothea Benton Frank and Karen White."
—*Booklist*

"Filled with quirky characters and a lot of heart . . . A story that readers will want to savor."
—*RT Book Reviews*

"Boykin's Faulkner-esque regionalism heightens the interest . . . A little sentimental, a little raw, and a lot local, Boykin's *The Wisdom of Hair* is a thoughtful but breezy poolside read—or fireside read."
—*Fort Mill Times* (SC)

"A beautiful and highly engrossing novel that I was unable to put down."
—*Romance Junkies*

"A story of change and empowerment, love and forgiveness, and the ability to find strength within one's self and those who care about you."
—*Book Queen Reviews*

"In the tradition of Wendy Wax's *Single in Suburbia* and Ann Napolitano's *Within Arm's Reach* comes the Southern tale of Zora Adams, daughter of an alcoholic Judy Garland impersonator."
—*Library Journal*

A
PEACH

OF A
PAIR

KIM BOYKIN

BERKLEY BOOKS, NEW YORK

BERKLEY

An imprint of Penguin Random House LLC
375 Hudson Street, New York, New York 10014

This book is an original publication of Penguin Random House LLC.

Library of Congress Cataloging-in-Publication Data

Boykin, Kim, date.
A peach of a pair / Kim Boykin. — Berkley trade paperback edition.
p.   cm.
ISBN 978-0-425-28199-4
I. Title.
PS3602.O95P43   2015
813'.6—dc23
2015007538

PUBLISHING HISTORY
Berkley trade paperback edition / August 2015

PRINTED IN THE UNITED STATES OF AMERICA

10 9 8 7 6 5 4 3 2 1

Cover photos: woman © Muna Nazak / Trevillion;
polka dot oval © Oksana Gribakina / Thinkstock
Cover design by Judith Lagerman.
Interior text design by Laura K. Corless.

Penguin
Random
House

For Mom and her sister, Leila.
For my sisters, Joan and Jenny.
And for Columbia College sisters everywhere.

Acknowledgments

I'm not sure Nettie's story would have gotten written if it weren't for Janet Cotter, who shared her love for Columbia College with me and introduced me to the true sisterhood the college is known for. Debbie Chick, librarian extraordinaire, at the Kershaw Country Library in Camden, South Carolina, thanks for your invaluable contributions to this book. Thanks also to Tilara Monroe and Jayne Bowers, who were generous with their time and thoughts on Camden in the 1950s. To Laurie Funderburk, owner of Books on Broad, thank you for supporting my work and pointing me in the right direction during my research.

As always, huge thanks to Doni Jordan, my dear friend, who planted seeds for this story without knowing it. Thank you, Paul Mask, assistant director AFNR and assistant dean extension administration agriculture, at Alabama Cooperative Extension System/Auburn University. I'm incredibly grateful for your thoughts on Alabama Agriculture and what Satsuma might have been like in 1953.

Thanks forever to HRH and Pulpwood Queen, Kathy Murphy, for suggesting I contact Jane McConnell when I was looking for folks who grew up in Palestine, Texas. While Jane's a Dallas gal through and through, she was kind enough to introduce me to some wonderful folks who shared their love for Palestine. Sara Nell Bible, Ann Lynne Bailey,

ACKNOWLEDGMENTS

Lee Brown, and Tomé Nell Gregg, you have my deepest gratitude for sharing memories of your hometown with me. You all have such fabulous names; I'm definitely stealing them for a book one day.

I'm so grateful to Jane Tuttle at the J. Drake Edens Library at Columbia College and the reference librarians at the Palestine Public Library who were wonderful resources to me. Same goes for Stuart Whitaker and his incredible photographs of Palestine. His commitment to the history of his hometown was a godsend. While Stuart told me the Redlands Hotel was not used as a hotel in 1953, I used a smidgen of poetic license and set a scene there anyway because I like the name.

Heartfelt thanks to Shari Bartholomew, a cardio care nurse who knows her way around a heart and a good book, and to Denise Stout Holcomb, booklover, and friend.

I'm one lucky girl to have Leis Pederson for an editor and Kevan Lyon as my agent. Y'all rock! Last, only because I love to give him a hard time, thanks to my brother-in law, Dr. Darrell Boykin, for being my go-to guy whenever I have medical questions. You're the best.

1

Thursday, March 26, 1953

Mail call," old Miss Beaumont bellowed into the commons room, and a flock of girls descended on her like biddies after scratch feed. Except for me. Normally, I would have been right there with them, clamoring for news from home. But since Mother called right after the tornado hit last month to say everyone back home in Satsuma was still in one piece, there hasn't been a single word from anyone. Not even Brooks.

It was bad enough that Hurricane Florence blew through in September and smashed much of Alabama to bits. Six months later, just when everyone was getting a handle on putting my hometown back together, a tornado roared through, undoing Satsuma all over again. And while I wanted Miss Beaumont to bellow my name, I was sure the folks back home were too busy with the cleanup to write.

On good days, the silence was unsettling, and on bad days,

it turned my stomach inside out. But I knew better than to complain.

Three and a half years ago, I'd been dying to get out of *the armpit of Alabama* to study music and accepted a full ride to the most exclusive women's college in South Carolina. Funny how, back then Satsuma, even Alabama herself, seemed too small for me. Now, all I can think about is moving back home, and it won't be long, just eight weeks till graduation.

I missed my mother and Sissy like it was the first day of my freshman year. And if I let myself think of the very long list of the people I love who have stopped writing me since those awful catastrophes, I would never stop crying. And Brooks. Loyal, faithful Brooks, who loved me enough to let me go away to college, saying he would wait forever if he had to for me to be his bride. The thought of how much I loved him, missed him, made my heart literally ache with a dull pain that left me in tears.

I was sure Brooks was working himself to death, helping rebuild Satsuma, because that's the kind of guy he was, always building something. At Christmastime, he proposed, a promise without a ring, but a promise from Brooks Carter is as certain as my next breath.

Miss Beaumont called the name of one of the catty girls who are jealous of me because I am the only 'Bama belle at Columbia College. Maybe in the whole state of South Carolina. She cut her eye around at me, waved three letters, relishing the fact that I had none. My roommate, Sue, had one clutched to her chest, praying for more as hard as I've prayed for word from home. Something. Anything.

Sue had badgered me to call home. Collect. I knew my family would accept the charges, but I was afraid of the news that must be so terrible, nobody could bring themselves to call the pay phone in my hallway. So I waited for letters. I craved them as much as I dreaded them.

Since I went away to college, Mama and Sissy, who just turned nineteen last month, have written me every week, sometimes twice a week. Nana Gilbert and Grandma Pope wrote just as often, always slipping in a newspaper clipping from home, sometimes a dollar bill, whenever they had it to spare. With nineteen cousins who are all tighter than a new pair of shoes, I could always count on letters from them. One day I received twenty-two, a record at the college; it was better than Christmas. And Brooks, my beloved one true love, his letters were always like Christmas and the Fourth of July rolled into one.

Brooks loves and knows me better than anyone. He should; we'd been sweethearts since the fourth grade. While it has been a little rough with my studying music and education here in Columbia, and him back home in Satsuma, Brooks has been the most wonderful, understanding man in the world. Of course when I got the scholarship, he wasn't at all happy, but he knew I was working toward our future. Me a teacher, maybe even a church pianist too, him running the feed store his daddy left him.

Lots of girls here have diamonds and are getting married the moment they graduate. But Brooks and I are waiting until next summer. He said it would be a good idea to get a year of teaching experience under my belt before we're wed. He's always so sensible like that, forward thinking, which I am not.

"Sue Dennis," Miss Beaumont yelled. Sue snatched the letter from her and cocked her head at me, reminding me to be hopeful. But I knew there would be nothing for me, not until Satsuma was put together again. And it must be bad back home, much worse than Mother let on for the news from home to have stopped altogether. As awful as that was, the worst part was knowing in my heart why.

I shook my head at Sue and forced a thin smile.

"Nettie Gilbert," Miss Beaumont called like the world had not just ended. I kept my seat on the kissing couch in the commons room. Sue jumped up and down for me, squealing, but for the life of me I couldn't move. She grabbed the letter from Miss Beaumont's withered old fingers and flew to my side.

"It's from Brooks," she gushed. "I just know it is."

But I knew it's wasn't. Mother's letter-perfect handwriting marked the front. I turned it over to see the flap she always sealed with a tiny mark, *xoxo*, but there was nothing. Someone was dead, their long obituary folded up inside. Someone so precious to me, no one, not even my own mother, could bear to break the news to me.

"Open it," Sue said. She'd already read her first letter, from her beau back home in Summerville. Her face was still flush. Sometimes we read our letters to each other, but lately, she'd kept the ones from Jimmy to herself since she visited home last. Even though their June wedding was right around the corner, I suspected they did the deed the last time she was home, and her letters were too saucy to share.

On the last night of Christmas break, I'd wanted to go all the way with Brooks and would have if Sissy hadn't fetched us from the orange grove. We'd taken a blanket there to watch the sunset. It was a perfect night. As crisp as a gulf night can be in December. The perfect time, the perfect place, but Sissy, who could never leave Brooks alone, insisted we play Parcheesi with the family. When I protested, all it took was a *Mother said* from her, and Brooks was folding up the blanket, putting it back in the knapsack along with my chance at becoming a woman.

"I'll be at your graduation before you know it," he promised when I gave him a pouty look. "And next summer, you'll be my June bride," he whispered like it was naughty. His breath sent chills down my thighs and made me hate Sissy, just a tiny bit.

At Christmastime, I saw the devastation from Hurricane Florence firsthand, but after the tornado roared through Satsuma a few weeks ago, I knew it was much worse. When I'd called, Mother had sworn everyone was okay. But I knew if something were wrong, if someone were terribly injured, she'd try to keep a tight lip, at least until I graduated. Partly for me because she loved me, and partly because I would be the first on both sides of my family to get my degree.

Mother had tried college, and then got married the summer after her freshman year. But I also know part of my mother was still angry at me for going so far away when I could have gone to 'Bama, which did *not* have a decent music program.

"Come on, Nettie, read it," Sue chided. But my heart refused to let my hands open the letter; I passed it off to Sue as she drug me back to our room.

"Sit," she ordered, pushing me gently down onto my bed. "You're being silly. It's something wonderful, I'm sure of it," she gushed, reaching for her letter opener. She slit the top of the envelope, pulled out a small white card, and offered it to me again.

Tears raced down my face, my neck. When I pushed it away, a sheet of lined notebook paper folded into a perfect rectangle escaped from the card and fell to the floor. Sue snatched it up while scanning the card. Her smile faded, and her face was ghostly white.

"Oh, Nettie," she whispered, unfolding the letter from my mother.

"It's Brooks, isn't it?" She nodded. "Oh, God."

I threw myself across the bed, sobbing. Brooks was dead. I would never see his beautiful face. Hear his voice rumble my name. Feel his arms wrapped tight around me, making me feel adored. Safe. Loved. The life that we'd planned would never amount to anything more than just words whispered between two lovers.

"Nettie." Sue lay down beside me, stroking my hair. "My sweet Nettie, you need to read this."

I couldn't. I buried my face in my pillow. She whispered how strong I was, how life wasn't fair, how very sorry she was my heart was broken to bits, and held me until I was all cried out. After I don't know how long, I shook my head and looked at her. "I just can't believe Brooks is dead."

Sue gnawed her bottom lip the way she did when she was taking a test. "He's not dead, Nettie." Her hand trembled as she put Mother's letter in my hand. "He's getting married."

"What?" I jerked the page away from her, and the card fell onto my lap. Neat white stock with two little doves at the top. Mother might have been a farmer's wife from Satsuma, but her well-worn etiquette book sat atop the Bible on her bedside table. And as far as Dorothy Gilbert was concerned, they were one and the same. Except the invitations weren't sent out months in advance. They'd been done so quickly, they were not even engraved, and the wedding was four weeks away.

Brooks's name should be below mine, but it was below Sissy's— Jemma Renee Gilbert, glared at me, *cordially inviting* me to her wedding. Worse yet, *the parents* of Brooks and Sissy were cordially inviting me too.

"This must be some kind of a sick joke," Sue whispered. "How can they do this to you?"

She read my mind and uttered the words I could not bring myself to say. How *could* they? *How could Brooks?*

My hands trembled so hard it was difficult to read the impeccably neat handwriting.

Dear Nettie,

It might seem cruel to send this letter along with a proper invitation, but I couldn't bring myself to call you, and I wasn't given much notice regarding this matter. I also know you well enough to know you would have to see the invitation to truly believe it. Although I do regret not having enough time to have them engraved.

I'm sorry to be the one to give you the news about Brooks and Sissy. I love you, Nettie, and I love your sister. I'm not condoning her behavior or the fact that she is in the family way, but you are blood. You are sisters. No man can break that bond, not even Brooks.

There's money and a bus ticket paper-clipped to the invitation. I've checked the schedules. You should be able to leave Columbia on Thursday the week of the wedding after your morning classes and get back by Sunday night. I know how you hate to miss class, and if you are also missing some wonderful end-of-the-year party, I'm sorry. So very sorry.

But the milk has been spilled, Nettie. Come home and stand up with your sister. She needs you. She's a wreck, and it makes me worry about the baby.

Just come home.

Love,
Mother

2

Sue dressed me in a mismatched skirt and blouse and put rouge on my cheeks, trying to make me look like I hadn't lost my mind right along with my heart. She held her mouth open, concentrating as she put her lipstick on me, a color that clashed with my auburn hair. Normally, I would have said something about her unfortunate color choices, in a very kind way. Not like the mean girls who made fun of her for being colorblind. Sue made the universal sign for me to blot, and I did. I looked ridiculous, but I didn't care.

"I'm not going," I whined and plopped back down on the bed I hadn't moved from since that awful letter came four days ago.

Every day since, Mother has called the pay phone just down the hall from my room. Sue told whoever answered it that I was indisposed. Too many phone calls from meddling parents had always bound us all together, the mean girls with the sweet girls, the plain with the fancy, and me, the 'Bama belle. Syrupy-sweet lies rolled off of our tongues, and we never thought twice.

Normally, I'd worry about the lies, the threat of my mother coming all the way from Satsuma to tan my hide, but I didn't care. About anything.

"Okay. So, you're going to go into Dean Kerrigan's office and you're going to tell her?"

Sue had gone over this a million times since I was summoned for this appointment, since I missed my senior recital Friday night. She waited for me to fill in the blank.

"I've had the flu." She nodded, waiting for the rest of the lie. "And I didn't go to the infirmary because—"

"Because you didn't want to get anybody sick." She smiled at me like I was one of her soon-to-be first-grade students. "And since I—I mean since *Sue* had already had the flu . . ."

My bed covers were a rumpled mess and were calling to me. Sleep was the only cure for my broken heart. In my dreams, Sissy never came to the orange grove the night Brooks proposed. He and I went all the way so many times, our bodies were a blur. And there was no Sissy. She didn't exist. Nothing existed, just me and Brooks. Until I woke up.

"Look at me, Nettie. Focus." Sue turned my face to hers. I loved her to bits for caring so much, for loving me so much, but right now I would have knocked her senseless and crawled back under the covers if I thought Dean Kerrigan wouldn't send someone to my room to fetch me. Knowing the dean, she would come herself.

"Since my roommate already had the flu," I whispered.

"There. We're going to be a little late, but you look perfect," Sue said. "And don't forget to say you're sorry. *At least ten times.* Just sprinkle them into the conversation so that you can graduate, Nettie. I want you to graduate, and I know deep down you want that too."

No, I just wanted to go to bed. Forever.

The whole way to the dean of students' office, Sue held my hand. When we entered the administration building, I could barely hear someone in the music building next door practicing on one of the concert Steinway grand pianos. The beginning strains of Chopin's Nocturne Opus 48 Number 1 in C minor, the haunting expression of grief that could not be contained with red bricks and mortar.

I'd wept that first day I touched those keys. After wearing out a secondhand no-name upright back home, sitting down on the sleek black bench and touching the ivory keys had been surreal. An equal mix of giddy and awe. The way Brooks always made me feel.

I turned around to walk in the opposite direction, but Sue pulled me back. "Come on, Nettie. Don't throw away the last four years. Not for a man. Not for anyone."

But Brooks had thrown away the last ten like they were nothing. Like I was nothing. Dean Kerrigan opened her office door, most likely to come look for me. She nodded at Sue to leave, and without a word, I walked into her office.

She closed the door behind me. "Please, sit, Nettie." She motioned to the small couch. She sat down beside me, took my hands in hers, and smiled. "Now, tell me what's going on."

"I'm sorry." *How many times did Sue say I should tell her?* "I'm sorry. So sorry." *But I was not at all sorry.* "Flu. I'm sorry. The flu, I had—"

"A girl like you doesn't miss her senior recital because of the flu, Nettie. Talk to me so we can figure out how to make this right, so you can graduate. You've worked so hard."

"I had the flu, I—" The last word dissolved into a whine that set my chest heaving. Tears streamed down the thick makeup Sue plastered on my face to make me look normal, perky.

Dean Kerrigan wrapped her arms around me. "That's it, dear; let it out." She smelled like my mother, like vanilla and rose water, or maybe I just wanted Dean Kerrigan to smell like her. To be her.

She always kept a stack of handkerchiefs on her desk in a little wicker basket for just such occasions. After I got over being a silly freshman, I always felt more like a peer to my professors than a student, even to the dean herself. Many times I'd smiled at that basket, sure I'd never need its contents to make a tearful plea or confession to Harriet Kerrigan, and now, I was on my third handkerchief.

"All right," she said gently. "That's enough, Nettie. You only get thirty minutes of my time to feel sorry for yourself, my dear." My breath stuttered when I laughed, still unable to look at her. She crooked a finger and tilted my face up to meet her gaze. My chin quivered, the tears building again. "No more tears now; we're going to work this out."

Dean Kerrigan's amber eyes were warm and full of love for me, for every girl at the college. Everyone adored her because she cared so deeply.

"I'm sorry," I whispered. "I'm so sorry."

"I want you to graduate on time," she said. I shook my head violently. "You might not feel like it at this very moment, Nettie, but I know you want that too."

"But I don't." If ten years with Brooks meant nothing, graduation meant nothing. "I know I'm supposed to make an excuse for missing the recital, but I'm not going to do that."

"I wish you would." She smiled. "Just a tiny excuse to show me you care."

"I want to withdraw from the college." I'd never quit anything in my life, but suddenly it seemed like a stupendous idea.

"Nettie. I've watched you play, the way you become the music. You're good enough to be much more than a music teacher if you wanted." Any other time, I would have basked in her accolades and played them off in an *aw shucks* kind of way that would only bring more. But I didn't respond at all. "What happened to make you give up on your dreams?"

"It doesn't matter what happened; I need to leave."

"To go home?"

"No." Another revelation. I didn't ever want to go home.

"What will you do?"

"I don't know." But I refused to go home and watch Sissy's belly grow with Brooks's baby, see them together at mandatory family dinners.

"You realize if you're not a student, you'll have to leave the campus, don't you?" she asked, like that would make me come to my senses.

The college had been my home for the past four years, many of the girls my sisters. I had twenty-seven dollars and a bus ticket to my name, nothing to pawn and nowhere to go. "Of course."

"You're a Columbia College girl, Nettie. That means something, and I won't let you throw it all away." She rose and went to her desk, a beautiful piece that was not like the boxy stuffy ones the other professors had. She put on a pair of blue horn-rimmed glasses, took three yellow forms out of her desk drawer, and placed carbons between the pages. "You're taking a temporary leave of absence," she said as she wrote, "due to a family matter. The busybodies over at the registrar's office will want to know what that is, but I won't tell them, and neither will you. This will make them think the worst, but let them. I want you back in September to finish your degree, Nettie. That's more than enough time to work out whatever has you running scared."

"Thank you; I'll be back." While I felt terrible about Sue asking me to lie, there I was lying to a woman I loved and respected.

She pulled the carbons out, handed one of the forms to me, and put the other two in her Out basket. "It breaks my heart that you're leaving. But take some time to mend your heart and come back. Not for your parents or for me; do it for yourself, Nettie."

3

EMILY

Emily pressed the jelly glass against the door and strained to listen, but Lurleen's voice was so feeble, Emily couldn't make out what she was saying. But she could hear that nitwit doctor's voice loud and clear.

"Miss Lurleen, things are going to get more difficult, and Miss Emily can't take care of you by herself," Doctor Remmy Wilkes said like *Emily* was the difficult one. "You all are going to need some live-in help, and, no offense, ma'am, but I think you'd be hard-pressed to find somebody around here to take the job.

"Yes ma'am," the doctor said. "I do intend to tell Miss Emily everything. Yes, ma'am, I believe it's for the best. But for now, I want you to rest as much as you can. I'll come around to check on you tomorrow."

Emily heard him putting his things in his bag and hurried toward the living room but didn't make it to her chair before the doctor opened

Lurleen's door. She wanted to wipe that look right off of his young face as he closed the door so quietly, like her beloved sister was already dead.

Shoot, Emily remembered changing this man's diapers in the church nursery, and here he was doctoring her and Lurleen. Well, if the Eldridge sisters weren't already as old as dirt, that made them so. And the doctor, all prematurely gray at his temples; that didn't make Emily feel any younger as he walked down the hall to tell her something he thought she didn't already know about her own sister.

Emily gave him a hard look to remind him that she *knew* more than he could ever hope to, *and* she never forgot anything. Yes, she would remember this one all right till the day she died. Little Remmy Foster Wilkes Junior, long before he became Dr. Remmy Wilkes. Him and his knack for playing innocent while his friends got punished for all sorts of tomfoolery.

Why, he and Pete Mason put three of the biggest bullfrogs in Kershaw County in the baptismal font and flat ruined that poor Mixon baby's baptism. Had a liking for reptiles of all sorts. Cleared the church one communion Sunday with a shoebox full of garter snakes, and let poor old Pete and that little Belcher boy shoulder the blame. Yes, Emily never forgot a thing and he knew it. *Oh, and another thing, he was not a good baby.*

"Miss Eldridge," his voice sounded like an undertaker's. Gave her the chills.

Emily straightened herself and smoothed the front of the new housedress she bought at Karesh's Fashion Shop for 25 percent off. A Kleenex fell out of the sleeve of her sweater. She always kept one stuffed there because she was forever forgetting to check her pockets. What a mess a wad of tissue made going through the wash, little bits of paper all over creation. *My Lord.*

"Miss Eldridge," he said, and stooped over to pick up her tissue at the same time Emily did and they almost knocked heads. "I need to talk to you about Miss Lurleen's condition. Why don't we sit down over here." He motioned to the settee.

The last time a man asked Emily to sit down on the settee was three years from the day that she retired from the Kershaw County school system. Couldn't believe she ended up buying an entire set of *World Book Encyclopedias* she had no use for. The fool print in those books was so small, they should come with a reading glass.

Emily ignored Remmy and sat down on the wingback chair instead. He shrugged, which was *so* rude, and then joined her, sitting in Lurleen's chair. Emily kept her eyes locked on his to make sure he knew she didn't want to sit and listen to him. He reached out and put his hand on her shoulder like he was trying to figure out how to say whatever he thought was so *g.d.* important.

"Miss Emily, Miss Lurleen's heart condition is getting worse, a lot worse. She needs to go to the hospital, but she refuses. Says she wants to die at home, and, to be honest, I don't think she's going to live much longer."

"You think my sister is gonna die?" Oh, the restraint it took not to smack this one. "Lurleen cheats death like a cat, always has." So mad, she could spit, Emily shoved his hand off of her shoulder and looked the little pissant straight in the eye. *"You are wrong."*

Before this little fellow was a gleam in his grandma's eye, Lurleen had a bad case of scarlet fever, and her barely six, no, nine. They said she was going to die then, and she didn't. The second time was when she fell off the top of the carriage house trying to walk the peak of the roofline on a dare from their baby brother, Teddy, God love him. And the third time, Lurleen was trying to learn how to drive that fool Oldsmobile. Closed her eyes every time one of those big old trucks whizzed by, and ran that contraption right off the road and into the ditch. Took out a row of mailboxes on more than one occasion. Never did learn how to drive, but then neither did Emily.

Some dust on the piano caught Emily's eye. Lurleen was always in charge of dusting, although she could never dust worth a lick. Emily took the tissue out of her sleeve and got up off the chair. It was a nice firm one, not like the chairs they made these days that were so soft, you had to struggle to get up. She swiped at the spots Lurleen would have gotten if she wasn't feeling so poorly, but you know how a tissue is, seems like those fool things are made of dust. Only a good dust rag would fix that ugly mess.

"Miss Emily," he said as she tottered off toward the kitchen to get the rag. "I wish you'd sit down so we can discuss this. If you can talk her into going to the hospital, I can prolong her life for a while, although I can't say how long. But what I am most concerned about is you. You're going to have to face the fact that Miss Lurleen is going to die, and make some adjustments."

"Young man, *be ashamed of yourself.* Why I wiped your b-u-t-t when you were just a little thing and here you are, coming in *my house*, presuming to tell me *you* know Sister better than me? Don't you think *I'd* know if Lurleen was going to pass?

"Miss Eldridge."

Oh, there he goes, trying to smooth things over like he had *not* just insulted her beyond all mortal bounds. Next, he'd try to humor her. *Lord, have mercy on my soul, but I despise that in a man.*

"I know you've known me since I was born, and it's hard to hear something like this from somebody who was fortunate enough to have you as a church nursery worker and sixth-grade Sunday school teacher. But I'm certain that Miss Lurleen's heart is about to give out on her. The sooner you accept that, the sooner you can help her get her affairs in order."

"Why, I *never*. What kind of doctor are you anyway? Just giving up on Sister like that. Didn't you take some sort of oath?"

He completely ignored the question, opened his black leather bag, and dug around until he found a pen and a pad. "Now, I'm going to give Miss Lurleen a prescription for some pills."

"*Don't you ignore me, Remmy Foster. I'll call your mother.*"

"Miss Emily, my mother and my father are deceased as you well know." He let out a tired sigh. Of course Emily did know about his parents, everyone did. That accident, the whole town gushing about Remmy taking over his father's practice so dutifully. But Emily could always read this one; she knew he wanted to be elsewhere and, at the moment, Emily wished he were anywhere but here.

"Miss Eldridge, I really am doing the best I can, and that is to say the best that modern medicine can do. These pills will make Miss Lurleen more comfortable, but *they will not cure her.*"

"Well then what in the name of Mary and Moses would she take the fool things for? I declare, I just don't know about you doctors these days, passing out God knows what kinds of drugs, and *nobody's* getting any better from them. *Especially* Lurleen."

He stood and looked at her like he was really going to make Emily believe all of his foolishness. "You're going to need some help to take care of her. Live-in help. Miss Lurleen agrees, and I told her I'd have my receptionist put out some feelers, maybe place an ad for y'all in the newspaper. Miss Lurleen asked me to help screen them, and I'm happy to do so if that would make things easier on you or make you feel better. I'm sorry to be the one to tell you all of this, Miss Emily. Really, I am."

Well he ought to be, for saying such things. Emily heard Sister calling her. He picked up his bag and said he was sorry again. Like *that* meant something. Why, Emily had a good mind to call his mother anyway, g *damn it. Forgive me, Jesus.*

Emily never used to swear, unless it was absolutely necessary, especially when she worked as a teacher. She was afraid that the words would become second nature and when one of her students started sassing off, she'd say something she'd regret. Something that might get her fired. But lately, Emily cursed, a lot and for good reason. Especially when that so-called doctor was about.

But she believed if God really thought long and hard about her situation, He'd agree wholeheartedly that swearing was completely called for under the circumstances, if not a necessity. And He probably appreciated the fact that the swearing was mostly in her head.

"See yourself out, Remmy. You're doctoring is as worthless as rubber lips on a woodpecker."

Even without the half smile that played at his lips, he was a handsome man, for a pissant. Why, if Emily were his age, he definitely would have turned her head. When she was a young girl, Emily was quite the looker. All she had to do was snap her fingers, and she'd have a dozen boys begging to be her beau. She touched her hair like she was twenty-one instead of seventy-one. She didn't feel *that* old, but sometimes, when she walked by a mirror, she was flabbergasted to see the wrinkled face looking back at her. Most days, she didn't feel a minute over twenty back when she was the belle of the ball, and her mother had to beat her suitors away with a peach tree switch.

"Emily, for goodness' sake. Where are you?" Lurleen called as the door closed behind Dr. Remmy Foster Wilkes. *Bah.*

"Coming," Emily yelled, because the old girl's hearing was not what it used to be. She tucked that prescription into her pocket and then remembered the way her mind slips when she does the wash. She took it out and stuffed it up her sleeve along with a clean tissue.

"Hungry?" Emily looked in the refrigerator to see what she could fix for lunch.

"Just a little bite, maybe something sweet," Sister hollered. Oh, yes, she was quite feeble until it was *sugar time*.

Emily warmed up some squash and onions from dinner last night on the stovetop along with a fried pork chop from the day before. She set a piece of loaf bread on the plate and a dab of tapioca pudding for Lurleen's ever-loving sweet tooth and started to the bedroom. But then she remembered the tea, and the fact that she poured the last glass for that *g.d. doctor.*

Hurrying back to the kitchen, she put two cups of sugar in the pitcher, not three like Lurleen did, and put the kettle on. She sat down at the kitchen table and looked over an old magazine and waited for the pot to call. The old girl must have dozed off, because she was quiet, for a change. But Emily couldn't read a thing without her glasses.

They were not in the fruit bowl where she always kept them. Had Lurleen gotten out of bed during the night and straightened up? Emily absolutely hated it when she did, because Lurleen could not put one *g.d.* thing back where it belonged.

The kettle let out an earsplitting whistle. Emily let it go on for a little to wake the old girl up. A few seconds later, Lurleen hollered for her dinner.

"You're not some kind of invalid, Sister. Get out of the bed." Emily rinsed out her mother's good crystal tea pitcher. "Why I'm fixing and doing for you when you can fix and do for yourself is beyond understanding. And having live-in help? Well, if you're not dying, which you certainly are not, you've lost your mind."

"Emily, I'm too sick to argue. Please. I'm hungry," she huffed. Lately, Sister was really good at sounding weak and pathetic. Why, she'd never been either of those in her life.

"No. You're just spoiled," Emily shot back, but not loud enough to be heard. Completely rotten from all those times everybody made over her because they thought Lurleen was going to die.

"She's too mean to die," Daddy had said, while at the same time slipping her a little sack of candy from Zemp's Drug Store.

Truly, she was not mean, but that was what Daddy always said when any of his children got hurt and started to whine, even Teddy. Like the time Tilara Jones's old milk cow stepped on Emily's foot and broke it. The pain was so great, Emily cried and cried and begged Jesus to take her home. When Daddy came to pick her up from the Joneses' place, he just laughed and told Emily she was too mean to die.

Emily poured the hot tea in the pitcher and stirred the sugar until it dissolved. Lurleen always let it sit for a while, which just turned it into a syrupy mess. She said lemons cut the syrup, but they don't. How Lurleen could drink it that way was a great wonder. It was *not* good tea.

With the glass and dinner plate on the tray, Emily headed down the hall, even though Lurleen could come out here and sit and eat with Emily if she had a mind to. But she took to bed after church, three weeks ago Sunday. Emily didn't let on that she knew Lurleen was okay. She just played along and fussed over her. Sister loved that almost as much as her syrupy tea.

4

NETTIE

Sue has cried enough for both of us; still, through my tears, my roommate looked like a kaleidoscope. A very lovely clown dressed in an orange poodle skirt, a blinding red blouse with a Peter Pan collar, a chameleon green sweater draped over her shoulders.

"Don't go." Her voice tailed off into a whine again.

"We've been through this, sweet girl. You know I can't stay." I stroked her hair, taking in the scent of the Chanel No. 5 her boyfriend splurged on for Valentine's Day. She puts a dab behind her ears every day, but only on her wrists on Sundays. "I'll be fine."

"Come home with me, Nettie. You can share my room until the wedding. Mama and Daddy want you to come. Please do."

Sue was the oldest of five girls and one lone boy they all doted on. Their home was as tumultuous as the tiny plot sandwiched between two orchards back home. Four houses squeezed together. Mine, Nana Gilbert's, Aunt Opal's, and Uncle Doak's.

"You're going to graduate and go home and marry Jimmy. And I—" Daddy had always called me the queen bee, said I came into the world so sure of myself. But for the first time in my life, I didn't have any idea what came next or what to do. Nothing was certain. Everything was broken, but I'd be damned before I'd let Brooks or Sissy or Mother break me. "You'd better get going, Sue. You have class."

She nodded and ran her hand over the top of my suitcase. "But a bed at the Y, Nettie?"

Dean Kerrigan had been kind enough to see to it that I had a place to go. I knew she had lived at the Y when she first moved to Columbia, a lot of the single teachers at the college still did. "You make it sound like it's some sort of flophouse. It's not." She nodded, giving my arm a gentle squeeze. "Now go to class. I'll be here when you get back. Promise."

Going through the motions of packing felt good. Better than wallowing in heartbreak. The rest of my belongings fit easily into the yellow Samsonite wardrobe Daddy gave me for high school graduation. I'd already taken most of my things home at Christmastime.

I stiffened at the memory of Brooks touching me in the orchard that night. The way his breath felt on my neck as he told me how much he loved me. Wanted me. Was that how he seduced my sister? Or had my sister's childhood crush grown into something feral and devious, something that was bigger than her? I shook my head, trying to get the image of Sissy's face out of my mind, that prissy sly smile when she'd interrupted Brooks and me that now *obviously* had nothing to do with Parcheesi.

"Damn you, Sissy." I'd never sworn out loud in my life, and yet the words tripped off my tongue. "Damn you and Brooks." And the baby? Brooks's baby?

A wave of nausea dropped me to my knees. Gritting my teeth, I would not damn that child, but I wouldn't shed another tear over the fact that it had taken a place in my family. My place.

Checking under the bed, I pushed the rumpled twin away from the wall. Doris Shelley's pink sweater fell to the floor. I had no recollection of taking it off the day my world came to an end, no recollection of much of anything after reading my mother's plea for me to return home to Satsuma. *For Sissy*. But there it was, shoved between the bed and wall, as soft as cotton candy, pink, with little white pearl buttons.

I folded it neatly and got to my feet to get back to the business of moving on. To where or to what I had no idea, but moving forward was imperative. The only way not to feel the gaping wound Sissy and Brooks had made inside me when they made that baby.

Since Mother's letter, the rumor mill at the college had been gushing with all kinds of scenarios, which Sue felt duty bound to squelch. But her efforts only served to make things worse, and made nice girls like Doris feel sorry for me. I hurried down the hallway, the sweater clutched to my chest. Returning it seemed almost silly; I knew she'd never ask for it back.

For most of the school year, everyone had heard her tearful conversations with her boyfriend on the hall phone. He was handsome, a frat boy at the University of South Carolina with a sporty black convertible. A lot of girls thought Doris let him do her wrong because his family came from money and hers didn't. She knew he was catting around, but she always took him back. I'd always wondered how she could forgive him, just like that.

Could I offer a polite acceptance if Brooks apologized, begged me to take him back? After all, I was still Dorothy Gilbert's daughter, bound by blood and good manners. Would I take him back? I placed the sweater on Doris's pillow along with a heartfelt thank-you note and hurried out of the room, grateful she wasn't there. I couldn't have taken another mournful look from her piercing blue eyes that said she knew exactly what it felt like to be me.

Pages on the hallway bulletin board ruffled as I pulled Doris's door to, advertisements with neatly cut fringes with phone numbers written in perfect script. Requests for transportation, ads for students who wanted to get a jump on finding a summer job. Hurrying home to Brooks the moment summer vacation began, I'd never had any cause to peruse the board. But with only a few dollars and a bus ticket to my name, I'd definitely need a job.

The telephone rang at the opposite end of the hall. A girl dashed out of her room to answer it. I could feel her eyeing me as I studied the board. Summer work babysitting an infant? Definitely not. Three offerings for camp counselors? Nothing that lasted for more than a couple of weeks. Lifeguard? I was a horrible dog paddler and couldn't save anyone without drowning myself. Besides, I'd heard the girls go on about the cute boys from USC who lifeguarded at Sesquicentennial State Park and the city swimming pools, and wanted no part of that.

Caregiver? I'd helped nurse Nana Gilbert through a horrible bout of the croup once; I could do that. But the position was in Camden, not Columbia. I took the advertisement off of the board, stuffed it in my pocket, and hurried back to my room. Justine, the cattiest of the mean girls, was on the phone, looking at me, twirling the phone cord around her finger. Her smile devious. "For you," she said, dangling the phone toward me.

After Dean Kerrigan filed the paperwork, one of Justine's catty minions who worked part-time in the registrar's office broadcasted that I was withdrawing from school. The only pleasure I had in this horrible mess was that it was killing every last one of them to know why.

Justine was a well-sculpted beauty who was never without a date and there was a good reason for that. While the rest of us dressed like young girls in poodle skirts and tasteful sweater sets, Justine, the ringleader of the mean girls, wore cotton peekaboo blouses with tight skirts and high heels. All of us had covered for her on more than one occasion.

Just a few weeks ago, when she didn't come back to the dorm after a fraternity party at USC, our housemother, Miss Beaumont, was on a mission to find her and wasn't about to give up until I stepped in and assured her Justine was at the library. On a Saturday morning. Studying. Something Miss Beaumont knew probably was not true, but she liked me, trusted me, and my word was good enough for her.

"I'm not here," I whispered to Justine, eyes pleading for her to follow the unspoken code we all shared.

She slid her delicate hand over the receiver and couldn't look any more like the cat who ate the cream. "You haven't had a phone call in over a month, Nettie, and it finally rings for you and you aren't lunging for it? Must have something to do with your leaving school."

"Please, Justine, I'm not here."

"Oh, but you are, though not for long I'm told," she gloated. "Tell me why you're leaving, and I'll tell them you're at supper."

"Justine," I said, begging her to lie for me the way I had for her a thousand times.

"Oh, this is too rich. The perfect 'Bama belle in a tizzy, leaving school so suddenly. Who got you knocked up, Nettie? Because your precious Brooks sure isn't the daddy." She might as well have punched me in the stomach. "Who is it? One of the boys from Fort Jackson? From USC?"

My heart pounded out of my chest. "Justine. Please."

She licked her bright red lips and took her hand off of the receiver. Her smile put the Devil to shame. "Here she is, Mrs. Gilbert," she said, slapping the phone in my hand.

"Hello? Nettie, honey? Hello? *Hello?*" I could picture my mother by the telephone table next to the blue platform rocker in the living room. Sitting on the edge of the seat, reading glasses dangling on the end of her nose. "Nettie Jean Gilbert! You speak to me this instant," she ground out in a motherly tone that had always made me snap to.

But how could she love me and command me to attend Sissy's wedding? How could she welcome Brooks into our family after what he did to me? And how could she choose Sissy over me? Because of a baby?

"Mother." The word sucked the air right out of my lungs; my stomach roiled.

"Oh, how the mighty 'Bama belle has fallen," Justine laughed. "And I'm enjoying every minute of it."

I gave her a hard look, opened the door next to the phone, and stepped inside; the cord reached just enough for it to close. Thankfully neither Patrice nor Halley, nice girls, the only two Catholics at this Methodist school, were not in their room. The girls shared a bulletin board beside the door, decked out with pictures of their sizable families. Not a single one of them looked traitorous, but then Sissy had never looked that way. Mother certainly didn't either.

"Nettie. You listen to me, young lady, you—"

Nobody really stops to notice that solitary moment when the apron strings snap. The bile that had crept up my throat was replaced by fury that had simmered under heartbreak for days.

"No, Mother, *you* listen to *me*." She gasped at my tone. "When you phoned me after the tornado, I waited thirty-two days believing something horrible had happened, that Brooks was dead. I heard nothing from anyone, not even you, until I got your primly worded letter and an invite to Sissy's wedding, demanding my presence. My blessing."

"I don't expect you to bless this union, Nettie. After the tornado, everyone around here was out of sorts, especially with it coming on the heels of the hurricane. I'm not making excuses for Brooks or Sissy, but the milk has been spilt, Nettie."

"Enough with the spilt milk. My sister *stole* my fiancé. There is no spilt milk. There's betrayal. And a baby I want nothing to do with. I don't ever want to see Brooks or Sissy again. And how could you possibly think I'd stand up at their wedding? Condone what they did, what they did to me?"

"Nettie. Lower your voice."

"Why, Mother? Because you don't want people to know Sissy didn't follow proper etiquette? Did she miss a step in the chapter on how to felicitously betray her own sister? Or did she just skip straight to the point of no return when she got pregnant with my fiancé's baby?"

"Rail if it makes you feel better, but Sissy isn't entirely to blame."

"You're right. I don't just blame Sissy. I don't know what happened between her and Brooks; all I know is that Sissy has wanted him to notice her since she was old enough to tag after me. And she finally got him."

"You can pile all the blame on your sister, Nettie, but it takes two people to make a baby. What about Brooks?"

"Brooks is none of your business."

"None of my business? Young lady, I am still your mother."

"No, you're not my mother. You chose. Between your daughters. You chose."

"Maybe if you had a daughter with a baby on the way you'd understand that I didn't choose."

"Is the baby in danger?" I snapped.

"Why, no. Nettie, honey, I'm just trying to do right by that baby, and if it means having you here for Sissy, so be it."

"No, Mother. It's up to Brooks to do right by the baby; it's up to Sissy. But you? *Expecting* me to attend their wedding, all but ordering me? You might as well have sent me an engraved invitation to watch them do the deed."

"*Nettie Jean Gilbert.*"

"I'm done with Brooks and Sissy and, when and if you take a moment to consider my feelings, I hope you'll understand that I'm done with you, Mother. Good-bye."

I threw open the door to hang up the phone. Four mean girls tumbled into the room; seven others surrounded Justine.

And now they knew. Even Justine who prided herself on taking everyone around her down a notch so that they admired her as much as they feared her, looked rattled by the truth. In that moment, she blinked at me, no predatory smile, just a look that closely resembled pity.

"Oh, Nettie," one who was slightly less slack-jawed whispered.

I didn't want or need their pity. I slammed down the phone and Debbie Sizemore, who was forever on the phone with her mother, reached for it. "I have another call to make," I ground out. Debbie jumped back like I'd taken a bite out of her meaty hand. "In private."

Pulling the ad out of my pocket, I dialed the number and retook my place in Patrice's room with the door closed. The operator put the collect call through. Finally, a woman's voice on the other end answered; she sounded testy, although not as furious as me. "I don't know any Nettie Gilbert; I won't accept the charges."

"Please. Don't hang up," I said.

"Sorry, ma'am," the operator said. "She's declined the call. Nothing I can do."

"I'm Nettie Gilbert. I'm calling from Columbia College about the caregiver position."

The woman on the other end heard my plea and accepted the call. "Thank you," I breathed.

"Least I can do for a fellow C-Square girl, but make it snappy. I placed the ad for my brother, and he's a real stickler about the phone bill. I'm Katie Wilkes, by the way; I run Remmy's office and his life. God knows he'd deny it until his dying day, but he needs it."

"Pleased to meet you, Katie, but I thought there was a caregiver position available."

"Remmy's a doctor; he's looking for live-in help for the Eldridge sisters. To be honest, he says Miss Lurleen could go any day. So she, as well as the job, might be gone by the time school's out."

"But I'm available now." Was I really as desperate as I sounded? Absolutely.

"Oh, so you're a graduate," she laughed. "Science major?"

"I'm a music major. And education. Taking a leave of absence," I added hastily.

"Music?"

"If you need references, I can give you my professors' names. Oh, and Dean Kerrigan will vouch for me for sure."

"Not sure how a music major is going to work out. Do you have any experience?"

"I've cared for the elderly." Not a complete lie. "Extensively." The three days nursing Nana Gilbert, who never got sick, felt extensive.

"Wonderful. And to have another girl from the college in town, even better."

But what would be required to help someone who was really sick? Dying?

"Maybe I should—" Reconsider? Hang up?

"Of course room and board are included, and if nothing else, the job will definitely be interesting. The sisters are a peach of a pair, although Miss Emily can be a real pill, and Miss Lurleen is— Well, you'll see."

"Katie—" Now that I thought about it, the lifeguard job really sounded good.

"Pay's thirty dollars a week."

Room and board? A decent stipend? But something in the hollow of my stomach said this was a bad idea. An inkling of what I'd felt the last morning at Christmas break when Brooks took me to the bus station and said good-bye. That feeling hadn't jibed with what had happened in the grove the night before, so I wrote it off to too much of Mother's biscuits and gravy for breakfast. Did I know then something was wrong?

With my huge clan, I'd always flitted around whenever I was home on break, seeing everyone, holding court, and loving the attention I got. Had I missed something? Had Brooks gotten jealous of my divided attention, or worse, bored? But did it really matter what had happened to make him stray? Knock up my sister?

My sister. The words still burned, torching every shred of faith I ever had in Brooks, in my own mother, and my father who'd remained silent in all this. Him I understood because he'd hoped and prayed for farmhands and never really knew what to do with two prissy daughters. But I'd lost faith in my own sister. In myself.

It was irksome just how intermeshed Sissy and I were, held together by sticky, dried blood. But now the wound was fresh, open, and it had nothing to do with what Sissy did to me. Everything to do with her absence, the hole I knew would always be there, and I hated it. Didn't want to feel the loss that had grown since I'd opened the invitation to her wedding; it was much easier to concentrate on her betrayal.

"The last bus from Columbia gets into Camden around six; station's just a couple of blocks from the office on Broad Street. I'll put in a good word for you. You come on by after Remmy finishes up for the day, and he'll talk to you. He thinks you're the one for the job, I'm sure he'll want to take you by to meet the sisters."

Cashing in my bus ticket to Satsuma would get me to Camden and back with enough left over to hopefully not have to dip into my twenty-seven-dollar kitty.

"And you'll have supper with us. Stay over if you like," she added.

"Oh, I couldn't impose."

"But I insist," she laughed. "It's the least I can do for a C-Square sister. So you'll come?"

"Yes, thank you, Katie; I'll see you tomorrow."

When I opened the door to hang up the phone, the catty mean girls had gone to spread the word far and wide, no doubt that the mighty 'Bama belle had indeed fallen. What they couldn't know was just how meaningless the pedestal I'd been on my whole life really was. How I'd crawled over my own sister to get there, fought to stay up on it, making damn sure everyone loved me. And if they didn't, I flirted and cajoled until they did. Maybe that was why my charms never worked with Justine and her brood, because there is only so much room on that lofty perch, and even the most genteel Southern belle will fight to the death to stay there.

5

LURLEEN

With Mama and Papa and Teddy gone, even during the years Emily and Lurleen lived under the same roof and did not speak, it had always been just the two of them. Lurleen, the strong-willed, practical one; Emily, the delicate flower.

The house was quiet, save the whisper of Emily's steady breath. There was something comforting about the gentle *puh puh puh* sound she'd made in her sleep for as long as Lurleen could recall. She should wake Emily and send her to her own room to rest. If sleeping the night in that wingback didn't kill her, it would surely make her wish she was dead come morning. But with Sister's head reared back and the moonlight streaming in the window, all Lurleen wanted was to hear that comforting sound a little longer.

She smiled at the unnatural glow the moonbeams made on Emily's face. What was it now? Woodbury beauty cream? Wasn't that the latest miracle Zemp's Drug Store was peddling? Probably not. Lurleen never kept up with such foolishness, but Emily was always the first in line to draw from the fountain of youth. It was one of the things that made Lurleen sure Emily would marry one of her many suitors. She never did.

The one thing Lurleen regretted most in her life was the seven years she lived under this roof and did not speak to Emily. She'd pretended Emily didn't exist, but that was just wishful thinking after the accident. If she could go back and change just one thing in her life, she'd change those years of silence. So much anger and blame, all directed at Emily, and yet her sister had loved her through every second of it.

Emily drew in a deep breath and snorted herself awake. "Lurleen?" Her voice trembled with the certainty that one day she would call Lurleen's name and there would be no answer.

"I'm wide awake. You were snoring again," Lurleen said, because she'd rather hear Emily incensed than worried.

"I do not, nor have I ever, snored," Emily huffed, running a hand through her tight silver curls. She patted her face, making sure her miracle cream was evenly disbursed.

"Remmy said Katie's sending that girl around tomorrow. Says she's a sweet college girl, and I want you to be nice to her, Emily."

"I do not want someone in my house. Going through my things and yours. She's *not* coming." Both hands on the arms of the chair, she leaned forward to punctuate her decree.

"Well, it's my house too, and I want her here. Get some rest so you won't be so cranky and you'll be presentable." Not that Lurleen gave a hoot in hell about what Emily looked like when company came calling, much less potential hired help, but she knew Emily cared a great deal about appearances.

"We don't need any *g.d.* help. I can take care of you just fine," she huffed.

"I don't know where this swearing thing of yours has come from, but it is most unbecoming." Lurleen tried to sound terse, but it took too much effort and came out more matter-of-factly. "There's no sense in both of us dying, and, you taking care of me round the clock is going to kill you dead."

"I'm fine. Perfectly fine, and I'd be even better if you and that blasted Remmy Wilkes would stop flustering me with all this talk about dying, which *neither* of us is going to do."

There was so much conviction in Emily's voice, Lurleen wanted to laugh at her steely desire to change the laws of nature. Everyone was born to die, some sooner than others. But arguing with Emily, especially when she was pretending to be riled but was really terrified, was pointless and would only serve to put her in even more of a tizzy.

"Go to your room, Emily. Get some rest."

"After what that fool Remmy said about you—" Her voice broke. "Why, I've a good mind to stay here just to prove that little pissant wrong."

Remmy Wilkes certainly didn't tell Lurleen anything she didn't already know, and had known for months. But the ache she felt in her chest had nothing to do with her heart condition.

Every morning, since Lurleen took to her bed, she'd intended to have a serious talk with Emily, but she'd kept putting it off, thinking it was much too early in the day to broach the subject. Bringing it up at lunchtime would surely cut into the nap Emily pretended she didn't take after her afternoon soap opera. Broaching the subject before bedtime? Bad dreams. The truth was, there was no good time to talk about dying. But Lurleen had put it off long enough.

"I am going to die, Emily. The doctor said so, and you keeping vigil by my bedside won't change that."

"Don't," she hissed. "You hush this instant. If you think you can just up and die on me, Margaret Lurleen Eldridge, you've got another thing coming."

"My heart is giving out, and I'm fine with it." More than fine to go to heaven, to hug Mama's neck, and Daddy's. To finally see John again. Even after all the years, she felt the loss of him deep inside of her from a place that did not heal.

"Then I'm coming too," Emily declared.

"This isn't you tagging along to a picture show, Emily. This is death. It's final. You don't get a say in it any more than I do."

"No, this is just you scaring me. You always loved to frighten me. You and—"

Emily didn't dare speak Brother's name, and as much as Lurleen thought she'd made peace with what happened so very long ago, the jagged memory sliced into her. It wasn't the tightness in her chest or the pain that made Lurleen hold her tongue. It was the constriction in the middle of her throat, an unseen hand, holding back words that would only leave Emily brokenhearted when Lurleen was gone. And what good would those words do now? No more than they would have a half century ago.

6

REMMY

Remmy Wilkes's shadow stretched long across the floor of his father's study, his only companion for another sleepless night. The house was dark, silent save for the occasional groan of the old place. The sound was comforting, although it shouldn't have been. He hated the old house, the legacy that held him prisoner, as much as he hated the constant sense of wanting that had followed him around since the accident.

There was a time when the yearning had gripped him with the ferocity of polio, crippling him, suffocating him. He'd wanted the life he'd planned for himself in Charleston, wanted Katie to be married and chasing a couple of her own children around. He wanted his parents to be alive. And in the darkest recesses of what his father had begrudgingly called Remmy's brilliant mind, when he couldn't have any of those things, he'd wanted to die.

But his sister had kicked his tail. For weeks after the accident all he did was sleep, and Katie gave him that for a while. Then she parked that damn wheelchair at the bottom of the stairs and fussed until he got out of bed. When he wasn't fit to practice anything, much less medicine, she'd booked appointments and made him drag himself down to the office. She was counting on him falling back into practicing medicine the way their father did and his father before him. And, much to his surprise, he did.

The house groaned, whether in agreement or to protest, Remmy wasn't sure. He turned on his desk lamp, opened a drawer, and pulled the letter out from his friend. Doctor Cecil Rutledge had made good for himself working at Baptist Hospital in Columbia. He and Remmy had been study partners and had double-dated occasionally. Of course for med students, that meant almost never. They'd worked their hind ends off to graduate at the top of their class, Cecil edging Remmy out by a half a point, something his mother lauded and his father shrugged over.

Remmy scanned the letter again, glad Katie hadn't opened it like she usually did with all the mail that came to the office. Cecil's promise that the job at the hospital was as good as his would have set her off for sure, and there was really nothing to get up in arms about. Not now anyway.

The job at Baptist Hospital opened up in two months when one of the senior physicians retired and one of his underlings moved up, leaving a space for Remmy if he wanted it. Not a lot of time for Remmy to find another doctor who was a good fit for Camden. But there was always someone fresh out of med school, usually with a bride and a couple of kids in tow, who was looking to buy a small-town practice, settle down, raise a family. After all, that was how

Remmy's grandfather ended up doctoring Camden until the day he died and Remmy's father took over.

A whip-poor-will that had taken up residence in the peach tree out back called to Remmy, one insomniac to another. He ran his thumb over the engraved stationery. This was what he had always wanted; he should be thrilled, but what about Katie? He owed her and would gladly give her every penny from the sale of the practice. Give her whatever she desired. Anything, except his settling for the life he never wanted.

EMILY

Emily sat at the instrument that had remained silent for over fifty years. Even after all that time, it still pained her to run the rag across the keys of her mother's piano. Brother's piano.

She snaked the dampened cheesecloth over the keys, taking great care they did not sing. But her hands were old, her touch not as sure as it had been all those years she'd cared for the piano, keeping it silent. Even now, she could still hear her mother's instructions. *There's a fine art to dusting the spinet; it must be done carefully and often.* She honored the voice in her head, running the cloth in the direction of the fine wood grain. *Always in a straight line, never in circles.*

Her hand trembled more than usual when she got to the upper keys. She could see Brother so clearly, head thrown back, laughing at her attempt to play Chopsticks with him. Teddy had inherited Mother's gift for playing by ear. Since he was six, he could peck out a tune after listening to a song on the radio. By the time he was twelve, he tore up the keys, putting his own design on songs like "Won't You Come Home Bill Bailey" and "Tell Me Pretty Maiden." He was Mama's delight, especially so after Daddy died.

But then everything went to hell, and there was no more music, and all that was left were two broken sisters.

What happened to Teddy was Emily's fault, and she'd paid for it a thousand times over, losing her mother to a broken heart. And the seven years Lurleen lived in the same house as Emily but didn't speak to her, didn't take anything from her hand. The shunning wasn't a religious edict. Goodness no, they were raised Presbyterian. But Lurleen had taken right to the practice. Even with the gravity of events, Emily was sure it couldn't last, but she'd been wrong.

Emily's finger slipped, pressing one of the keys. She braced for the forbidden sound. There was none, just a dull thud to match the ache in Emily's chest for the time she never had with Mama and Teddy, for the time she lost with Sister.

"Emily," Lurleen called, her voice weak, strained.

"Don't holler. Use the *g.d.* cowbell I gave you," Emily called back.

"Emily!" The bell clanged.

She closed the hinged lid and pushed off of the piano, her gait unsteady. As annoying as the bell was, Emily was grateful every time it rang. She crossed the living room and headed down the hallway to what used to be the sitting room but was now Lurleen's bedroom; Sister hadn't made it up the stairs to her own room in weeks.

"I heard the phone ring a half hour ago." Just those few words left her short of breath. "Who was it?"

"That pissant Remmy Wilkes."

"He's not a pissant," Lurleen snapped without sounding like she was breathing her last. "He's a fine doctor, as fine a doctor as his father. God rest his soul."

"He called to say a girl's coming around to meet us. I told him not to bother." Yes, she'd snapped at the man and was more than happy to put the fear of God in him so he would forget about this foolishness. She was quite capable of taking care of her sister, thank you.

"Well, he won't listen to you. I told him, he finds someone he thinks will do to send them by." Lurleen gulped for air. "But before I die of thirst, do you think you could bring me a glass of tea? I'm beyond parched. And for the love of Pete, put some sugar in it this time."

7

NETTIE

The bus was crowded and smelly, thanks to the unseasonably hot spring day. When it stopped in Blaney, an older woman got on and sat down across the aisle from me. As I was saying hello, a serviceman plopped down next to me, no greeting to myself or the old woman. I looked straight ahead, the *LIFE* magazine I'd splurged on clutched to my chest. I'd picked it up on a whim because fellow redhead Elaine Stewart's cover photo was powerful and sultry, beautiful. Inspiration for my new life. But it wasn't until I got on the bus that I'd realized the starlet was in the news because she was going home to visit her folks.

Not me, Satsuma was the last place I wanted to be.

The name on the man's stiffly pressed khaki uniform read *Gerwaski*; he was minimally decorated. A private maybe?

Even with Fort Jackson in the general vicinity of my all-girls school, I knew surprisingly little about army boys. Most likely because I was promised to Brooks and never paid attention. Girls who did go for the boys in uniform seemed to yearn for white-hot love affairs that burned until their beau was shipped elsewhere and they found another. Though there were a few girls, some army brats themselves, who selected boys by taking in their stripes before they looked at their handsome faces.

As the bus rumbled along, the private caught my eye and nodded. "Ma'am," he said, his accent clipped. Definitely not from the South, and, with those bedroom eyes, definitely flirting.

Sitting over the rear axel, the ride was less than smooth, oftentimes swaying the two of us hard against each other. Each time the private's smile got a little wider, his eyes a little softer, coaxing me to blush or return his greeting. I nodded back but gave him no encouragement. I could feel him staring, smiling, waiting for my face to go hot. Brooks used to do that all the time, especially in church. Making me blush and think things that felt normal but the reverend called un-Christ-like.

Across the aisle, a baby cried. Instinctively I glanced to see the little butterball sitting on his mother's lap, his fat fist shoved in his mouth, teething for all he was worth. Every cell inside me clinched when the baby smiled at me, making my heart swell and then deflate with the truth; I would never have that with Brooks. I didn't want to smile back at the baby, but then he did this thing covering his eyes with a full-on grin that made me think boys come into the world knowing how to flirt. When he attacked his fist again all wide-eyed and happy, I realized I was smiling, grinning.

"Private First Class Gerwaski, ma'am. At your service," he said like I was watching him instead of the baby.

"Hello." That was all I gave the private, but he seemed sure it was an invitation to try a little harder.

"And you are?" He waited patiently for me to break into a smile and flirt back. When I didn't, he added, "The prettiest girl I think I've ever seen." And I didn't even blush. I was immune to his charm, his chiseled face, his bedroom eyes.

"You're not going to talk to me, pretty girl?" His smile was full on and would have made the collective student body of Columbia College sigh. He might as well have being making eyes at the old woman across the aisle, who harrumphed at his efforts. She shook her head with a steely glare meant to ward off the private's unwanted attention, but he either didn't notice her or didn't care.

Content to wait me out, I could feel him grinning at me until the bus hit a bump in the road. "Where are you headed?" He nodded at me with that amorous stare, still flirting.

"To see my *boyfriend*," I lied.

"Lucky guy." He smirked. "You'll have to forgive me. You're just so damn pretty, and I didn't see a ring on your finger."

I shifted in my seat and faced the window, hoping that would shut him up.

"I'm going to see my girl," he said less flirty. I had no idea why he thought he needed to tell me.

When the bus stopped in Lugoff, the private nodded and got off. "Good riddance," the woman across the aisle muttered.

I smiled at her, but the whole exchange made me wonder if my mother had watched Brooks flirt with Sissy. Of course my sister had been flirting with Brooks since she could walk, so Mother was no stranger to the practice. While I truthfully didn't want to know how it happened, I couldn't stop myself from wondering, from screwing the knife in so deep, it had disappeared into my back and clean through my heart.

Thankfully, the bus finally rolled onto Camden's Broad Street. It was a large town, compared to Satsuma, small compared to Columbia. I got off the bus and waited for the driver to unload my small yellow suitcase. It felt odd taking it to a job interview. I wasn't quite sure what to do with it when I got to Dr. Wilkes's office farther down Broad, so I left it on the stoop along with a prayer that it would be there when I got back.

I stood on the threshold of a small reception area, dressed in my very best lemon yellow Lorette skirt and white cotton sweater set. A lovely girl, not much older than me, was behind the desk on the telephone. When she glanced up to see me, her face lit up, so much so that I looked behind me to see if her gaze was directed at someone else. She was beautiful, petite, with a stylish short black haircut and impish brown eyes. She was dressed in a smart, fitted cap-sleeved pullover the color of robins' eggs. The front yoke had a delicate ecru starburst design around the collar, making it look rather glamorous for a receptionist.

"Yes, well I need to get off the phone; we have other patients who might be trying to call to get an appointment, you know." She shook her head and rolled her eyes at me, waving me into the office. "Of course I believe you're sick, Mignon. Truly sick. Why, you just saw Remmy a few days ago. Heard you tracked him down at the dime store lunch counter and he wrote you a prescription right there on the spot.

"Maybe you should give yourself some time to get better, make sure that works before you try something else. Oh, and *definitely* stay home. Goodness knows, you might be contagious. Wouldn't want half of Camden to come down with whatever you have this week now, would we? And don't you worry one bit; I'll be sure and give Remmy your regards. Feel better." The receptionist ended the call with a smirk.

"You must be Nettie. Don't be shy, come on in," she said, but didn't rise to shake my hand. Good thing since I was as jittery as dying June bug. "You are staying overnight aren't you? I don't see a bag."

"Oh, yes." I blushed and reached back for my suitcase.

"Great. I can't wait to hear what's going on at the college. I graduated cum laude, class of forty-nine," she said brightly. "Same year Remmy graduated med school." Her smile faded into a thin line for a moment. "I absolutely adore dear old C-Square." Her lips turned up, although her smile didn't quite reach her eyes.

I nodded and moved to her desk, where a wheelchair was folded up, tucked away on the other side. I let out a deep breath, steadied myself and executed a good, firm handshake. "Pleased to meet you, Katie, and thank you for your very kind invitation to spend the night."

She folded her other hand over our clasped ones and gave me a genuine smile. "So glad to meet you, Nettie Gilbert. You'll have to excuse me. While I'm normally quite professional on the phone, there are a lot of husband-hunting women in this town, of which Mignon Coffey is one. They only see two things about my brother: he's single and a he's a doctor."

I nodded. "Is she going to be okay?"

"Mignon? Well, if I don't kill her for calling the office every five seconds, yes. My brother says she's a hypochondriac, but she's really a desperate flirt who will never get her hooks in Remmy if I have anything to say about it," Katie said. "Trouble with my brother is he's too good. If he charged for every coquette after him, we'd both be rich, but he sees patients all the time for free. Checks in on the

Eldridge sisters most every day. Rarely bills them for anything, but then he doesn't bill the likes of Mignon for tracking him down for a *prescription*," she said, making bunny ears around the last word.

She wouldn't have to worry about me; I certainly wasn't on the hunt. But I did glance at her hand to see she was unmarried. Surprising, such a beautiful girl, young and vivacious enough to make any man forget about the chair. Before I could offer to help, Katie gave the wheelchair a jerk to unfold it, lifted herself into the seat, and started down a long hallway.

"Pretty girl like you, Nettie, you must be engaged. Pinned?" So, she'd noticed my left hand as well. I was glad she was ahead of me so she couldn't see my face burning.

I'd been promised to Brooks since the fourth grade when he took a skinny brown pine needle off of the playground, braided it into a ring, and married me during recess. Couples got married, divorced, and then remarried by the time the last bell rang at the end of the day, but not me and Brooks. For as long as I could remember, he'd always been mine, and it was impossible to even think about living in a world where I didn't have him. A world where he belonged to my sister, who'd either bewitched him or had been bewitched by him.

I wanted to believe it was Sissy who threw herself at Brooks so often, she wore him down. After all, I *knew* him; at least I thought I did. I'd always been as certain of him as I was my next breath. But maybe I was wrong and in my prolonged absence, he had seduced my sister. The thought made me lightheaded. Moving down the hallway, I realized I wasn't breathing. When I took in a deep breath, Katie craned her neck around for an answer to her question.

"Not pinned or engaged," I said, and meant for my tone to be light, conversational, but it sounded serious. Final. She nodded with a thin smile that made me think she was well acquainted with heartbreak and knocked on the door at the end of the hallway.

"Remmy?" She didn't wait for him to answer, just pushed the door open. "This is the young lady I told you about from the college. Nettie Gilbert, my brother, Remmy."

The office was a wreck of files and papers strewn across the desk. A little flustered, perhaps with his sister, the man rose and shook my hand. "Pleased to meet you, Miss Gilbert."

Remmy Wilkes's smile was beautiful and as wasted on me as the flirty private's efforts. He made a halfhearted attempt to straighten some of the papers on his desk before taking off his reading glasses and rubbing the bridge of his nose. He looked remarkably younger without his glasses. As he moved some books out of the only other chair in his small office, he caught Katie rolling her eyes.

"Pigsty," she said under her breath.

Remmy narrowed his eyes, ignoring her insult, but I could feel him wanting to shoot back some brotherly retort. "Have a seat, Miss Gilbert," he said with a lazy drawl meant to put me at ease.

I'd been so distracted by my own calamity, the realization that I'd never interviewed for anything in my life came from out of nowhere. I had been courted by colleges, able to pick and choose. I'd never had to worry about impressing anyone to get what I wanted, much less what I desperately needed. The pulse at the base of my throat kept perfect time with my wildly beating heart, and I was sure he noticed. When I touched the place, his eyes shifted back to mine. He smiled and sat back in his creaky leather chair that needed a good oiling, and pressed the tips of his long fingers together.

I could see why eligible ladies in this town would feign illness to see Remmy Wilkes. He was undeniably handsome with his jet-black hair, a tiny bit of gray around his temples. He had the same eyes as his sister. Chocolate brown. Smart, but with little creases around his that said he was a good bit older than me. Maybe eight or nine years.

While I was not the least bit interested in him, I couldn't help but notice his hands. They were beautiful. Musician's hands. Long fingers stretched wide, more than enough to comfortably span an octave. They seemed a waste on a small-town doctor when they could be gliding across the keys of a concert piano.

While my fingers were short, making me work twice as hard when I played, Remmy's were much like Brooks's, the same hands I was sure our children would have. Back home, sometimes when Brooks and I were alone, he would sit behind me on the piano bench, his legs tight around my hips, his big hands barely on the tops of mine but completely covering them as they floated across the keyboard, making music together. Had it always been just me making music? No, it was Brooks too, nuzzling my hair off of my neck, pressing kisses there. Making me arch into him.

"Miss Gilbert?"

I shook the memory out of my head and was grateful to see the good doctor had his beautiful hands in his pockets. "That's a good skill you've got there, tuning folks out. It'll come in handy for this job," he laughed.

"I'm sorry." My face burned bright as I sat up extra straight and gripped my pocketbook a little tighter. "You were saying?"

"About your qualifications, Katie says you're a crackerjack caregiver. Lots of experience," he said like he had his doubts.

"Yes, I have some experience." Which didn't seem like a huge lie when I spoke to his sister over the phone, until now. But, with leaving school, I was desperate.

Leaving school? Good Lord, what was I thinking? Of course, I wasn't thinking at all, but I couldn't go back now. Not after the show I put on yesterday for Justine and her biddies. Could I ever go back to the college? Could I ever go home? The last thought made me wince hard, but Dr. Wilkes just kept yammering on, rearranging the mess on his desk like he was tidying up on my account.

"As you can imagine, with the sisters being old maids, always living together, Miss Lurleen's illness has been hard on the both of them."

For the first time since Mother's letter arrived, I felt a tiny sliver of the whole horrible truth that I hadn't just lost Brooks, I'd lost my only sister. Forever. "Of course it is." My eyes stung. I blinked hard and prayed to God to let me get out of that office without bursting into tears.

"That's pretty much the long and the short of the job." Of which I hadn't even heard the first detail, but did it really matter? I needed the job; Katie had talked me up, and the way she made it sound, it was as good as mine. "I'll be honest with you, Miss Gilbert, the sisters are at best difficult. By no means am I trying to ward you off, but no one around here wanted the job, mainly because the pay isn't much more than four dollars a day."

"And room and board," I confirmed rather desperately.

He nodded, studying me. "Katie says you're taking a leave of absence from the college. It's a little late in the semester for that, isn't it?"

"I assure you, Dr. Wilkes—"

"Remmy. Please."

"Yes, it is late, but if that's a concern, let me assure you, I'm a straight-A student with an impeccable record, and I'm extremely hardworking."

He nodded, studying me, long fingers pressed together again. I hoped he was either too much of a gentleman to demand to know why I was leaving school or too anxious to fill the position to care.

"Look, Miss Gilbert, as much as I'd like to hire you, something tells me maybe this job isn't for you. It's going to be hard work, and I know the college is, well—" He actually smirked.

If he thought the diplomas behind him intimidated me, two belonging to him and two to his father, both from the College of Charleston and the medical college there, he was dead wrong. Even though there would be no sheepskin for me, I was proud of my school.

"Columbia College is not a glorified finishing school, if that's what you're implying, Dr. Wilkes."

"With all due respect, Miss Gilbert, my sister is an alumna. Sidled up next to the army base and USC, not to mention its connection to Wofford, which as I'm sure you well know is all boys, the college is known for being a good place for a girl to get her MRS degree."

"Maybe it was like that *way* back when you were in school," I snapped, my backbone suddenly appearing.

He laughed, his eyes dancing with that same impish look I'd seen in his sister's. "I'm sure you are quite capable, Miss Gilbert. I didn't mean to insult you, and if I did, I'm truly sorry." But I got the distinct feeling Remmy Wilkes liked riling me as much as he did his sister. "What say we ride over to Laurens Street, you meet the sisters, and if you still want the job, it's yours."

EMILY

Emily sat beside the bed for most of the day with the small embroidery hoop, working on a monogrammed pillowcase. Her sister's face was peaceful, but Emily was taken aback by how very old

Lurleen looked. Yes, Sister had never looked after her appearance like Emily did. Not even when John was living. Now, her skin had a ghostly pallor and her gray hair, always unruly, even when they were girls, was even more so. The dark circles under her eyes that were still clear and beautiful, the prettiest azure blue, resembled spent tea bags. Matching lines above and below her lips looked as if invisible stitches had once sewn her mouth shut.

Emily's chest squeezed tight as she pushed away the memory of Lurleen's silence.

Glancing at the clock intermittently, Emily prayed the old girl would stay settled until well after four. She continued the neat, even stitches even though the tightness in her chest was still there. Maybe it was from thinking about Lurleen's condition, her age, maybe it was from thinking about John. Something Emily hadn't allowed herself to do in a long time, and, sitting next to her sister's bed it felt wrong.

Emily rested the needle on the taut fabric and rubbed her eyes. Just a few minutes before the hour, Lurleen's eyes were closed, her breathing almost normal.

Pushing herself out of the wingback, Emily laid the hoop in the chair, moved quietly to the door, and closed it behind her. She hurried down the hallway. Glancing at herself in the mirror, she was struck hard by how she looked nothing like her sister. A tight feeling gnawed at her heart.

For far too long, time had literally flown by. Lately, it seemed to have quickened its pace, unraveling what little Lurleen had left, and there was nothing Emily could do about it.

These days, it was the small comforts that kept Emily sane, kept her focused on the here and now. A good piece of saltwater taffy, maybe a fine chocolate, her needlework, the little feral kitten she sometimes spied out back by the carriage house. She tuned the old radio to her favorite program, her guilty pleasure since it aired eighteen years ago, and sat down on the wingback, pulling the footstool from underneath. Propped up and comfortable, she allowed the announcer's voice to sweep her away as he crooned the introduction to *Backstage Wife.*

Now, we present once again, Backstage Wife, *the story of Mary Noble, a little Iowa girl who married one of America's most handsome actors, Larry Noble, matinee idol of a million other women—the story of what it means to be the wife of a famous star.*

Although Lurleen knew about Emily's addiction, Emily would never admit to another soul how much she craved the story. Once, when their preacher chose the unholy hour of half past three in the afternoon for a visit, Emily hadn't so much as offered him a glass of water, much less ice tea and a slice of pound cake or whatever sweet she happened to have on the cake plate that day. Emily didn't want to be rude, but having a congregation full of women, the reverend should have known better than to visit during soap opera hours.

Although that particular pastor had preached against most everything good and worthwhile, including soap operas. There was nothing morally wrong with the program. On the contrary, each time a determined unprincipled vixen tried to get her claws into Larry Noble or an unscrupulous gentlemen pursued poor Mary, the couple always remained fiercely loyal to each other.

Emily closed her eyes as Mary made her daily declaration of love to her husband, hungry for his answer, the clever way Larry always romanced the words.

"Oh, darling," his handsome voice crooned. "You're so beautiful.

You walk into the room and I don't see anyone but you. Why, I'm the luckiest guy in the world to hold you in my arms every day, Mary Noble. You're the best thing that ever happened to me." Emily sighed, drifting away with his words.

When the doorbell rang, she awoke with a start to hear the monotone drone of the local farm report. Across the room, through the lace panel over the front door, Emily recognized the outline of Remmy Wilkes and a woman in a yellow skirt and white top. Annoyed she'd slept right through her program, she reached across the table and turned the radio off. If Lurleen wasn't here, she'd sit quietly and wait for them to go away, but Lurleen had been resting so peacefully, more so than she had in a long time. Emily hated for them to ring the bell again and wake her.

She shoved the footstool under her chair and smoothed her hair as she made her way to the door. She yanked it open to find Remmy Wilkes smiling annoyingly at her, and a young woman with red hair, so wide-eyed, it looked like her green eyes might pop right out of her head.

Before Emily could say a word, the cowbell clanged down the hall. "I'm coming." Emily glared at Remmy, letting him know he'd better stay put. "I hope you're happy, Remmy Wilkes; she's awake."

"I'm sorry to wake Miss Lurleen," he drawled, hat in hand with that mischievous smile that said he knew Emily had been cat-napping.

"If that's Remmy, send him on back." Lurleen's voice was unusually clear. "And send the girl back too." She punctuated the command with a deep sigh that could be heard all the way down the hall.

Remmy nudged the girl's back, and she walked into the foyer with a wisp of a smile until she saw Brother's piano and blushed like she knew all the secrets the spinet held. She was beautiful. Tall, willowy, gorgeous long auburn hair. She moved with the grace of a dancer, and she and Remmy made quite a handsome pair, although neither of them seemed aware of it. The girl smiled tentatively, but Emily gave her a look to let her know exactly what she thought about her unwanted presence.

"Miss Emily, I'd like you to meet Nettie Gilbert. Nettie, this is Miss Emily Eldridge." While Emily and the girl exchanged tight, barely cordial greetings, Remmy placed his hat on the rack like he owned the joint. "If it's okay with you, I'll look in on Miss Lurleen," he drawled, pretending to ask for Emily's permission. It didn't matter that it definitely was not okay; he shifted his black bag to his other hand and gave the girl another nudge toward the hallway.

8

LURLEEN

Lurleen unbuttoned the buttons and then loosened the tie at the neck of her nightgown. She looked away from Remmy as he pressed the stethoscope against her chest, under her breast. The young girl he brought with him looked away too, giving Lurleen an illusion of privacy. The girl seemed nice enough, although she hadn't said much since Remmy introduced her. He moved the disk around for what seemed longer than usual.

"'Bout the same," Remmy said, pulling her gown together. Lurleen was never the type to expect miracles. She retied the satin ribbons and nodded. He put his stethoscope in his bag, and dug his fist into his back and stretched like he was getting old before his time. "I suspect the best way to go about this is to just leave y'all to it. I'll keep Miss Emily company until Nettie thinks she's ready to take her on," Remmy laughed, but the young girl didn't seem to find him humorous.

Lurleen noticed the girl's fingers kept moving in a funny way, but the same pattern over and over again.

Lurleen nodded at Remmy and he excused himself. "You're nervous, Nettie."

"No ma'am," the girl answered before Lurleen could tell her not to be.

"You are," she pointed to the girl's hands. She clasped them behind her back, where Lurleen suspected she was doing the same thing.

"Runs," she blushed. "When I'm nervous I play runs, even without a piano. They're soothing to me . . ." Her voice trailed off. "But I noticed you have a piano," she added hopefully.

"It's been broken for some time now." A little of the light left the girl's eyes. There wasn't any point in explaining why the piano remained silent. "Remmy says you're a college girl in Columbia."

"Columbia College. I'm taking a leave of absence." The words sounded rehearsed, making Lurleen wonder if the girl was expecting. Why else would she be leaving college so suddenly? If she was in the family way, as slender as she was, she couldn't be very far along. Surely Remmy would have mentioned that, if he knew. But, with Lurleen not long for this world, the idea of leaving Emily with this young girl was surprisingly comforting. The very idea of a baby toddling through the house, delightful.

"Where's home, Nettie?" Lurleen asked.

"Satsuma. Alabama," she said.

"Never heard of it."

"It's a farm community, satsuma oranges mostly. Pecans. Cotton. Corn." She went on to give an account of her hometown that might have come from a brochure, but it was clear she was dancing around something. Maybe the child?

"And you're what, nineteen?"

"Almost twenty-one."

"I suppose Remmy told you all about me. That I'm dying." She nodded solemnly, meeting Lurleen's gaze. She liked that. Lately, most people who came to visit didn't look Lurleen in the eye at all; even Emily had had a hard time with that. "And you understand you're here for Emily as much as you are here for me?" Another nod.

"My sister is not easy," Lurleen said. "And I'm no picnic either."

"I'm not looking for a picnic," the young girl said, "just a job and a place to stay."

Did someone run her off without even the decency to take her to a home for expectant girls? Emily would recognize her weakness in a second, tear her apart, and Lurleen would have no peace in this world or the next. And wasn't that what all of this hired help malarkey was really about, leaving Emily with someone who would take care of her when Lurleen was gone?

While the thought of dying alone didn't bother Lurleen one iota and was almost comforting, the prospects of leaving Emily to that destiny tormented her.

"My sister will try to run you off like a stray dog, but I want you to promise me you won't go."

"I won't let her."

"It's always been just the two of us, or it has been for so long; this job won't be easy. Emily can be vexing and confounding. Overbearing too, and those are her very best qualities." Lurleen caught her breath but barely. "Sister has a jealous streak a mile wide, so believe me when I say she will make it her job to make you quit."

The girl stood extra straight and squared her shoulders. "I said I'd stay, and I meant it."

"You're young and pretty, and I'm under no delusions that you'll be here forever. But, if you're going to take this job, I'll ask one more promise. After I'm gone, I want you to stay with Emily for a while. She would never admit it, but Emily is going to need you."

"Of course, I'll stay." She nodded solemnly.

"Just don't leave the second I'm dead."

The girl's head snapped back for a moment but her look said she had a sincere appreciation for Lurleen's frankness, maybe even admiration. "I won't. You have my word."

"All right then, you're hired."

She looked surprised, shocked actually, which was a little disconcerting. Maybe Lurleen should have taken some more time, not hired the first person who walked through the door out of sheer desperation. But time was something Lurleen didn't have.

"Thank you. You won't be sorry," the girl promised.

"I believe I won't."

"When shall I start?" she asked.

"Tomorrow morning, I suppose. Seven o'clock, if that's all right with you. I can have Remmy send for your things if you like; of course I'll cover the cost. Unless you want to go back to Columbia to fetch them yourself, say your good-b—" Lurleen's breath was cut short. She closed her eyes and waited for the moment to pass. When she opened them, the girl was looking fearfully at her. "Don't worry, Nettie Gilbert. I'm not dead yet. But listen to me, making this move sound so final." Of course it was final. Death was final. "Columbia's not so far, much closer than Alabama, that's for sure." Nettie didn't laugh at Lurleen's attempted humor.

"Sending for my things would be lovely," Nettie said, sounding relieved that she wouldn't have to go back to the college. "Then I can get right to work."

Lurleen had always loved puzzles, especially the walking, talking kind. And she took as much delight in knowing what made someone tick as she did the process of drawing them out. Odd, since Lurleen had been in her shell for so long, old long before her time. A crushing loss will do that, but that wasn't what stole Lurleen's youth. It was the anger she carried for so long, anger that didn't go away when she started speaking to Emily again, that still resided in the hollow of her belly without a purpose. Carried so long, it was an immovable part of her.

"That would indeed be lovely," Lurleen said, looking forward to puzzling out Nettie Gilbert.

EMILY

Emily developed her intimidating stare her first year of teaching, when she was stuck with a slow class full of hooligans. They were used to riding roughshod over everyone, much like Remmy Wilkes was accustomed to getting his fine way, but Emily could rein them in with a single look and have them shamefully contemplating their shoelaces in no time.

But what did this pissant do? He just kept yammering, laughing like he was thoroughly entertained. Even crossed his arms to show he was unaffected by her look.

"I believe it's been a while, Miss Emily. Aren't you about due for a checkup?" he asked.

That did it.

"Why Remmy Wilkes, it's bad enough you practice your worthless medicine on my poor sister, while charging a pretty penny, I might add. But you have the gall to sit in my living room, drink my good tea, which I'm seeing now was a mistake to offer you, and drum up business? Well, I guess you have to pay for that fancy red car somehow," Emily huffed.

"Miss Emily, as much as you don't want to believe it, I do care very much for you and for Miss Lurleen," he said, his usual condescending tone noticeably absent. "I'm a good man and a good doctor and I'd really like it, appreciate it really, if you could find it in your head and your heart to accept the fact that I'm here to help you and your sister."

"And how do you presume to do that, when you can't heal her?"

"There's a lot of things I'm not in charge of, and believe me, if I could heal your sister, I would before your next heartbeat. I truly wish I could, but, at this point, it's up to the good Lord, not me. What I can and will do is keep your sister comfortable until her time comes. I've promised her I would do as much, and she wants that. I know you don't have any peace right now—"

Emily sucked in a breath and spat out the words. "There can be no peace without my sister."

He nodded. Every pretense of highfalutin doctor gone. "But I hope you will be able to find some just the same."

The door opened, and the young girl walked down the hallway with a smile that was meant to win Emily over. So young. So beautiful, a kernel of jealousy dug hard into Emily, making her wish she'd stopped time in its tracks that morning John came to the house to fetch Lurleen. If Emily could change anything, even the fact that Lurleen was going to die, she'd take those moments back. Change them. Do something different. Right. The memory of John's beautiful face was so close, the effects of what Emily did so massive, far reaching. It was too much to bear.

"Nettie," Remmy said softly, his tone washing over Emily, bringing her back to the present.

"Dr. Wilkes," the girl said like she was trying to maintain her distance.

"I'll just take my tea and sit on the porch," he said. "Let you all talk a bit."

The girl nodded but did not watch him go. Just stood there, pocketbook in hand, looking down at her penny loafers, most likely waiting for Emily to ask her to sit. Well, at least she had manners.

"Please," Emily said, nodding at the settee. "I guess between my sister and that nitwit doctor I'm overruled."

The girl looked at Emily, head held high, not taking the bait. "Miss Lurleen has asked me to stay. Work for y'all, and I'm delighted. And grateful. She also says you're going to try to run me off," she said evenly.

Emily winced for such a brief portion of a second, she was sure the girl didn't see. Running her off was the plan. But now, coming from this girl's lips, it sounded more sinister than sensible.

"I promised your sister that I'd stay on, and you should know that a promise isn't something I take lightly. I will be Miss Lurleen's nurse, your hired help, but above all, if you let me, I will be your friend. So, you can try to make me leave, but there's no way in—" *Hell*, Emily finished the thought for her, eyes slightly narrowed at the girl's tenacity. "I won't go."

Emily nodded and waited until the girl looked her in the eye. It took a while after screwing up the courage for that little diatribe, but there they were. Sparkling eyes Emily was sure were full of secrets. She knew this because they matched her own.

9

NETTIE

"But why?" Sue whined.

"It's better this way." Right now, I felt strong. Going back would only serve to remind me why I was leaving, and I couldn't bear to see the pity in Sue's eyes, that same look on my friends' faces. Certainly Justine was over her momentary lapse of sympathy. She probably had the catty minions standing watch for my return while Justine sharpened her claws. As horrible as it was to disappoint and maybe even hurt Sue, I was relieved I wouldn't have to succumb to their torture yet again.

"I'm going to miss you so much, but I want you to be happy." She sniffed and made a lame attempt to laugh it off. "I really don't know what I'm going to do without you. The room is so empty already."

"Donna Ciriello's been dying to get out of her room since Sharon joined the mean girls. She'd love to move in, and you love Donna. She's such a sweet girl."

"She is, but she's not you. I love you so much, Nettie, it hurts that you're leaving. Why you're leaving. I'm worried about you."

"Please don't be." I swallowed back tears and wheeled around to see Remmy watching me. I swiped at my eyes and attempted to smile, pleading for a few more moments of privacy, but he didn't move. Oh, yes, Katie had said he was a stickler for the phone bill and goodness knows how long I'd been on. "I have to go now, but I'll be there to stand up with you and Jimmy at the end of June. Promise. I love you, Sue."

"Then don't say it. Nettie. Don't say good-bye." She gulped the words, sobbing. "Never say good-bye."

"I won't. We're sisters." I set the phone gently on the cradle and turned to see him still there. "I'm sorry. My roommate is a little long-winded." I grabbed my purse and pulled out a few bills and put them beside the phone. "Three dollars should more than cover the cost of the call. If it's more, please let me know and I'll pay you the rest."

"Put your money back in your pocketbook, Nettie Gilbert." He smiled. "Cora May says dinner's ready, and she doesn't like to be kept waiting."

He motioned toward what was a beautiful dining room with tall walnut wainscoting that matched the glossy dark floors. Just above the wainscoting, the walls were a lovely candlelight yellow. Connected by a fancy ceiling medallion, a glorious chandelier hung over a long mahogany Chippendale table with ten chairs that could easily seat fourteen guests. A large oil portrait of horsemen in red coats ready for the hunt hung over a long buffet on one side of the room, and four smaller paintings of a horse in various stages of a jump were on the opposite wall.

An older woman, maybe in her sixties, ran her hand over the tablecloth. She was pretty, with a heart-shaped face the color of black coffee. Striking amber-colored eyes scrutinized fine china bowls scattered across the table full of mashed potatoes, field peas, fried okra, creamed corn. A silver butter dish and a tray of biscuits were the centerpiece. At the head of the table, a beautiful roast beef was swimming in gravy. And, after not having an appetite for days, I was suddenly hungry.

"Dinner looks delicious," I said, making Cora May smile.

"You have one of Cora May's biscuits," Katie said, pushing her wheelchair up to the table. "You'll think you've died and gone to heaven." She pulled into an empty space and transferred herself to the dining chair on her right, glancing back at the chair, a silent command for Remmy to wheel it away.

"Aw, Miss Katie, how you do go on. But everybody knows it ain't my biscuits that'll take you to the back side of heaven's gate; it's my cornbread. For sure."

"I can attest to that," Remmy said, holding my chair.

"Thank you," I said, ignoring that his hands lingered on my chair for a moment before he pushed Katie closer to the table.

"Won't you stay and eat a bite, Cora May?" he asked.

"Thank you, Remmy, but I best get on home. Darnell will be wanting his supper."

"Everything's wonderful, Cora May. We'll take it from here. Thank you very much," Remmy said, sitting down and placing his napkin in his lap.

The woman nodded and gave his shoulder a squeeze, then Katie's.

"Love you," Katie said.

"Love you too, babies," Cora May said, taking one last look at the table.

Remmy served the roast beef and the bowls were passed around. While Cora May's biscuits were indeed heavenly, they weren't as good as my mother's or my grandmothers' back home.

"I'm so glad you stayed, Nettie. It's so nice to have another girl in the house." Katie smirked, as she heaped her plate with friend okra.

"What are you talking about? Between you and Cora May, I'm outnumbered," Remmy drawled, passing the peas to Nettie. "Don't believe her for a second, Nettie; those two are forever ganging up on me to get whatever they want."

"Why, Remmy Foster Wilkes, you take that back," Katie said playfully. "Cora May and I have never conspired against you. Not once. Except of course when you ordered that awful blue suit. You should have seen it, Nettie; it came all the way from Chicago and was so ugly, I had Cora May burn it."

"I loved that suit." Remmy smiled.

"You have rumpled old pajamas that look better than that suit," Katie laughed. "I considered it my sisterly duty to save you from yourself."

"Enough about the one poor clothing choice I've made in my life," Remmy said, making Katie nearly choke on his words. "What did you think about the sisters, Nettie?"

I didn't know Remmy or Katie well enough to tell them what I really thought, that Emily was rude, overbearing and Lurleen was at best brutally honest. "They were nice."

Remmy and Katie looked at each other and burst out laughing, making me wonder what I'd gotten myself into.

"My apologies, Nettie," Remmy said. "Of course the sisters are nice."

"In their own way." Katie punctuated the thought with a huge grin.

"I spoke to Miss Lurleen before we left," Remmy said, fully recovered but with that inherited Wilkes smirk. "She mentioned she would like to have your things shipped to their home."

"Oh, I'll call Dean Kerrigan's office and arrange it first thing tomorrow," Katie piped up. "She's such a dear; I haven't spoken to her in ages. She wasn't in when I called to have the advertisement put on the bulletin board. It will be great to catch up with her."

"That's okay," I blurted out, my heart racing. I knew Dean Kerrigan would keep my secret, but I wasn't so sure about the girls who worked part-time in the administration office. Of course, after my tirade with Mother, everyone knew my sordid tale, and some would be only too happy to share it with Katie. "My roommate will mail my things."

"Nonsense," Remmy said. "I'll just swing by the college tomorrow and pick them up. I'd planned to visit a colleague at Baptist Hospital anyway."

"Oh, I'd like to see that, a dormitory room's worth of girly chattel in that red sports car, flying down the highway. Besides." Katie narrowed her eyes. "You have appointments tomorrow."

"Only until two o'clock; that's plenty of time to get there and back, and I'm sure Nettie is anxious to get her belongings, settle in."

"It's not much, really. Just a suitcase, a few boxes of clothes, some mementos," I said. "They don't warrant a special trip; they can be easily shipped."

"I'm sure they can," Remmy said, pouring himself more tea. "But I'm more than happy to do it for you, Nettie."

The glow from the brotherly-sisterly banter left Katie's face and was replaced with a look that resembled the one I'd seen when she was talking to the husband hunter. Katie turned her attention to her plate, head down, quiet. Diagnosing her mood, her brother threw out a playfully arrogant line about the college, much like the one I'd snapped at him for earlier. He looked hopeful his sister would take the bait. She didn't. Neither did I, and the remainder of the dinner was noticeably silent.

Remmy

Nettie had protested when Remmy sent the girls to porch sit while he washed the dinner dishes. Come morning, Cora May would fuss at him for sure, but that was okay. He thought the menial task would take his mind off of the call he'd gotten from Cecil, but it didn't. Tomorrow Remmy would interview for the job he'd always wanted, even if it wasn't in Charleston.

But he wasn't fresh out of med school, like Cecil was when he started working there. No doubt the powers that be would wonder why he hadn't plowed ahead with his career, sold the practice in Camden right off the bat, and moved on with his life.

From the porch, Nettie Gilbert laughed at something Katie said, and he found himself smiling at the sound. Seemed like the girls were having a good time, and Remmy was glad. He loved his sister, but lately, her moods could change quicker than the dark April sky that had just opened up, making him wonder if everything that had happened was finally catching up to her.

He picked the meat platter up out of the soapy water and rinsed it off, running his hand across the surface until it felt clean. Lightning flashed. Katie squealed and then giggled. Even when she was little, she hated the thunder but loved to watch the sky light up with angry streaks. The memory of her running full tilt through the house for her bed made him freeze for a few seconds. He could almost see her on her belly, legs windshield wiping back and forth while she watched the long window for the next flash.

After the accident, Katie hadn't missed a beat when she was confined to that wheelchair. Maybe her losses were finally catching up to her. It wouldn't surprise Remmy; there was not a day that went by that he didn't think about those last perfect moments in his life, the day he graduated from med school. Mama, Daddy, and Katie had come to Charleston to watch him accept his diploma from the Medical College of South Carolina. He remembered looking into the crowd and finding his mother, who was always such a crier, but even more so that day.

She and Daddy were sitting in the row closest to the stage, so that when he shook the dean's hand, he could see Mama boohooing. Daddy was of course as stoic as ever and still smarting because Remmy had finally told him he wouldn't be taking over his practice in Camden, but Daddy had beamed just a little when Remmy waved his diploma at them. And Katie had been so beautiful that day; she'd even drug her fiancé, Jack, to the show.

Poor guy had to endure a car trip with Mama and Katie planning the wedding, *then* had to sit through a boring graduation ceremony. Afterward, Mama had made Remmy pose for a thousand pictures. He still had the one Jack took of the four of them, the one where Daddy actually smiled. He kept it tucked away in his sock drawer.

That last moment frozen forever on Kodak paper, when Mama and Daddy could still draw breath and Katie's legs still worked. Before Remmy became the country doctor he never wanted to be.

He'd paid dearly for surviving the tragedy without so much as a scratch: the loss of his parents, not taking that job he wanted in Charleston. But no more so than Katie. Jack had been injured, but walked away from the accident, and when he found out Katie was never getting out of that wheelchair, he'd walked away from her too.

Even four years after the accident, Remmy still couldn't bring himself to change the shingle above the neat red brick building a few doors down on Broad Street—Dr. Foster Wilkes, MD. It would feel too much like surrender. But he would never surrender to this life in Camden.

He stacked the last bowl in the drain, threw the towel on the counter, and let out a tired sigh. Before he left the office to take Nettie over to the Eldridges' house, he'd gone over the files Katie had set on his desk; he'd done it more out of habit than necessity. He knew tomorrow would shape up to be no different from any other day. Mrs. Casper was coming in for her bursitis. The Johnson triplets, who always came down with whatever virus was going around all at the same time. He'd shuffled through the others to find all of them unremarkable. He'd had to reschedule his appointments after lunch to meet with his friend Cecil, hopefully before the interview. It would be interesting to hear what he had to say.

Mignon Coffey's file had been on top of the stack along with a note from Katie. *This wretched woman called today, six times. I'm tempted to turn her in to the authorities for harassment.* He smiled at Katie's tenacity, although sometimes he wished she would give that protective streak of hers a rest. Mignon was nice enough. Pretty. Had a little hypochondria, that's all. But Katie despised her.

Maybe he shouldn't have gone out with Mignon, but that was for him to decide. He didn't care how much he loved his sister, he was not going to discuss his love life with her. She meddled enough as it was.

He headed down the hallway that led to his father's office, sat down on the ancient leather chair, and propped his feet up on the desk, something that had always killed his father, even though he did the same thing all the time. After Remmy took over the practice, he used to sit here and believe the life he'd planned for himself before the wreck was still possible. It wasn't long before Charleston seemed as far away as California. China. But this new opportunity in Columbia was just what he needed to finally practice surgery again, and with Cecil there, it would seem like old times.

Until then, he was still right where his father wanted him to be. He blew out a breath, dialed the number, and waited. The phone rang so many times, he sat up and shoved his hand in his pocket and pulled out his car keys, ready to go over there.

"*Hello.*"

"Mr. Buck?" He breathed out a sigh of relief. "This is Remmy. Just checking in."

"No. You're just calling to see if I'm dead yet. We'll I'm not, so you can hang up now."

Remmy smiled, grinned actually, and returned his feet to the place on the desk where the finish had been worn slightly away from the backs of three generations of Wilkes shoe leather.

"You feeling all right?"

"I was until I had to get out of my chair during this storm and answer the blame telephone. I told you to stop calling me every day. You're a doctor; you ought to have something better to do."

"Than annoy you? No sir, I can't think of anything better to do right offhand," Remmy laughed.

Sometimes calling Buck was the best part of his day. But Buck was eighty-five with a laundry list of infirmities. One day Remmy was going to call and there would be no answer, no sweet spot in his day.

"Did you take your medicine, Mr. Buck?" Silence. "If you think I'm annoying on the phone, I know you don't want me to come out to your house in this rain and watch you take it. Now lay the phone down and go take your pills."

"*You*, treating me like a five-year-old," Buck huffed. "I have underwear older than you."

"Well, stop acting like you're five, and go take your medicine."

Remmy held the phone away from his ear in anticipation of Buck slamming the handset down on the telephone table. He heard the familiar clunk and then the sound of the old man shuffling off. A few minutes later, he was back. "You're a pain in my ass, Remmy Wilkes."

"Yes, sir. Good night, Mr. Buck."

A bolt of lightning flashed. Then a thunderclap made the girls squeal before the whole street went pitch black. "Getting candles," Remmy hollered. He felt his way out of the office, down the hallway, and back to the kitchen. He opened the junk drawer and felt around for the flashlight, then located a couple of tapers and some matches. He turned the flashlight on, grabbed some matches and a couple of empty Mason jars out of the pantry, and pointed the beam toward the porch.

"Give Nettie the light," Katie said as the screen door closed behind him. "We're going to tell stories till the electricity comes back on."

Remmy handed her the light and lit the candles, dripping wax in the bottoms of the jars and then standing the candles on end and holding them in place until the wax cooled. He sat down in the rocker across from Nettie. "Hope you've got a lot of stories. Last time we had a storm like this, the power was out for a couple of days," he said.

Nettie had seemed so serious earlier at his office, the sisters' house, on the phone with her roommate and hadn't relaxed much more over dinner, especially after Remmy offered to fetch her things. He liked seeing her laughing, having a good time.

But when Nettie held the flashlight under her chin, an attempt to look eerie before she broke into laughter, Remmy's breath caught in his chest. Earlier, when she'd walked into his office he thought she was pretty enough, even more so when he'd riled her. But the way the light caressed her face, she was breathtaking. Striking, green eyes, red hair falling down her back, full lips she kept trying to draw into a thin line. But then they would turn up just before she started laughing. She held the light with one hand and talked with the other, long, fluid, graceful strokes. And as smart as Remmy was, he felt moronic for not noticing right off the bat how truly beautiful Nettie Gilbert was.

"This meeting of the C-Square girls is officially called to order," Nettie announced. Remmy pretended he was getting up to leave, but it would have taken more fortitude than he had to do so. He grinned at her and was rewarded when, for a fraction of a second, the tiniest flirty look crossed Nettie's face before turning her attention to his sister. "The honorable Katie Wilkes presiding," Nettie said, passing the light to Katie.

NETTIE

It is normal, maybe even inbred for a Southern girl to flirt, but I wanted to slap myself silly for the unguarded moment I gave Remmy. The last thing I wanted was some kind of dalliance with any man, most notably one who seemed to have his pick of the most eligible girls in town.

I hadn't really thought about my life after Brooks, but after meeting the sisters today, I was sure I didn't want to be an old maid. Not that it would be so bad to be without a man. No, I was sure I would endure spinsterhood quite nicely. But, without a sister? Maybe Katie would consider joining ranks with me. Almost twenty-five, she didn't seem the least bit concerned about having a man around. Didn't mention them once, which was quite different than the girls from the college who seemed to minor in everything and major in boys.

While Remmy washed the dishes, I'd come right out and asked Katie if she was seeing anyone special. The girl didn't even blush, just laughed that hearty laugh of hers and changed the subject. No, Katie Wilkes was much too busy, too happy, to be concerned with a man and the pitfalls that came with one.

"So, is Miss Ludy still with the PE department?" Katie asked. "I was so terrified of her my freshman year, that booming voice. 'Nobody gets their period three times in one month, now get out there on that field, Wilkes.'"

"She is indeed still there, and everyone adores her, although the freshmen still fear her. I know I did until I realized how much she loves all of us, and the college. We're lucky to have someone of her caliber."

"A PE teacher of high caliber. Just how high would that be?" Remmy teased.

"She won six medals at the First International Track Meet in Paris in 1922, two of them gold. And she helped pave the way for women to compete in the Olympics, Dr. Wilkes. Is that high enough for you?" Nettie sassed.

"Ignore him, Nettie. Please tell me Dr. Babble isn't at the college anymore. He was old as dirt when I was in the chorus," Katie said.

"Oh, no. My freshman year, he retired, and Mr. Darr took over. He's from California; looks just like Eddie Fisher but with a James Dean pompadour. He's quite handsome.

"I played piano for the chorus. You should have seen the girls staring at him all dreamy like. I understand when Dr. Babble ran the chorus, girls had to be threatened or bribed with extended curfews to get them to participate. When Guthrie Darr took over, he had to turn students away."

"Ooh, Guthrie Darr. Even his name sounds handsome. And looking like Eddie Fisher? I'd sign up in a heartbeat," Katie said. Maybe she wasn't the best prospective partner for my spinsterhood.

"What kind of name is Guthrie Darr," Remmy teased. "Sounds awful flimsy to me."

"I assure you, he is not flimsy, but he is quite dreamy," I said.

When Remmy smiled at me, my face went hot, and there was just enough light from the candles and the flashlight to see he was watching me, and he was enjoying himself. I moved the candles in the Mason jars on the small table toward him and Katie, glad to retreat a little further in the darkness.

"Why, the whole school, and not just the students, practically pledged their undying love to him when they dedicated the class of fifty-three yearbook to him. My roommate, Sue, worked on the dedication for two weeks; I heard it so many times, I cold recite it in my sleep. *To Guthrie Darr for his winning personality, his sincerity, and true friendship. You add a new note to the music of our lives.*" I barely got Sue's painstakingly written tribute out without laughing. She would have been mortified, but it had been funny to watch the whole school swoon over the likes of one man. "Every girl truly adored him."

"Even you, Nettie Gilbert?" Remmy clutched his heart, flirting hard enough to put the private on the bus to shame. "Please. Say it isn't so."

Remmy was dreamy in his own right, and without a single quality I'd consider in a man. No, the next man in my life, if there ever was one, would be everything Remmy Wilkes and Brooks Carver were not, and above all, he would be faithful. Even if that meant he was unfortunate looking and as dumb as a sack of hammers.

"Knock it off, Remmy," Katie snapped playfully, but with an edge in her voice. "This is girl talk and if you're going to play the peanut gallery, you can go straight to bed."

"All right. All right," Remmy said. "I'll just sit here and listen, but honest to God, it's hard to take you ladies seriously when y'all make that place sound like Nirvana. There had to be some drawback."

"It practically was," Katie said. "And there were no drawbacks, except for freshman year when dates were chaperoned."

"Oh, it's changed with the times," I said. "Freshmen can double-date now, after second semester, of course."

"Because it's harder for two girls to get themselves in trouble than just one? That makes perfect sense." Even in the dim light, he'd seen my face fade and knew he'd struck a chord.

"*Remmy Wilkes*, don't talk about such a delicate subject in mixed company. It's uncouth," Katie chided.

"It's not uncouth; as a licensed physician, I'm entitled to talk about the human condition, not judge it," he said, looking at me like he hoped to see my smile return. I turned toward Katie and allowed my hair to curtain the side of my face. "That's for the busybodies and gossips, of which I know you are not one, good sister. And if you were, with all you know from folks coming and going from my office, I'd have to fire you."

"You'd never fire me. Not in a million years, and you're just jealous because you went to the lowly old College of Charleston," Katie teased.

"Ah, yes. Poor me. Going to a real school that was founded in seventeen hundred and seventy rather than what? Yesterday?"

"Eighteen fifty-four is hardly yesterday," Katie said.

"*We sing the praise of her we love*," I pitched the song too high, and came down an octave. "*We lift her name in song. White gleaming as the stars.*"

Katie joined in our alma mater with a beautiful rich contralto voice that sounded so much like Sue's it would have made me cry if Remmy hadn't chimed in, loud and awful, making both Katie and I shout our alma mater over his. "*Her gentle heart has made her great; her breath is love, she knows no hate. Her faith that God controls her fate makes great our own Columbia.*"

We all broke into laughter that competed with the raging storm, and I realized that was the first time I'd really laughed in weeks. "On that horrible note, if you don't mind showing me to my room, Katie, I'm going to bed," I announced. "I have to be at the Eldridges' at seven."

"I'll show you to your room," Remmy said, opening the screen door. I followed Katie into the house. "I'll drop you off tomorrow too," he offered, unaware of the look his sister gave him, for just a moment.

"It's close enough to walk; I'll be fine. But if you'd drop off my suitcase when you bring my things from the college, I'd greatly appreciate it."

"Of course. Come on now, I'll show you to your room upstairs." His hand brushed across the small of my back like it had at the sisters' house, only this time it lingered, guiding me to the stairs. "Good night, sis," he called. Katie didn't return his words.

10

NETTIE

Thankfully, I'd unfolded my good Ship 'n Shore blouse and hung it up last night so it only looked like I'd wallowed in it rather than slept fitfully through the night in it, but I suspected Miss Lurleen wouldn't care. Miss Emily was an entirely different story. Yesterday, among other things, I'd noticed her housedress was perfectly pressed, each tiny pleat steamed into place. She wore earbobs that made her lobes an angry red when she snatched one of them off to massage her ear. And her shoes were not sensible for someone her age, but Miss Emily seemed like she didn't feel ancient and certainly didn't want to look that way. She had an air about her that said she'd always been beautiful, worshiped.

Miss Lurleen was sturdy. I suspected she had been a beauty in her own right when she was my age. But she was the kind of woman who wouldn't have cared one bit, compared to Miss Emily, who likely craved attention as much as she savored it.

I slipped on the yellow skirt I'd worn the day before. Buttoning my baby blue cap-sleeved blouse, I remembered what it felt like to be adored, to be someone else's wonder, Brooks's wonder. No matter what had happened between now and the night in the grove, I knew Brooks had loved me then. I pinched the tender skin of my underarm just below my elbow, a trick my applied music professor taught me when I was learning a new song.

The pain was supposed to create an aversion to the excitement, the nervousness I felt at learning a new piece and flying through it. Pinching the underside of my arm made me slow down, and the marks weren't easily seen. After Professor Parker suggested the idea my freshman year, I was black and blue for weeks, but I quickly learned to temper my nerves, keep my thoughts in the proper direction.

I pinched myself again and vowed I would every time my mind strayed from my job at the Eldridges' to unruly thoughts of Brooks or Sissy, my parents or my old life. And most especially every time I was tempted to sass or argue with Miss Emily, my thumb and forefinger would painfully remind me to redirect my thoughts so that I could keep my job. I raised my arm and took in the angry red mark, praying that would be the last one and ready to sally forth into my new life.

REMMY

Remmy had every intention of seeing Cecil first and then swinging by the college to pick up Nettie's things, until he woke up smiling, thinking about her. He wrote it off to the fact that she was smart and funny and beautiful. The fact that she slept two doors down from him last night probably had something to do with it too. Whatever the case, she'd been on his mind all day, and the closer he got to Columbia, the more he wanted to know her story. The one she wasn't telling last night on the porch.

Pulling into the Columbia College main entrance, he glanced at his watch. He was definitely cutting it close if he was going to make it to Baptist Hospital on time. He got out of his car and headed off to look for the administration building, ignoring the girls rubbernecking as he walked past them. That was one of the things he remembered about Katie going here, even the most homely guy could feel like a god at an all-girls school. He remembered grinning at the girls when he'd come to visit and Katie whacking his shoulder, ordering him to stop encouraging their adoration. But he was a guy, and guys liked that sort of thing.

He stopped at a flock of students perched on the lawn, maybe twenty, some giggling, some of them sighing, trying to catch his eye. "Good afternoon, ladies. Which way to the admin building?"

"That way," a portly brunette said. "I can show you if you like." And then ten other girls offered to show him too.

It was toward the end of the semester, the time Remmy had always poured it on at the College of Charleston in order to get the grades he needed to get into med school. But instead of looking serious, halfway studious, most of the girls looked at him like it was open season for the Sadie Hawkins ball.

"Thanks. I'll find it." Remmy nodded.

He found the building, hurried up the steps, and followed the signs to the dean's office. A cute blonde with a face as round as a dinner plate blushed the moment he entered the reception area.

"Hello, I'm Dr. Wilkes. I'm here to pick up some boxes for Nettie Gilbert. I was told Dean Kerrigan would have them ready to go."

"Are you *that* kind of doctor?" The girl sounded like a bubblehead.

"A *medical* doctor? Yes." Remmy hated his condescending tone that sounded so much like his father, who always insisted on being called Dr. Wilkes by everyone. Remmy's mother said it was because his father had worked long and hard for the title and wanted to be recognized as such, but it always felt like his father was proclaiming he was better than everybody else, including Remmy.

"Oh, so, Nettie really *is*—" The girl paused. "You know. Because I'd heard it was her sister— Wow, Nettie's *expecting?*" She whispered the last word.

Nettie was expecting? That explained the glow he'd been sure was a reflection of her natural beauty, her abrupt departure from this place that didn't feel any more like an institution of higher learning than it did when Katie went here. "Not that it's any business of yours. Now, about Miss Gilbert's things."

"Yes, sir." The girl snapped to, went into the dean's office, and rummaged around before reemerging. "The boxes aren't here. Let me call Miss Beaumont, the housemother for Nettie's dorm; she knows everything about everything."

The girl plucked a yellow pencil from behind her ear, dialed the number, and waited. "Eve? Hi this is Ginny at Dean Kerrigan's office. Someone's come to fetch Nettie Gilbert's things. A *doctor.* Yeah, I know can you believe it? He says some boxes should be here but they're not. Any ideas?" She paused and shoved the pencil back into place and waited. "Can you ask Miss Beaumont if she knows?

Oh, she is? I think she makes up that story about going to the doctor for her bursitis. I think she has a boyfriend. No. No kidding.

"Every time I go into Tapp's Department Store, I see her at the lunch counter, and she hasn't bought a thing. Well of course I know you don't *have* to buy something. But like I was saying, Miss Beaumont was looking all goo-goo eyed at the soda jerk, you know that old guy with too much hair? Yes, I know isn't that a scream. The last time I was there, and you know I shop every Saturday, religiously, whether I buy something or not— Ooh, I forgot to tell you, I found this little yellow sweater set with the cutest—" Remmy cleared his throat and the girl nodded at him. "Anyway, it's a divine outfit, and as I was leaving, I saw Miss Beaumont at the exact same spot, and—"

"Miss?" Remmy clipped, glancing at his watch. Cecil would be pissed if he was late for the interview, and Remmy wanted that job.

"Oh, yes. Do you know anything about Nettie's things, Eve?" Remmy didn't return her conciliatory smile. Moments later the girl started up again. "Well, tell Sue, she has to. He's here now. Waiting rather impatiently I might add." She whispered the last words into the phone just loud enough for Remmy to hear. "Hey, don't say that; it's not fair. Nettie was always nice to us. No, for pity's sake, don't alert Justine and her minions. I don't care that Bettie and Gina have been nice to you lately, they're mean girls. They're not your friends. Even if you share this little tidbit with them, they'll dump you soon as they get what they want. What do they want? Why, you're a crackerjack at mathematics. All right then. I'll send him over now. Thanks, Eve. Hey? You wanna go to Tapp's Saturday?"

"Miss," Remmy barked, making the girl jump a mile. "*Please.*"

"Gotta go." She hung up the phone and propped her chin on her hands, her expression a cross between coquettish and apologetic.

"Sorry. You can pull your car around to East Dorm. Eve will try to pry Nettie's things away from Sue and you can be on your way. By the way, how is she?"

"Nettie is fine," he said as uncomfortably as if one of the busy-bodies back home had asked him to discuss one of his patients. Of course Nettie wasn't his patient, and for some reason, that bothered him.

"Nobody could believe what happened to her. I mean, she's Nettie Gilbert, for Pete's sake. It's just so sad, a nice girl like her ending up that way."

Nettie certainly didn't look like she was expecting, but if these girls knew, that meant she was more than likely a couple of months along. And in the family way, she'd be in no shape to deal with the Eldridge sisters six months from now, maybe even sooner. Maybe there wasn't any point in taking her things to Camden. Maybe she'd just go back to wherever she came from, and why did that bother him?

When he'd interviewed her, there'd been moments when the determination in her eyes had bordered on desperation. Maybe she had nowhere else to go. Remmy had seen that time and time again with unwed mothers and he hated it. No, he'd do what any good doctor would do for Nettie Gilbert. Help her as best he could, see to it that she knew what to do to remain healthy for herself and her baby. But it niggled at him, some guy taking advantage of Nettie, not doing right by her. A girl like her, she must have fallen hard for him to end up in her predicament, and surprisingly, that bothered him even more.

The girl stood and returned the pencil to the cup on the desk. "I'll just get my sweater and show you where to go."

Remmy waved her off. "Thank you for your help; I'll find it myself."

"Oh, wait. You need to know how to get to East."

"I'll find it," he repeated, wanting to just get the hell out of there.

He saw a yardman and asked for directions to Nettie's dormitory, and it did not take three years and a running commentary about shopping at Tapp's to get a straight answer. Remmy jogged back to his car and was pulling into a space behind the building a few minutes later. A bevy of women whistled from above. He looked up to see two dozen girls in bathing suits on the roof, smiling down on him.

It wasn't so long ago that he and Cecil used to pass by the girls' dorms at the College of Charleston to try to catch a glimpse of the girls sunbathing on the roof in their skimpy suits. He doubted Nettie was one of those rooftop girls, not if her porcelain skin was any indication. He gave a half wave, ignored the giggles and catcalls as he headed into the building.

Waiting at the front desk was a tearstained young woman with the saddest expression Remmy had ever seen, yet she was dressed utterly cockeyed so that each piece of clothing she had on clashed with the other. A large yellow suitcase was sandwiched between her and two overflowing pasteboard boxes she had in a death grip. A half dozen or so dresses on hangers were draped over the boxes, and she was looking at Remmy like he was Simon Legree.

"You must be Sue." He extended his hand. "I'm Remmy Wilkes," he said, leaving the doctor off. Still, she didn't let go of the boxes. "Thanks for bringing Nettie's things down. I know she's looking forward to getting them."

Truthfully, he knew nothing of the sort, but he felt a little like he was trying to talk this girl off the ledge; his tone certainly sounded that way. She nodded and raked her arm across her runny nose. "Nettie is my best friend."

"Of course." Remmy nodded. "She's a very nice girl."

"We always took care of each other. *Oh.*" She waved her hand frantically in front of her face to swat away her tears. "I'm just going to miss her so much. And I worry about her."

Remmy was worried too; he knew how this worked, and it was a damn shame. Girls like Nettie going into hiding. Shipped off to some home for unwed mothers under the pretense of an extended vacation to visit a long-lost aunt who didn't exist. Even worse were the girls Remmy knew for a fact were held prisoner in their own homes. While their parents made up some story about them being away from home, the girls were forced to stay away from the windows. And, if that wasn't bad enough, when they finally went into labor and had to leave the house to be delivered, they were made to lie down in the car with blankets thrown over them.

The shameful way those girls were treated was far and away more immoral than some poor girl getting herself pregnant.

"I'll take care of her," he swore before he realized. He had no cause or claim to take care of Nettie Gilbert, but he would do this for her friend, for every young girl who showed up at the hospital when he was in med school, terrified and ashamed. For Nettie. "I promise."

"What Brooks did to her—"

So, that was the bastard's name. Brooks. A single syllable, curt and cold; he even sounded like a pompous ass. Well, good for Nettie, getting away from a guy like that. He didn't deserve her.

Sue snarfed and lifted one of the overflowing boxes. "Allow me," Remmy said, taking the box from her. He made two trips to the car and put the top up so Nettie's things wouldn't be full of dust and pollen when he got them back to Camden.

"Thanks. For doing this," Sue said. "Give her a hug for me." She straightened herself and attempted to smile. "Tell her I love her, but please don't tell her I told you about Brooks."

"I won't," he lied. Of course Remmy wouldn't mention the bastard when he talked to Nettie about her delicate situation. But at some point he would broach the subject, of course before the baby came, to let her know not all men are alike. Although the ones like this Brooks fellow certainly were.

"Thank you," the girl said, the last word dissolving into a whine before she fled upstairs.

Remmy barely made it to the hospital on time. The facility was impressive and Cecil was happier than a punk in a pickle patch showing Remmy around, bragging every five seconds over the latest medical equipment. The hustle and bustle of the place, the pretty nurses. Just prior to catching up with Cecil, Remmy had spent an hour interviewing with Dr. Cheatham, the chief physician, hearing more of the same, except for the part about the nurses. Then Remmy and Cecil ended up in the cafeteria downstairs where the food was actually good, and Cecil's claim about the nurses was verified.

"Now that you've seen the inside of a real medical facility again, what do you think?" he'd asked, all puffed up, knowing this was exactly what Remmy had always wanted.

Remmy shrugged, surprised he wasn't bowled over by the place, even though it really was top notch. "It's nice."

"Nice?" Cecil pushed his plate away, lit up a cigarette, and took a long draw. "Sport, you're a surgeon, not some damn country doctor. You're wasting yourself on Camden when you could be here, doing what you were meant to do."

Remmy's father had balked at the idea of Remmy specializing in anything other than family medicine. By that time, Remmy was at the top of his class and it didn't matter what his father thought. He'd do whatever he damn well pleased, and he was meant to be a surgeon. That's what the teaching physicians had said during his residency in Charleston; that's what he knew in his bones. And yet his bones were in Camden, right where his father said they would be if he had anything to do with it.

"You said the job doesn't start until July; I'll give it some thought."

"Well don't think too long; they'll be making a decision in three weeks, four at the most. You're not the only candidate they're looking at, sport, but maybe this isn't your first interview to get back into surgery." Cecil shrugged and exhaled a cloud of smoke. "You talking to the boys in Charleston?"

For four years, getting back to Charleston was all Remmy had thought about. But now, the idea of the life he wanted didn't throb inside of him like it had since the accident, like it was going to bust out of him and take over. Now the feeling was much less potent, but it shouldn't have been. This was the life he wanted. Wasn't it?

A pretty nurse with long blond ringlets sidled up to Cecil and put her hand on his shoulder. "Dr. Rutledge, you're needed in the operating room. Car accident, a bad one. Better come quick."

Cecil nodded, snubbed out his cigarette with a cocky look. "Duty calls," he said, nodding at Remmy, knowing that was the greatest enticement Cecil could have left him with. The feeling that Remmy should be in that OR, piecing a victim back together, felt like a tight fist around his throat, but an hour later, when he pulled up in front of the Eldridge sisters' house, the feeling was barely there.

11

NETTIE

I plopped down on the front porch swing, dog tired and completely exasperated after nine hours of dealing with Miss Emily. On the other hand, Miss Lurleen was kind and welcoming. Although she stayed in bed all day, she'd asked very little of me other than to fetch her meals, sweet tea, and read aloud from Marjorie Kinnan Rawlings's *The Yearling*. I'd read the book in school ages ago and remembered it being a tearjerker. Somehow reading it to a dying woman and knowing the ultimate demise of poor Flag made the story ten times sadder, and I prayed there was something uplifting in the stack of library books on Miss Lurleen's bedside table, something humorous. Maybe a nice romance.

While I was prepared for Miss Emily to badger me and try to run me off after I arrived this morning, she didn't say a word. Just handed me a long list of chores that obviously hadn't been done in years.

Dusting the chandelier. Wiping down the baseboards of her considerably large home. Waxing the floors. And those were the easy things. Each chore was performed under her scrutiny while she gave a running commentary of everything I was doing wrong. How you can dust baseboards other than by rubbing them with a dust rag is beyond explanation, but the undersides of both of my arms were black and blue and ached from reminding myself to hold my tongue.

Just before four o'clock, something magical happened. Miss Emily turned her soap opera on and passed right out. I looked in on Miss Lurleen to find she was sound asleep too, and was grateful to have a moment to myself. I slipped out to the porch with a tall glass of sweet tea and the *LIFE* magazine I'd splurged on before I left Columbia.

I pressed the glass against my forehead and picked up the magazine, but I was too tired to read or even look at the pictures inside. The homeward-bound starlet staring at me on the glossy cover should have been inspiration for what I could be. Cool. Confident. A sultry redhead. Definitely nobody's doormat. Even if the pennies in my loafers were my last two cents, I'd bet a movie star like Elaine Stewart wouldn't lose a minute's peace over the likes of Brooks Carver or Sissy or Mother or Daddy.

Closing my eyes, the muddled sound of Miss Emily's soap opera droned on in competition with her snoring. She was resting up no doubt to make another go at working me to death. Well, anything, even hard labor was better than being the girl everyone pitied at school, and I couldn't imagine the looks I would get if I were back in Satsuma.

Remmy's sporty car pulled up to the curb out front. He gave a half wave and a smile, pulled one of my boxes out, and headed up the walkway. "Hey, Nettie," he called. When he got close enough for me to get a good look at his face, I wanted to run or scream, but I couldn't move. *He knew.*

Disappointment was etched into every strong line of his ruggedly handsome face. He made two more trips to the car before sitting down on the swing beside me and attempting a conciliatory smile. "Hey," he said softly.

"Remmy." I really tried not to snap, but between Miss Emily's crusade to send me packing and knowing Remmy Wilkes knew everything and felt sorry for me, anything less was beyond my restraint. Good etiquette, however, was etched into my being. "Thank you for fetching my things," I added tightly.

"That bad, huh?" He smiled and pushed off on the swing so that my feet were no longer anchored. "Figured as much."

"Miss Lurleen is fine, if that's what you mean." The floor brushed my feet, and while every smidgeon of good sense told me to stop the motion, part of me felt good and free and relieved. Even though I'd only carried my burden for a few days, I was tired of wearing it like an ill-fitting party dress. The pity party was over. No more slipping back into *what if* or nursing the *whys.* If I wanted people to treat me differently, I would have to be different, and starting with Doctor Remmy Wilkes was as good a place as any.

I straightened, stretching my backbone, laying it straight against the back of the swing. Moving forward, I put my feet flat on the floor, making it zigzag until Remmy's long legs stopped it completely. "So you know my secret."

He winced a little at my tone and then attempted a smile. "I have a feeling I could know you for a million years, Nettie Gilbert, and never know all your secrets. But, yes. I know."

"It doesn't change anything. Miss Lurleen likes me a lot, and even if you tell her, which I hope you would be a gentleman and would not, I don't believe she would send me packing."

"I'm not worried about that right now; besides, she has such little time left, I don't know if it would even make sense to tell her." He resumed the motion of the swing, moving so slowly; the toes of my shoes barely skimmed the floor. "I'm more worried about you. How are you feeling?"

"Why do you care?"

"Aside from being a good doctor? I suspect it has a lot to do with you being a pretty girl, a nice girl who doesn't deserve what she's been handed. So, I'll ask you again, how are you feeling?"

"About as good as one can feel in this situation."

"Are you sleeping well?"

"I will tonight. Apparently Miss Emily put a lot of thought into planning my demise."

"Death by housework. That's a new one."

"Surely there must be something in all those medical books you have on the subject." He laughed even though my attempt at humor sounded bitter. And I'd had enough of the bitterness too, but, honestly, I was too tired to move. "I would offer you a glass of tea, but I'm afraid I'd wake the beast."

"That's all right," he drawled, picking up the magazine between us on the swing. "Doing some heavy reading?"

"I do read, if that's what you're implying. You'd think after your shameful performance of your school's alma mater last night, Remmy, that you'd have given up on trying to take a Columbia College girl down a notch."

He laughed, chocolate brown eyes flirting, announcing to the world that Remmy Wilkes, however refined and reserved he appeared on the outside, was trouble. "It was just a joke, Nettie; I am in no way implying you're not smart or that this girl"—he ran his long finger across the starlet's photo—"has anything on you."

"Other than being a movie star, of course." And the guts to go home. "She's probably not tired or overworked. At least she doesn't look it." No, she looked like a girl who did the deed often and enjoyed it, and it gave me a small consolation that I'd never seen *that* look on Sissy's face. But I had seen a glimpse of it on my own, the night Brooks and I came so close to making love in the grove.

"Fair enough, but I do have a prescription for what ails you. A little further over to the right on the radio dial, there's another soap opera that comes on after the one Miss Emily listens to." He laughed when my eyebrows nearly touched my hairline. "I know this because I have a lot of women patients, I hear them talking about which program is best. Just switch the channel while she's asleep. My guess is Miss Emily will keep right on dreaming, and it'll buy you another hour's peace." Just as he looked at his watch, the music came up on *Backstage Wife*, and the announcer began wrapping up the broadcast.

"And what do I say when she wakes up to a different story entirely?"

"Women like Miss Emily, once they get to a certain age, when they question themselves, they do it internally. They don't want folks to think they're getting old. More than likely, she'll think she changed the station herself."

I couldn't help but smile at the very idea of Remmy trying to help me outfox Miss Emily, and, when I did, that swoon-worthy crooked grin of his grew wider. I was completely unaffected; however, I was grateful for the suggestion. Grateful enough to tease him, just a little. "Why, Doctor Wilkes, that's down right diabolical. Do you scheme like this with all your patients?"

"Only the pretty ones." He shrugged and got up from the swing. "You stay here and get some rest. I'm gonna test my theory." He disappeared into the house while I drank sweet tea and pondered Remmy Wilkes knowing my secret.

Oh, who was I kidding? How could there be any secret when the entire student body of Columbia College knew my sister was carrying my fiancé's baby? And I was reasonably certain that even Miss Emily in all her demonic glory wouldn't expel me from her house for being a woman scorned.

Moments later, I heard the slippery baritone voice of a different announcer, catching listeners up on another soap opera. I have to confess I was elated when I didn't hear Miss Emily's shrill voice, demanding I walk up the wall and scrub the ceilings until they gleamed. And I was also just the tiniest bit disappointed when Remmy didn't come right back out onto the porch.

About twenty minutes passed before he returned to the swing, with a very cocky grin on his face and having helped himself to a glass of tea.

"She's still alive? I haven't killed her yet?" I smirked.

"Miss Lurleen or Miss Emily?" he said.

"Both. Either." I set my tea glass on the small table beside me, ready to run in and see for myself.

"Don't get all flustered again, Nettie. Miss Emily has her head reared back, sawing logs. She may have some sinus problem going on from the sound of it. Wish she'd let me examine her here or come into the office so I could check her, make sure she's okay. Maybe you could help with that."

"If I demanded she never set foot in your office again, that might do the trick. And Miss Lurleen?"

"Well, you were right; she likes you." My face went tight at the notion of Remmy testing Miss Lurleen's opinion of me by sharing my predicament. "Relax, Nettie, I didn't tell her anything, and I won't. It's not my place."

He was lifting his tea glass to his lips when he caught sight of the underside of my arms. His brow furrowed as he set his glass beside mine. He didn't ask to examine me, he just did, pulling both of my arms straight, away from my body and turning my palms up. He ran his fingers over the tender angry skin. "Who did this to you, Nettie? Was it that Brooks bastard?"

In all my life, I'd never heard Brooks called anything but good and decent. But it wasn't Remmy's insult that unnerved me; it was his possessive tone that said he had a right to ask that question, one that went beyond being a good doctor.

I jerked my arms back and wrapped them around myself. "Not that it's any of your business, but no."

"Tell me who did this to you, Nettie? Good God, was it Miss Emily? Tell me who hurt you," he demanded.

"It wasn't anybody. I did it to myself," I snapped.

"Nettie," he whispered. "Why?"

"It's something I do, to break a bad habit or a bad thought, and I'm sure you can imagine from the looks of me I've had some seriously bad thoughts to squash and the day isn't even over yet. Honestly, I've never considered actually taking another life, but Miss Emily has a way about her that would make even the best soul question that line of thinking." I ran my hands over the bruises. They did look horrible, and if I'd seen the same on Sue or Patrice or any of my friends, I would have had the same reaction as Remmy. "I appreciate your concern, really I do, and I know it looks terrible. I promise I'll find a different way to deal with my frustrations, one that doesn't disfigure or mar."

"Let me take you out," he said firmly, which had nothing to do with anything, and made me feel even more uncomfortable than I already did. "Take your mind off of your situation, this job."

The idea was sweet and honorable, enticing even. But there was no way in hell I was going to get on Katie Wilkes's bad side, dating her brother. "Ah, but you forget, Dr. Wilkes. I'm stuck here, twenty-four hours a day, seven days a week until somebody dies. And, hopefully it will not be me."

He was unaffected by my attempt at humor. "Then sleep when the baby sleeps," he said evenly.

"I beg your pardon?" I hissed.

"I don't bring it up to be cruel, Nettie, but it's what a new mother has to do—what anyone learns when they care for someone who's ill. Relax for the first hour when Miss Emily's first soap opera comes on, change the channel before she wakes up, and then take a nap during the second hour. It'll help you cope. Keep you healthy. With any luck, Miss Emily and Miss Lurleen will be asleep before nine and you can have some time to yourself."

I had to admit that a nap sounded really good, and the sisters going to bed just after the sun went down, even better. So much so that I suddenly realized I was grinning from ear to ear.

"And while I'd never ask you to abandon your post," he added, "maybe you'd do me the honor of allowing me to porch sit with you on occasions. Like tonight for example. Say, around nine thirty?"

"A reward if your theory is correct."

"Precisely," he said.

"And is it proper for the good doctor to porch sit, unchaperoned with the new girl in town? I don't think your sister would like that at all."

"I'm a grown man, Nettie. What my sister thinks about where and with whom I spend my time is none of her concern."

"I'm sorry, have you met your sister?"

"Come on, Nettie. Say yes."

"All right then. But please don't tell Katie. I've seen her in action, and I don't want to get on her naughty list. She can be frightening."

"And on that ridiculous but accurate assumption, I'll leave, but I'll see you tonight."

There are certain words, phrases between a girl and a guy, that no matter what the circumstances are, whether good or bad, they demand to be punctuated with a kiss. Remmy's promise felt that way, even if I didn't want it to, even if I was the tiniest bit disappointed there was no kiss. He walked to his car, folded the top down, and waved before he got in and drove away.

12

NETTIE

Say what you will about Justine, high priestess of the catty mean girls, but if love is indeed war, she put General Patton and all of his strategists to shame. Without fail, she knew when to advance and when to retreat, and on her worst day, she could make Scarlett O'Hara look like mealymouthed Melanie. While the majority of my C-Square sisters jumped at the first proposal to come along, dating a boy never altered Justine one bit. Not the way it did other girls who seemed to kowtow to any single guy with a decent-looking pompadour and pair of penny loafers.

I suspect Justine came into the world knowing herself. She was the only girl who entertained eleven guys on the kissing couch in the commons room our freshman year. Of course not at the same time, but I wouldn't have put it past her. While girls like Doris Shelley were putting up with boyfriends who catted around and begging those cads not to break up with them, Justine called the shots. I wanted to be the girl who called the shots; I only wish I'd paid closer attention as to exactly how Justine wielded her power.

Miss Lurleen was asleep before eight thirty. I'd piled my hair on top of my head and soaked in the tub until I was sufficiently pruney. Miss Emily's room was dark around nine when I came out of the bathroom, and she was definitely snoring. Back home if Brooks was coming over, I would have spent hours picking out the right outfit, primping, something Justine certainly did. But I was too tired to preen for anyone, and besides, this wasn't a date. I left my hair on top of my head and slipped into a pair of denim pedal pushers and a navy gingham wraparound blouse.

Until I opened the refrigerator and poured two glasses of sweet tea, the house was dark save the hall light upstairs. Closing the door, the house was dark again, including the porch. After one day of Miss Emily working me like a Hebrew slave, I knew every inch of the house and made it out to the swing just fine with the scant light from upstairs.

I sat there for a few minutes, then moved to the glider, then the rocker like Goldilocks. The glider was directly across from the rocker but was squeaky. The runners on the ladder-back rocker were so worn down, the chair barely moved but did just enough to feel unstable, so I chose the swing.

Remmy came up the sidewalk, walking at a good clip. He was still dressed in his dark slacks and white dress shirt sans tie. Maybe this really was a date.

What was I doing? Other than the Eldridge sisters, Remmy and I had nothing in common. And he was old, not *old* old, but certainly a good bit older than me. Experienced I'm sure with the likes of powerful women like Justine. Probably not a good guinea pig to test my prowess, or lack thereof, on.

"Hey, Nettie," he said quietly, no kiss on the cheek. My body was aching and too tired to scheme properly, or anticipate his first move. Then he threw me off completely when he took the rocker. I was glad the porch was mostly dark so he couldn't see my face all flushed. I scooted into the middle of the swing. "Hey, Remmy."

"You're still alive," he laughed.

"Barely, but yes. How was your day?"

"Long." Silence. Crickets chirped to fill the gap. Absolutely nothing in common. "Started with Jimmy Setzler; he's six. Mom brought him in for a sore throat, and he bit the crap out of me."

"Why?" I laughed.

"After his mom whipped him good, even after I told her there was no need, the poor kid confessed his older brother told him I was a Communist spy set on snatching him and selling him to the Russian army."

"That's terrible."

"That's a big brother for you. When I was ten, I got in trouble for convincing Katie she was adopted. Had her going pretty good until she started to cry because Mama and Daddy had bought her from the gypsies. I'm not sure gypsies deserve the bad rap, but I sure got my hide tanned by Mama and then again when Daddy got home from work."

"That's terrible. They didn't have to punish you twice."

"I turned out all right."

"No, I mean what you did was terrible," I laughed.

"Katie turned out okay too. You have siblings?"

I nodded, but I don't think he could see me. "A younger sister."

"And you never did anything like that?"

"She's always been my shadow. At first, I accepted it, but when I got to be maybe twelve, I started to resent it. So I told her our house was haunted. I'd take her things, a hairbrush, her favorite doll when she wasn't looking and then blame it on the ghosts. My grandmother's and two uncles' homes were right by ours. I thought maybe she'd go running to one of their homes and stay there forever. But it only made her stick closer to me.

"One morning my mother couldn't find her car keys. When my sister burst out crying and told her the ghost must have them, Mother figured out what I'd done. She made me give everything back and apologize before she switched my legs good."

"Ghosts, huh?" Remmy chuckled. "So you lived in the middle of an orange grove? What was that like?"

"I call it an orange grove here because nobody here knows what satsumas are, which is what we call them back home. Satsumas are sweet, smaller than a regular orange, about the size of a mandarin and have a loose skin like a tangerine."

"You miss home?"

I missed the flat fields of billowy white cotton and the tall graceful plots of corn. I missed the gnarly-looking satsumas after they'd lost their leaves and their glossy green foliage when it was decorated with tiny orange balls. I missed the tall pecan trees but not picking them up for Mother and certainly not shelling them. I missed the place I had at home, the eldest grandchild and first of two girls that were treasured even though my father was trying for boys in hopes he'd have more farmhands. I missed my mother and wondered how I was ever going to look her in the eye again after reading her letter or the way I'd last talked to her. And Sissy, who had always been my shadow; I missed her most.

"Yes," I whispered, moving the swing slowly back and forth, the old chains groaning under my weight.

"It's in your voice." And I swear I felt his smile in the dark. "You wanna talk about it?" I thought he might come sit beside me, but he didn't, and wanting him to didn't make me feel very powerful at all. I had no idea what Justine would do in a predicament like this. The truth was she wouldn't be in a situation like mine, but I suspected if she were, she'd be tight-lipped about it, change the subject.

"It must be a little strange taking care of patients who've known you since you were born."

"Indeed, it is strange and frustrating, too. Parts of it are nice."

"Do you like being a doctor in your hometown?"

He blew out a breath. I wasn't sure what that meant, but I could feel he wasn't comfortable with the question. "Since I met a certain redhead, I'm liking it a whole lot better." He laughed, but his tone said there was more to it than that.

"So just yesterday, before that redhead came along, you didn't like it much?"

"I've wanted out of Camden since I took over my father's practice. Even interviewed for a job at Baptist Hospital yesterday, which by the way Katie doesn't know about. Other than the fact that the job isn't in Charleston, it's what I've always wanted."

"What's in Charleston?"

"What isn't in Charleston? Food that could put Cora May's to shame. And if you tell her I said that, I'll deny it till my last breath. The culture, so many things that made me feel like I belonged there."

"And you never felt like you belonged here, in idyllic Camden?" I teased.

"When I was a kid, yes. I just never wanted to settle here; it felt too much like I was living my father's life and not mine. How about you? Do you like it here?"

"Very much, although the strangest thing happened today," I said.

"So what happened, Miss Gilbert, that was so very strange?"

"A reporter from the *Camden Chronicle* called and asked if the sisters had any news."

"And how is that unusual?"

"I just thought it was odd she was calling to scare up news."

"The *Camden Chronicle*'s kind of a big deal."

"Okay, but why was she calling here for news?"

"You had a chance to look at a paper yet?"

"Does using it to clean windows count? Because I did my share of that today."

"It was probably Appie Speed Watkins who called; she writes a little bit of everything including the Camden Chatter column. It's kind of a society column. My mother used to get a call every week, Katie takes the calls now. As a matter of fact, Katie talked to Mrs. Appie this morning; I'm pretty sure you'll see your name in next week's paper, unless some other big news eclipses your visit."

"My name?"

"Something like, 'Last Thursday, Miss Nettie Gilbert, a resident of Satsuma, Alabama, as well as a student at Columbia College, visited Miss Katie Wilkes, also a CC alum. After a superb roast beef dinner prepared by Cora May Johnson, the two sat on the Wilkeses' porch during the recent power outage and argued the superiority of their school to no avail with the esteemed Dr. Remmy Wilkes.'"

"That ranks as big news? Kind of disturbing," I laughed. "What about President Eisenhower or Communist aggression?"

"They don't have anything on the Camden Cotillion Club let alone the society page. So you know what this all means, don't you?" I shook my head. "You're big news, Nettie Gilbert."

13

EMILY

A week ago, Miss Priss showed up for work like she was dressed for church, but not today. In dungarees and a cotton shirt that was no longer crisp or white, she'd positively made the bathroom tile gleam, while answering the cowbell every time it clanged. Yes, it shouldn't take much more of that to send the girl packing.

And Emily was reasonably sure something was going on between the girl and the good doctor Wilkes, which would explain why he stopped by every single day. Of course that had to be why. It couldn't be because Sister was worse. And then Remmy had confounded Emily, who admittedly was eavesdropping, and probably Lurleen too when he'd said Sister *should* get out of the bed unless she wanted to die sooner. But getting out of her bed might indeed kill her. Honestly, how any institution of higher learning gave that man a diploma to practice tiddlywinks much less practice modern medicine was beyond her.

"*Emily*," Lurleen hollered, ringing the bell.

Well the old girl must have forgotten about her hired help. Emily turned on the radio. *Backstage Wife* would be on any minute. She hurried down the hall to the bathroom, where the girl was scrubbing twenty years' worth of mineral deposits off of the toilet with a pumice stone. "The bell tolls for thee." Emily smirked at her clever remark that earned the tiniest hint of a sneer.

The girl threw the stone on the floor, making spatter marks on the outside of the toilet. "And you'll clean that up when you come back," Emily said.

She rinsed off her hands and pushed by Emily without a word, and Emily couldn't blame her. The girl's attempts at kindness and humor the first few days had been rebuffed so often, she didn't try anymore. But she did use the breaks Emily gave her to sit with Lurleen, read to her. And Lurleen seemed to really like the girl's cooking, because she'd cleaned her plate every meal, which she hadn't done in weeks. It was a slap in the face to Emily, although she was so pleased with Lurleen's appetite, she had no intention of complaining.

"She wants you," the girl said flatly, without a smidgeon of manners.

At five minutes to four? What was Sister thinking? If she made Emily miss her story . . .

She entered the room to see her sister propped up on pillows in freshly pressed cases, sheets with every single wrinkle pressed out, not just once, but, after Emily pointed out the error of the girl's ways, twice. "The girl said you wanted to see me."

"She has a name. It's Nettie, and she's sweet and helpful, and a very good cook, I might add," Lurleen barked. "Close the door."

Emily sucked in a breath and dug her fists into her hips. "Are you saying I'm not a good cook?"

"I'm saying you're a bitch."

Emily's heart lurched hard against her chest; she closed the door and spun around to glare at Lurleen. "What did you say to me?"

"You heard me. I've only said that word one time in my life, and I won't say it again."

"You've lost your mind."

"No, but I believe you have. And keep your voice down or so help me Emily, I'll never speak to you again."

The words children say all the time but don't really mean, that adults say without thought, settled between them. Emily hated the threat, the reminder of that horrible time in their lives when Lurleen didn't speak to her.

"*You*. Working that poor girl like a rented mule. What in the world is wrong with you? She's here to take care of me and help you. She promised me she wouldn't let you run her off, but honest to Pete, if I were her, I would have reneged on that promise without a second thought. And in her condition; she's—"

Emily blinked at Lurleen and pretended to be unaffected. She was wounded, but she'd die before she let it show. Lurleen droned on, her tone hushed until Emily couldn't take it anymore. "Oh, pish-posh, Lurleen, what condition? She's hired help. She's doing it for the money."

"She's doing it for me," Lurleen hissed. "And I think she's expecting."

"Expecting? Well, then she's got to go. We can't have some way-ward woman in our home."

"She's not wayward, and don't say a word about it because I'm not one hundred percent sure. What I am sure of is she's not going any-where. She's staying right here for as long as she likes. So I'm asking, no, I'm *demanding* that you stop acting like the Pharaoh's taskmaster this instant."

"Sister, you're in no position to be making demands," Emily snapped.

"Don't make me get out of this bed and haul that sweet girl up to you face-to-face so you can see what you're doing to her. It's not right, Emily, and I won't stand for it."

Emily bit her lip to keep from saying what she was really thinking. Lurleen swearing at her. Lurleen taking up for the girl, gobbling down her cooking like she hadn't eaten anything worth having in weeks. Who did she think she was? "I don't want her here. You knew that, that *g.d.* doctor knew that, but did you listen to me? No."

"I don't care what you want, Emily. Her being here is for your own good and mine. But as tough as she is, you're wearing her down to the nub and I won't have it."

Emily looked at her watch. She'd already missed the prologue of her story, and now Mary Noble's sweet voice sounded in peril. Without a word, she turned on her heel and left Lurleen's room, slamming the door before taking her place on the wingback beside the radio. She pulled the footstool out and propped up her feet, trying to forget about how horrible Lurleen had been to her and trying to decipher what had already happened in the story.

But she was so angry with her sister, even sweet Mary Noble couldn't save her. Emily picked up the girl's magazine and flipped through the first few pages. Larry Noble was being a horse's ass to poor Mary. It was a bad day all around for good women everywhere. But Emily had found that new soap opera by luck. It was a good story, although not quite as racy as *Backstage Wife*.

The girl came out of the bathroom. She hadn't eaten any lunch, not that Emily knew of. Was she expecting? She didn't look it, and if she was, it wasn't good for her to skip meals. Or perhaps work so hard. "Did you eat?" She looked at Emily like she'd suddenly sprouted nine heads. "You heard me. Did you eat today?"

"Breakfast," she clipped. It was after four, and she'd had nothing since six a.m.? That wasn't good. The girl eyed her magazine in Emily's hands. No, Emily had *not* asked for permission; this was her house. She'd do as she pleased. "But I'm not hungry," she added.

"Well, you *are* going to eat, even if it's just a little something. I don't know what you said to my sister to get her so riled, but I won't be accused of starving you." Emily raised her eyebrows. "So, even if it's just a piece of fruit, you'll eat. Is that understood?"

"Yes, ma'am, but I won't discuss Miss Lurleen with you," she said evenly.

Oh, the gall of that child. "Do as I say." Emily pointed to the kitchen. The girl disappeared and returned with a glass of tea and held an apple up for Emily's inspection. "I'll be on the porch until your soap opera is over. Then I'll finish the toilet."

"See that you do."

REMMY

Nettie?" She looked gaunt, almost comatose, and completely undone. "Are you all right?" Remmy hurried to the swing, dropped his bag, and sat down beside her. Her fingernails were broken and ragged, hands that were so graceful were now rough and chapped. Her long, beautiful red hair was in a sad ponytail, the tattered tie nearly falling out. "Honey, are you all right?"

"I shall not be moved," she said with such little conviction, Remmy was tempted to take her pulse. "And did you just call me honey?"

From nine until around eleven, he'd spent the last seven nights with Nettie, and they were the nicest he'd had in a very long time. She'd sat in the glider while he'd sat in the swing and they'd talked about music, which Remmy knew absolutely nothing about except he liked it, and Nettie seemed to need it to breathe.

She'd asked him about being a small-town doctor, which should have stuck in his craw, but Nettie had seemed utterly enchanted with his stories. She seemed to like him, but she was still adamant about Katie not knowing about his after-dark visits.

Remmy hadn't said anything to Katie because it was none of her damn business. Besides, he liked having those two hours to himself with just Nettie. She was smart and funny, and he felt her soft drawl in his bones. All good reasons to avoid talking to her about the baby. If she'd run from whatever her situation was with this Brooks fellow, she might run from him too if he pushed the issue, and that bothered him even more than the idea of that bastard fathering her child. Besides, he liked her and he wanted her to like him enough to trust him enough to tell him about the baby.

"I wasn't being forward. Honey." Remmy smirked, resisting the urge to tuck a strand of hair behind her ear. Instead he reached for her wrist. Her pulse rate was way too fast for someone resting. "You scared the hell out of me, Nettie. You just looked so—"

"Bedraggled? Thanks a lot, Remmy."

Yanking the tie out of her long, red mane, she shook her head, then arched her back and gathered it into a ponytail, securing it with the ribbon and raising her eyebrows at him. *Happy?* God, yes, and if she didn't look so tired, he'd ask her to do that again.

"Is that you, Remmy Wilkes?" Miss Emily called from inside. "Leave Nettie alone; she's resting."

"I'll be in to check on Miss Lurleen in a few minutes," Remmy hollered, smiling at Nettie.

"And that would be the first time she's addressed me by anything other than *girl*," Nettie said.

"So, she's still being a pill."

"Yes, but what she doesn't know is that it makes me even more determined to do my job, because Miss Lurleen is a dear. Or maybe she isn't but in comparison to her evil sister she seems to be."

"I take it Miss Emily didn't fall asleep during her story today."

"No, something has her peeved, something her sister said to her. I'm sure I'll pay for it later."

"Working yourself up like this isn't good for you. How are you feeling?"

"Tired." She blew out a breath and took a swig of tea. "Really tired. One minute I want to cry, the next I want to scream."

"That's normal."

"Well, thank goodness. Is wanting to strangle the life out of Miss Emily normal too?"

"Yes, but in your condition I wouldn't advise it," Remmy laughed. He knelt by the swing and took her slender ankles and put them on the swing. "Keep your legs propped up and rest a bit. Doctor's orders."

Just then Miss Emily pushed the screen door open. "Don't tell me you're forcing your worthless doctoring on this poor girl. Leave her be, Remmy Wilkes."

"I'll see you in a few minutes," he said to Nettie. She shrugged and pressed her glass of tea against her forehead and closed her eyes.

At just over six-two, Remmy towered over Miss Emily. He pushed by her, eyes narrowed, testing his own restraint. He went straight to Miss Lurleen's room and knocked on the door. "Remmy, is that you?" she called. She was sitting up in the bed reading the Bible. Her color was good. Breathing steady. Her face was definitely fuller thanks to the extra fluid that came with congestive heart failure.

"Hey, Miss Lurleen. You all right?"

"Well aside from the fact that I'm dying, yes. You always ask me how I'm feeling. Do I look particularly bad today?"

"No, ma'am, on the contrary." He took her pulse. A little high. "Except for some extra fluid, your color looks really good; you have a little spark in your eyes. Just trying to figure out what the difference is because whatever it is, you ought to do more of it."

"Well, I just lambasted my sister, if that's what you mean. That's why I'm sitting here reading the Bible and trying to repent. Honest to Pete, I love Emily, but she can unnerve me like nobody's business."

Remmy laughed and nodded. "She can, but I suspect it's just that protective streak of hers. Before I came to check on you, Miss Emily was fussing at me about bothering Nettie."

"And I was fussing at her about the way she's treating Nettie, working her to the bone. Being mean. It's shameful, and I told her I won't have it."

Remmy checked her blood pressure, then listened to her heart.

No change. "Your pressure is good, heart sounds good. Lungs, not so good. Are you still taking your water pills, your digitalis?"

"Yes," she clipped, and looked away.

He pulled the covers back to see her ankles were swollen and painful looking. The opal ring she wore on her right hand was cutting into her finger. "How's your appetite?"

"Nettie's a fine cook. I've been eating like a horse."

"And she's following the no-salt diet?" The old woman blushed hard. "Miss Lurleen? You know salt will kill you."

"Maybe, but I'm not dead yet."

"All right, I'll speak to Nettie about your diet."

"You try eating eggs without salt, Remmy, or anything that's not sweet and good. But if you do speak to her, it's not her fault; she didn't know I wasn't supposed to have this." Miss Lurleen opened her bedside table drawer and pulled out a saltshaker that was three-fourths empty. "I stole it from my lunch tray one day and haven't regretted it since."

"Well, I hope her giving you a salt block to lick isn't the only reason you're fond of her."

"No. She's a nice girl, and I hope she'll stay on after—after I'm gone."

"She is nice," Remmy said, putting his stethoscope back in his bag. He rolled the blood pressure cuff up and tossed it in too.

"After I'm gone, I want her to stay for Emily. And if she does—if she does, I want you to deliver her baby; I'll instruct Emily to cover the cost."

Baby? So Miss Lurleen knew about Nettie's condition. Could he treat Nettie Gilbert? Absolutely. But he didn't know how she would feel about that, and he knew she'd be better off in the hands of a specialist. "Miss Lurleen, Nettie might feel more comfortable seeing a gynecologist, and Dr. May's practice is growing; I hear she's a very fine doctor."

"Well, whatever Nettie decides, I'm sure she'll need to see someone soon. She hasn't mentioned her condition to me, maybe she's trying to hide it, but she can't hide it forever. And I want her to be healthy, and the baby, of course. That's why I ordered Emily to be nice, to go easier on her. She really is a dear."

"Funny, she said the same thing about you." Remmy smiled.

"Will you talk to her about seeing a doctor?" Miss Lurleen reopened her Bible.

"Of course." Tonight. When he was sure they'd be alone, he would. Even if it meant it would send her running again.

NETTIE

I'd begged off earlier when Katie called asking if I wanted to meet her at one of the restaurants on Broad Street for supper. She made me promise I'd come to dinner next Sunday at her house and said she wouldn't take no for an answer. As much as I liked her and would have welcomed having someone closer my own age to talk to, I was too tired to do anything other than work all day and flop in the bed. Well, except for visiting with Remmy. I was surprised at just how much I anticipated his next visit, which was probably very un-Justine-like, but I'd given up on being a vixen.

I liked it when he came to see me, not Miss Lurleen, who really was sweet, and certainly not Miss Emily, who had drawn in her claws after her conversation with her sister earlier. And yes, with the bathroom door open and hunched over the toilet, I'd heard a little of their conversation, but the moment Miss Lurleen called her sister a bitch, I stopped eavesdropping and closed the door. When Miss Emily emerged from the bedroom, she pushed the door open and gave me a look. I sure she was going to fire me on the spot. But she'd gone straight to her chair for soap opera time, and that was more than fine by me.

By dinnertime, she was much less combative, and even complimented the Apple Betty I'd made when I took it out of the oven. But the best part of Miss Emily laying down her cross was that Miss Lurleen rewarded her by coming out of her room for dinner. Of course she was completely out of breath and nearly collapsed at the kitchen table, but there the three of us were, enjoying a fine meal of chicken-fried steak and gravy and an array of lovely vegetables Miss Emily canned over last summer.

"Nettie," Miss Lurleen began. "You're a wonderful cook. Everything you've made has been delicious."

Her inflection implied there was a *but* coming. I was no stranger to criticism; every time I played for my instructors, I anxiously awaited their thoughts on how to make the piece better and, of course, how wonderful I was, which sounds conceited but is not. Every artist, or at least the ones I knew, thrived on accolades, but it was the ones who continued to better their craft beyond the accolades who were the true musicians.

However, my cooking was an entirely different story. I wasn't always gifted in the kitchen like I was at the keyboard. Even if I became the personal chef for the president of the United States, there were many past trials and even more errors that had given way to family jokes back home that would never die. So, I was a little sensitive about my cooking.

"Yes ma'am?" I set my fork down.

"Oh, honey, don't look so dejected." Miss Lurleen put her hand on mine. "I wasn't trying to say the food is bad."

"She's saying it's going to kill her," Miss Emily snapped, and after a stern look from her sister, she added, "*dear*. It's the salt."

"Yes, well, my sweet sister *could have* told you, but, apparently, she was trying to kill me too. Otherwise, she would have, but Remmy says I have to lay off the salt. And, as much as I've loved having it the past few days, surprisingly even more so than sugar, you should probably cook without it, and you and Emily can add it to your plates as you see fit."

"Oh, Miss Lurleen." I put my napkin on the table, unable to eat another bite knowing I'd almost killed that sweet lady. "I'm so sorry. I'll throw the box out to make sure I don't add it out of habit."

"No you won't. Lurleen has to watch her consumption. There's no need for the rest of us to fall on her sword," Miss Emily said, punctuating her words with the saltshaker. "And *you* finish your dinner. You'll need your strength."

"Because we're giving you the day off tomorrow," Miss Lurleen said. Miss Emily jerked her head around at her sister, eyes bugging out. "Emily and I both feel like you deserve it. Don't we, Emily?"

"I suppose," she said tightly.

I'd seen the list of chores Miss Emily had made. It was four and a half pages long, and some things were repeated as many as three times at various places on the list, like she'd forgotten she'd already added them. There were only two pages left, and you can only steam iron unmentionables so many times.

Oddly enough, the piano was not on the list, but then it already gleamed. It called to me, begging me to sit at the keyboard and play. I gave in once and touched the upper keys, but nothing happened. Just the dull thud of the hammer missing the brass strings altogether. Why would someone, presumably Miss Emily, take such good care of the outside but never the inside? This morning, before Miss Lurleen enforced the peace, Miss Emily caught me running my hand across the keys, but not pressing them. Right away, her stern look told me the piano was off-limits.

"Why don't I finish up any chores you have for me, Miss Emily, and then take Sunday afternoon off?"

"You're such a gem, Nettie." Miss Lurleen squeezed my hand.

"Yes, isn't she," Miss Emily said dryly. "Now eat."

I should have cared that Remmy Wilkes was coming calling, about how I looked or what I wore. I did, however, bathe out of common courtesy because I smelled to high heaven after attempting to turn over Miss Lurleen's garden by hand. When the head of the hoe finally broke off in the harsh clay, I almost got down on my knees and kissed the ground. Knowing full well that chore would be added to tomorrow's list, I didn't.

After a long soak in the sparkling-clean bathtub, I slipped on an old pair of blue jeans with a white cotton T-shirt and combed out my wet hair before taking my place on the porch swing. Perhaps I didn't care about my appearance because I felt comfortable with Remmy or because the porch was unlit. But there was no compulsion to impress him; he was just a friend who came calling, albeit after dark.

I saw him coming down the sidewalk, walking briskly, fading in and out of the light from the full moon that filtered through the clouds and ancient oak trees. Dressed in jeans and a short-sleeved shirt, he looked younger than he did in the crisp white shirt and black tie he normally wore. He waved at the dark porch, though I wasn't sure he could see me.

"Hey, Nettie," he drawled, bounding up the steps. I stood and for a moment it felt like he was going to kiss my cheek, but he didn't.

"Hey, Remmy," I breathed. We sat down in the swing, a switch from him sitting in the rocker across from me. "How was your day?"

"After I left here? Busy. Katie had me on a bunch of house calls. I finished up with my last patient at the office about an hour ago. Went home, took a shower, and came right over." He moved the swing back and forth slowly.

"You didn't eat? I bet Katie wasn't happy about that," I said, letting him control the rhythm.

"My sister is not my keeper, though she sure as hell thinks she is. It's good to shake her up every now and then to remind her of that."

"By missing a meal?" I asked. "There's probably a better way, like flat out telling her."

"I tell her all the time, but like most women, she hears what she wants when she wants."

"I should be insulted, but it seems wrong to punish you for being right. I made a lovely Apple Betty; would you like some?"

"Sounds good," he said.

I opened the screen door, taking care it didn't bounce in the jamb as neither of the sisters seemed to have a hearing problem.

Although with Miss Emily upstairs and Miss Lurleen in the back bedroom downstairs, it was doubtful they'd hear anything anyway. While I was doing nothing wrong with Remmy Wilkes, moving stealthily through the house, it felt that way. I eased the refrigerator door open, pulled out the pan, and scraped a generous serving into a bowl. I didn't bother with the horrible store-bought ice cream like Miss Emily and Miss Lurleen had with their desserts at suppertime. However I did pour him a glass of milk to wash it down.

Remmy was standing by the door when I returned, opened it for me, and took the bowl and cup, returning to the swing. I sat down beside him, knees pulled up to my chest, smiling as he devoured the dessert. In less than two minutes, he set the empty bowl on the table beside the swing and started on the milk. "You were hungry," I said.

"Didn't think I was, but it was really good."

"Thanks."

He raked his hands across the tops of his thighs. "So, how are you feeling?"

My laugh was soft and unintentionally flirty. "Why do you keep asking how I feel?"

"Aside from the fact that I'm a doctor and that's what I do?" The scant light revealed the faint outline of his face and a smile that made me wish the light from the hallway wasn't so stingy, because I really wanted to see Remmy Wilkes, smiling, relaxed, looking at me.

"Yes," I said, "aside from that."

"I don't know, Nettie; you're smart and funny."

As much as I didn't want or need any kind of romantic involvement, I liked Remmy Wilkes. "Really? I could say the same thing about you."

"I like you," he said simply.

The words wound tight around me, terrifying and exciting me in equal measure. "Oh."

He laughed, easing the tension until he took my hand, making my pulse skyrocket. "Relax, Nettie. Liking you is not a bad thing."

It wasn't bad; it was just foreign. Having another man hold my hand, move me with just a few words. Part of my brain said to say good night right then and there and send Remmy Wilkes on his way. The other part of my brain echoed back: Remmy Wilkes was beautiful and good. "No. It's not a bad thing," I said, unwinding my legs so that my bare feet were on the floor.

I have no idea where the notion came from. I suspect it was there since the day I met Remmy, but I thought I would die if I had to live another second without knowing what it felt like to kiss him. And in the most forward moment of my life, I leaned in and touched my lips to his. He let go of my hand and threaded his hands in my hair and took control of the kiss, our tongues tangling, our breath in perfect rapid time. I was shocked to the bone at how very much I liked kissing a man who was not Brooks Carver, or more precisely a man who was Remmy Wilkes.

I moved closer for more. He pulled me onto his lap and slid his hand to my bottom to hold me in place. I was breathless when we pulled apart and he pressed his forehead to mine. "Nettie," he whispered. "We have to talk."

Even though I'd had little to no experience with men, I was reasonably sure no good conversation ever began with those words. I scooted back to my side of the swing and drew my knees up to my chest again.

"And that's not a bad thing either," he said, taking my hand. "We've already established that I like you. It should be obvious that I'm attracted to you, and if it's not, let me just say that you're gorgeous, and I am very much attracted to you."

His conciliatory tone made my stomach dip. "But you're holding my situation against me. Aren't you?"

"Up until a few seconds ago, I was holding *you* against me, so no. But your situation does matter to me."

I jerked my hand away. "My *situation* is none of your business, Remmy."

"Maybe. But it matters to me. You matter to me. What I'm trying to say is, with the baby coming—"

Good God, was there no way to escape my sister and her infamous child? "*The baby* isn't your concern, Remmy."

"But I am worried about you, and I feel guilty that I'm partly responsible for putting you in a place where you're being worked to death. In your condition, you should—"

"*In my condition?*" What? Deserted? Scorned? Wait? My *condition?* "I'm not expecting, Remmy, if that's what you're implying," I bit out. "But my sister is, with my fiancé's baby, or my ex-fiancé."

There was a throbbing in my ears, my own heartbeat racing like a freight train. And if I could have pulled up the floorboards, I would have slid underneath the porch with the spiders and God only knew what else to escape Remmy Wilkes and the pity I felt radiating off of him.

"Nettie, I'm so sorry." He reached for my hand again, but I jerked away. "From what your roommate and some of the other girls at the college said, I just assumed—"

"*Incorrectly.*"

"Yeah." He leaned back in the swing and blew out a deep breath. "Okay. Yeah, I'm an idiot, but I have to be honest, I'm more than relieved."

"That I'm not knocked up?" I bit out.

"The world isn't kind to unmarried girls who are expecting." Ah, but Sissy had managed to remake the world so that it revolved around her and her baby. "I've seen it, and I didn't want that for you."

"So, what was your plan, Remmy Wilkes? Were you going to save me from the horrible world? Marry me?"

"There's no reason to be angry at me, Nettie. As for your question, I hadn't gotten that far yet. But I was going to make damn sure you were taken care of and that you were taking care of yourself. Do whatever I could for you."

"And that included kissing me and hauling me onto your lap?"

"Hey, you started the kissing, and make no mistake, I'm glad you did. I wanted to kiss you that first night I walked you to the guest bedroom at my house, but I was afraid that you'd think I was being presumptuous." My entire body pulsed with anger and embarrassment. "And if I'm being honest, Nettie, I'm glad you're not carrying another man's child. If there was anything that bothered me about your situation, or what I assumed your situation was, it was—"

"That I was damaged goods?"

"No. I didn't like the idea of another man touching you."

I stood for him to leave, but he didn't budge. "You should go, Remmy."

"I think I should stay, and you should tell me how you feel about this horrible thing that happened to you."

"Oh, so now you've gone from playing doctor to psychiatrist?" I hissed.

"This isn't about me, but you? You have a right to feel hurt, to feel betrayed; I can't imagine everything you're going through, but if what happened was enough to make you leave college a couple months shy of graduation, it must have torn your guts out. So, unless you ask me again, I won't go. You don't even have to talk if you don't want to; just sit back down and be with me."

14

EMILY

Not good for you to stay in bed all the time, Miss Lurleen, but it's equally important you don't overdo it.

As worthless as Remmy was, his words stuck in Emily's craw, making her feel hopeless. If Sister stayed in the bed and rested, she was going to die. If she got up and moved about, she was going to die.

Emily crawled into her own bed with her newspaper and a few magazines and let out a deep sigh. She cursed herself for forgetting her reading glasses, then realized they were on top of her head. She lowered them onto her nose and opened the newspaper.

More People Die by the Knife and the Fork Than by the Gun and Sword the headline screamed. Wasn't that the truth. Emily didn't like Nettie, but she had enjoyed her cooking and hadn't said anything to her about the salt for purely selfish reasons. She'd hated having to worry about feeding Sister something that might kill her as much as she hated trying to add enough salt to her own food because it was almost impossible to get it to taste right once it was cooked.

She turned the page to see the Camden Cotillion Club had had their annual soiree before the Carolina Cup this past Saturday. Photos of rich horse people from up North and local well-to-do Camdenites dotted the page. There was a time when Emily would have not just attended all those balls, but she would have been the belle. But at some point, even though she always kept up her appearance, it didn't matter that she was the belle. She stopped going to the parties, and the invitations ceased.

She skimmed the Camden Chatter column to see so many folks had entertained out-of-town guests for the Cup. For Emily, the Carolina Cup used to be better than Christmas, a week of parties that culminated with a day of steeplechase. The pageantry of fine thoroughbreds and beauties like Emily was unmatched. Not that she was well traveled and would know, but it had to have been the case to attract the rich horse people and the likes of the DuPonts, the Williamses, the Buckleys.

The beginning of the column always listed upcoming dinner parties and cocktail parties. Newell Bolton's wife and the Nortons and the Lawrences were forever entertaining. The last entry was surprising to say the least. *Miss Katie Wilkes entertained Miss Nettie Gilbert in her home last week for a lovely dinner to celebrate Miss Gilbert's recent employment and move to Camden.* Good Lord.

Emily tossed the newspaper onto the floor and picked up *LIFE* magazine. Humph. That girl probably bought it because the actress on the cover favored her a bit. Emily used to do that, imagine she was Lillian Gish or a blond Edna Purviance, especially Edna with those expressive eyes. She had been Charlie Chaplin's favorite actress; he was even going to marry her until he chose another star-let over her. Emily flipped through the pages and stopped short. *Miracle in Palestine, Texas,* the headline blared.

She read and reread the article. Miracles in Palestine? Wasn't that the general vicinity where all those miracles in the Bible took place? Well, it was Texas and not the exact same Palestine. Still, it was an answer to prayer, albeit God only knows how far away Pales-tine was from the great state of South Carolina. Emily had never asked anything of Lurleen, not really. Not since John died and their brother disappeared, and Emily knew she had no right to ask any-thing of her now.

The snaggletoothed five-year-old boy in the picture on her bed-side table smiled back at her. Brother. Teddy. Perfect and happy. He was such a beautiful child. Emily was five when Mama announced Emily wouldn't be the baby of the family anymore. She was so angry at her parents as she watched Mama's belly grow, hating the baby inside that was coming to steal Emily's place in the world. And Daddy, goodness knows he always wanted a son; if he got his wish, Emily knew she'd be a dull and distant gleam in her father's eye. Then Brother came into the world. Beautiful. Perfect. Screaming for attention, and for the next eighteen years, Emily doted on him. Loved him to bits until he disappeared on his birthday.

There was no search party when he vanished. It was like the whole town was wishing Teddy good riddance, and who could blame them? Everyone from Emily's friends, to the preacher, to Brother's teachers, knew it was wasted effort to look for him. For years he'd been as wild as he knew how, taking chances. Hoping to die.

At first, all of Camden pitied him, which seemed to fuel his anger. But after a while, the patience of friends of their family, neighbors, the police grew thin, and it didn't matter that Teddy's life was changed by an accident. It didn't matter that he was on a path to destruction that was all Emily's doing. And then Mama died and that was it; he was just gone one morning. No note, no nothing. Just gone.

Since then, a day hadn't gone by that Emily didn't wonder where he was, pray for him. She prayed he'd married. She prayed he'd found peace. She prayed that God would give her just a small sign to let her know whether her baby brother was alive or dead. And while it was always tragic for death to steal someone young and in their prime, somehow *not* knowing what happened to Teddy was far worse, a constant pain that was as fresh today as it was the moment he went missing so long ago.

Yes, Emily would give anything to have her prayers answered. But she suspected not having any answers, never having any real peace, was her punishment.

REMMY

Remmy sat for two hours with his arms wrapped around her. His shirt was wet from tears she'd shed. And it was sheer torture, not being able to do anything for her other than hold her. His reward came about fifteen minutes into her crying jag when she wrapped her arms around his middle and her body relaxed into his.

By that point, he'd already lost himself in Nettie Gilbert. The way she felt pressed against him, the smell of her hair, the way her breath felt on his chest. After a good while, she moved her head from side to side against his chest until he laughed and then she laughed too, and that was just about the nicest sound he'd ever heard. "Did you just wipe your nose on my shirt?"

She pulled away just enough to run her hand over the wet spot. "Sorry," she whispered.

"That's a first," he said still holding her tight.

"You've never entertained a tearful woman, Dr. Wilkes?" She settled back onto her place on his chest.

"I have, but I'm not sure any of them wiped their noses on me."

"Maybe they did but you didn't notice."

"Maybe I didn't notice because they weren't you." He kissed the top of her head. "Not to be a broken record, but do you feel better?"

She nodded. "I didn't think I had any tears left. Guess I was wrong."

"It was a shitty thing they did, and you're entitled to every tear, every feeling."

"Maybe it wouldn't be so bad if my mother hadn't sent me an invitation to the wedding—"

"Are you kidding me? You're not going, are you?"

"No, I'm not. To be honest, I'm not even sure Brooks or Sissy is worth crying over, but my parents? All my relatives who knew but remained silent?"

"Maybe your relatives didn't know," Remmy offered.

She shook her head. "There was always a myriad of letters from home, but they suddenly stopped. From everyone. They knew. They just didn't know what to say to me. Besides, it wasn't their place to tell me Brooks was a cheat and Sissy is—"

"What?" Remmy asked.

"Aside from being a fiancé-stealing coquette, she's still my sister, which, as much as I hate to admit it, that means something. Although not as much as it did before."

The breeze sent the clouds floating past the April moon, leaving it clear and bright. The scent of the tea olives that surrounded the stately old home was sweet, intoxicating. He stroked her hair, loving the feeling of her pressed against him, confiding in him. There was a closeness that wasn't there before. And, perhaps the biggest coup of all, she trusted him.

Before he met Nettie, he'd always believed contentment was stagnating, dangerous, and he'd known very little of it since he moved back to Camden. His entire life had always been about going after the next big thing in college, then med school, and it usually was not a woman. Remmy had dated around a lot but didn't have time nor the inclination to devote himself to one woman, who, as he well knew from his friends, would demand and divide his attention. And yet, with Nettie Gilbert in his arms she felt like home. Even Camden felt like home. Right now she could ask him for anything in the world, and he'd move heaven and earth to give it to her just so he could hang on to the feeling a little longer.

"I'm really sorry that happened to you, Nettie. But I'm glad it brought you here to me."

She tilted her face up to his and closed her eyes, a silent invitation he took with pleasure.

The next morning, Miss Lurleen's heart sounded good but her blood pressure was up after Remmy broke the news to her.

"She's not?" The disappointment in Miss Lurleen's voice equaled Remmy's euphoria that Nettie wasn't pregnant with some other guy's baby.

"What happened isn't for me to say, but no, she's not expecting." Remmy moved the stethoscope around, wishing her lungs didn't sound iffy. He pulled Miss Lurleen's gown back together and tossed the scope in his bag.

"But why not?" The woman was dumbfounded.

"That's not for me to say; what I will say is that she was wronged. The only reason I'm telling you is I didn't want you to say something to her about it, and, without meaning to, embarrass or upset her. She's had more than her share of both lately."

Miss Emily barged into the room without knocking. Remmy ignored her and continued his examination of Miss Lurleen, who looked at her sister like she was going to cry. "Nettie's not expecting, Emily," she said weakly.

"And here I was going easy on her," Miss Emily snapped.

"Well, don't go pulling your cat-o'-nine-tails out again. Don't you dare say a word to her that we thought she was in the family way," Miss Lurleen shot back. "And don't go getting any ideas about running her off; as long as I can draw breath, she's going to be here. And, if you're smart, Emily, after I'm gone, you'll keep her on for as long as she'll have you."

"Have me? Humph."

"Did you want something, Sister?" Miss Lurleen asked. "Because if you didn't, after Remmy leaves, I don't want to be disturbed."

"Yes, I have something very important to discuss later after Dr. Worthless leaves. However, the girl—" That drew a hard look from Miss Lurleen. "Nettie wanted to know if you were going to eat in the kitchen with us again."

"Thank her, please, but no. I'm feeling completely spent today."

"You got out of the bed and walked to the supper table?" Remmy asked, checking her extremities for swelling. "There's good and bad in that; hope it was mostly good for you."

"Good and bad?" Emily said. "Dr. Worthless here has now turned into Dr. Ambiguous."

"Good in that it's not healthy for her to stay in bed all the time. There's all kinds of problems that can arise, the least of which is bedsores," he said, looking at Miss Emily before he turned his attention to Miss Lurleen. "Did it tire you out? Leave you short of breath?"

"Yes, but I'm fine," Miss Lurleen said like she couldn't die quick enough.

For so long, calling Mr. Buck had been the best part of Remmy's day, but it paled in comparison to sitting on the Eldridge sisters' front porch with Nettie Gilbert. And rightfully so, but he was tired of feeling like he was sneaking around to see her. He'd tell her tonight he intended to date her properly, and if the sisters complained about Nettie taking some time for herself, he'd ask Cora May or Katie to sit with them.

Remmy had pretty much had his fill of sisters in general. Before he'd left the house to visit Nettie tonight, Katie had given him the third degree, and he'd given it right back to her.

"You're almost ten years older than her," Katie snapped.

"Doesn't matter, and my seeing Nettie is none of your business, Katie. I know that always turns you sour on any woman. Until now, I've barely tolerated your ordering me around, trying to maneuver people out of my life, but don't get any ideas this time because it won't work. I like her; she likes me. End of story." Well, he hoped that wasn't the end of the story, because he wanted to get to know Nettie and see how things would go.

Katie didn't say another word, just retreated to the living room and stuck her nose back in her book where it belonged, which was damn fine by Remmy. Next on his list was telling the sisters of his intention to date Nettie Gilbert, not that he had to. He and Nettie were both adults, but he planned on being around the Eldridge home a lot more and not in the capacity of a doctor, so it seemed like the right thing to do.

He hurried down Laurens Street, his body strung tight with the anticipation of seeing her again, holding her, kissing her.

When he got to the house, it was completely dark. He started up the steps, and couldn't wait to find Nettie on the porch waiting for him. But she wasn't there. He called to her, albeit softly, but there was no answer. He sat down on the swing and waited maybe an hour, or until it was apparent even to the dimmest man that she wasn't coming. He had been pressed for time when he'd visited Miss Lurleen earlier in the day; but Nettie had seemed fine then. This didn't make any sense.

Had Katie meddled and phoned her after he left the house, even after he'd warned her to stay out of his business? Had he unknowingly said or done something to warrant Nettie's absence? If he did, why hadn't she just called or told him to his face instead of just not showing? At that moment, Remmy, who always prided himself on being studious, wished he'd paid more attention to the women he'd dated in the past. Maybe then he could figure out what in the hell had Nettie Gilbert running scared.

15

LURLEEN

Emily was acting weird. More so than usual, and it was giving Lurleen the creeps the way she was cutting her eye around at Lurleen, trying to get up the nerve to say whatever it was she had to say. She'd never been like this before; she'd always been only too happy to just come right out and ask for the sun, the moon, and while the good Lord was at it, the stars. But something definitely wasn't right. Did she forget to pay the taxes? The insurance? Had those fools up and canceled their homeowners' policy again? She didn't have the time or the inclination for this, but whatever was wearing on Emily was big, so big, Lurleen couldn't keep her mouth shut.

"Just come right out and say it," Lurleen huffed.

"Say what?" Emily, ever the professional at playing dumb, used to be cute and coy, but now her routine was just annoying.

"Whatever that weight is on your delicate shoulders. Just say it."

"Are you ready?" she asked.

"For what? Breakfast?" Because she sure hoped there was more to it than toast and jam and cold coffee, which also told Lurleen that Nettie did not cook. "And where's Nettie; did you finally succeed in running her off?"

"I'm incensed," Emily snapped. "I told her I'd make breakfast this morning. This used to be a fine meal for you, but now that girl has poisoned your mind right along with your palate."

"She hasn't done anything of the sort, and I'm sorry if I misread you, Mata Hari, but you've been acting very mysterious, and, frankly, I'm too tired to put up with your eccentricities. So, for God's sake, just spit it out."

"To die." She swallowed hard, and wouldn't look at Lurleen. "Are you ready to die?"

"Why? Are you thinking of killing me?"

Emily's head snapped up. She looked horrified. "No, of course not. I just need to know."

"I've never been the one who had a problem with the idea of dying, Emily. That's you, but am I ready today, at this second? No."

She sat down in the chair beside the bed and began to wring her hands, a sure sign that all hell was about to break loose. But for the love of Pete, Lurleen didn't have the energy to fix one more thing for her sister. And what would Emily do when she was gone? Go to wrack and ruin no doubt without Lurleen here to keep the bills paid and finances straight, to shoo away every door-to-door salesman peddling a new and improved gadget that in truth wasn't worth two cents and a ball of twine.

Emily touched the magazine poking out of her apron pocket a

couple of times and went back to wringing her hands. As peeved as Lurleen was, the lost look on Emily's face stabbed at her already failing heart.

"Well, Emily," she began, her voice not entirely void of the frustration that had her wound tight. "I've lived a very long time. I know Jesus, so, I suppose, in some regards, yes, I'm ready to die." Emily's eyes went wide; she didn't have to say she wasn't ready to let Lurleen go, every fiber of her being was screaming the news, and Lurleen could neither change nor fix this for her sister. "Look, I don't have a choice here. My heart's about to give out, and not just because Remmy Wilkes says so; I feel it. I know I'm near the end."

"But how can you know what being near the end feels like if you've never been there before?" she asked, almost childlike, and started to cry because they'd been together forever.

Lurleen was well acquainted with what the end felt like. Losing John, seeing his beautiful body marred and lifeless had taken her to the edge, and she would have gladly leapt over it to join him in eternity if it hadn't been for Teddy. For four years his anguish kept her tethered to this earth, trying to protect her mother and Emily from his infirmities, trying to protect him from himself; there was little time to think about John. Then Mama died and Teddy left, and Lurleen hated the terrible trick time had played on her.

She'd been so busy worrying about her brother, grieving with her mother and then for her mother, she could barely see John's face when she closed her eyes. And there were no pictures of him; Teddy in one of his fits had seen to that. But she couldn't blame the child, not after what happened.

After Mama died, Emily cried every day for at least ten years; it was a wonder, so many tears inside of one woman. She must have inherited all of Lurleen's. No matter what, she and Lurleen loved each other. Even during the times when their sisterhood was all they had to cling to, they loved each other.

Lurleen never cried, and she hated to see Emily carrying on now. "Sister," Lurleen said, "this is something I can't fix. I'm old; so are you, and we are going to die one day. If I could do something about that, call down the rapture so we could go together, I would."

Emily always had a way about her, using her dramatics to massage a situation until it suited her, pouting and carrying on until she got her way. Then she'd perk right up, jabbering on about her prize like she had not shed one tear. Daddy always got so flustered with her, all she had to do was look like she was going to pitch a fit and he gave in. Yes, Emily was spoiled rotten now, and, heaven help the good Lord and the angels, she would be long into eternity.

She pulled the magazine out of her apron and spread it open over Lurleen's lap on the chenille bedspread. Lurleen blinked at the full-page ad for Tareyton Cigarettes. "Honestly, Emily, what good would starting a nasty old habit do now?" Emily pointed to the headline on the opposite page.

A picture of a good-looking man, young but with white hair just the same. *Miracle in Palestine, Texas: Faith Healer or Hoax?* Lurleen could only make out the headline because it was big, and she didn't have her reading glasses. Emily handed Lurleen her glasses. She didn't have to read far before she knew where this was going. A woman who was having some kind of heart surgery had gone to the silver-haired preacher's tent meeting and was completely healed. Even took medical tests afterward to prove it.

"I know how you hate snakes, but he's not that kind of healer." Emily's last words had her signature little whine that was just above a whimper. "And if he heals most anyone who comes, and folks come from all over, I know he'd heal you."

"I don't think so, Emily. The magazine is clearly questioning the man's practices, which explains the word *hoax* in such big print. I don't need my glasses to see this for what it is."

She ratcheted up her little whine and swiped at her eyes. Honestly, Lurleen *would* have to die to get a moment's peace. But surely even Emily had enough sense to know that Lurleen would never make it all the way to Texas and back, and how would they get there without a car and with neither of them ever having learned how to drive? Emily cued the tears that trickled down her beautiful old face like a water-fall. "Emily, I'm too tired to even think about getting better." Emily was so blasted stubborn; Lurleen didn't think it was possible, but here Emily was, crying harder.

"What do you want me to do? We don't have a way to get there, and what if we traipse across the country and I give out along the way? How are you going to get me home to bury me proper?" Besides, Lurleen would probably spoil before they lowered her into the ground at the cemetery beside Mama and Daddy.

"Well," she said, wiping her nose with a tissue, completely aware she had exasperated Lurleen into submission. "I thought we might take the bus out there. Maybe see the ocean along the way. You know you had the chicken pox in high school and never went on your class trip to Folly Beach. I remember you always fussing because you really wanted to see that ocean, and I've seen it, Sister. It's *really* pretty. And we'll be seeing the Gulf *of Mexico*, Lurleen; doesn't that sound divine?"

Emily might have been the schoolteacher, a crackerjack at geog-raphy, but even Lurleen knew Texas, much less Palestine, Texas, was at least a thousand miles away. She also knew Emily would carry on until she said yes. Lurleen shifted around in the bed her grandmother gave her, looked around her room at the pictures from three generations of Eldridges, her mother's antique chifforobe and basin stand. She'd done that a lot lately, look at her things longingly, thankfully, knowing she was going to die in peace in this very room. But Lurleen could see there would be no peace, because she'd be gallivanting across the country with her pouting sister, who wouldn't give a soul a moment's rest until they surrendered to her every whim.

"All right. We'll go," Lurleen said, knowing full well she would never see the ocean before she died.

16

NETTIE

I should have said something when Remmy stopped by to check on Miss Lurleen yesterday, but the moment I saw him standing at the screen door, I knew I had to avoid him at all costs.

Luckily, he was in a hurry to get to his next appointment. But it wasn't just his rushing off or my chickening out that kept me upstairs last night. It was the way my heart jolted that first moment I saw him on the other side of the screen door, the way my entire body hummed, the same way I felt whenever I saw Brooks. No, it was even worse.

Of course I knew from personal experience that thread of anticipation was as old as man and womankind. But look what that had gotten me. Pain. Heartache. Yes, and a newfound and healthy aversion to Remmy Wilkes. Because, after confiding in him, kissing him, and having him reignite feelings I was sure were forever dead, I knew I would never survive being hurt by him.

So, last night, I'd stood just behind the lace curtains at my bedroom window and watched him come up the walkway and disappear onto the front porch, where he stayed forever before finally leaving. And then I'd barely slept at all.

But I couldn't hide from him forever, not when he came by the house most every day to check on Miss Lurleen. No, the plan was to pull him aside somewhere in the house where I would have some measure of privacy, but not too private, politely apologize for standing him up. Thank him for listening to me, without mentioning the kissing, the caressing. Tell him I was not nor would I ever be interested in him. And, while I was at it, I would suggest he stick to the local girls his sister hated. For all I knew, if Remmy had told Katie he was spending his evenings with me, she had already lumped me into that category.

Now, he was standing on the front porch, waiting for me to let him in. My heart slammed against my chest in rapid succession, like a bird trying to escape the world through a closed window. "Nettie. A word with you, please," he said. "On the porch." He stepped back so I could open the screen door and throw my plan right out the window.

He was angry and something else, I wasn't sure. I swallowed hard, heart still out of control. I wasn't getting anywhere near Remmy Wilkes so that he could do that thing he does, listen, make me feel important, desired. I'd known the back side of all those things, and they were agonizing when they were suddenly snatched away. No, I couldn't endure that anytime in the foreseeable future. Maybe never. Was that what had launched the sisters into spinsterhood? If so, they'd better move over and make room for one more.

"Miss Emily, Dr. Wilkes is here to see Miss Lurleen." I said the words, looking straight at him, ignoring his request, and knowing with the mood Miss Emily was in she'd take the bait. She'd been stalking the house all morning, looking for a good fight. As much as she said she hated Remmy Wilkes, after she attempted to spar with him or if she was successful, she always had an extra spring in her step. Especially if she thought she'd bested him.

He opened the door, but I didn't budge. Any other man would have stalked away, but not Remmy. He just cocked his head to the side and stood fast.

"You see to him," Miss Emily shouted from her chair. "I have no use for the man." That would be the last time I depended on the support of a fellow spinster.

I stepped out onto the porch. Hands shoved into the pockets of my jeans, studying my bare feet. "You could have talked to me, Nettie. And, for the record, you can always talk to me," he said. "But you left me sitting on this porch alone. I stayed here and thought about why you'd stand me up, not even for a real date, and the only conclusion I came to is that you're a runner."

There was no arguing with that. Up until now, I'd always been sure I was the direct opposite. But I had left my home, my family, even Brooks the first chance I got and had taken a scholarship hundreds of miles from Satsuma. Why? Was I running then? What was I running from? Was it Brooks? Had I deserted him long before he cheated on me?

"Remmy, I'm sorry I stood you up; that was wrong. But, please understand I'm not ready to start a relationship, and that's where this felt like this was headed." With him, and those dark chocolate eyes, that easy way that could wreck my heart in a million ways if I wasn't careful.

"That's because it is headed that way, Nettie. You know it. I know it. What I don't understand is, what changed? What sent you running again?"

"I'm not, I—"

"You are."

"You'd better not be charging me to stand on my porch and talk to the help, Remmy Wilkes," Miss Emily hollered. She grumbled something unintelligible; the sound of her sensible shoes clicking toward the door was a relief. "Be gone, Remmy. Your services are no longer required. I've found a real healer and, soon, my sister will be as spry as a new kitten."

"Miss Emily." Remmy nodded, brows knitted together, looking at me as if I knew something about her claim. When I shook my head, he opened the screen door and came inside. "Until Miss Lurleen tells me she's no longer my patient, I'm obligated to see her. So, if you will excuse me." She gasped when he pushed past her, headed for Miss Lurleen's room.

"You," Miss Emily snapped. "Come with me. It may take both of us to remove him from the premises."

By the time we reached the bedroom, Remmy was already taking his stethoscope out of his bag. "How are you feeling?" he asked as Miss Lurleen opened her nightgown. "And what's this I hear about you getting a new doctor?"

"Me? I don't have another doctor," Miss Lurleen sputtered.

"We don't need a *doctor*," Miss Emily said. "We've got God on our side."

"You want to tell me what this is all about, Miss Lurleen?" He continued his examination, looking at me every once in a while. For support? To make me feel guilty? Weaken my defenses?

She let out a long, stuttering breath and retied her gown. "It appears I'm going on a trip."

"To be healed. Finally," Miss Emily added.

Remmy nodded, taking her blood pressure. "It's Emily's idea. There's this faith healer," Miss Lurleen said.

"So, where are you going?" He pulled back the covers to check her feet. "When are you leaving?"

"Palestine. Day after tomorrow, not that it's any of your business," Miss Emily snapped.

"That's an awful long way to go, Miss Lurleen." Remmy hung the stethoscope around his neck. "How are you going to get there?" he asked, looking at me like I had something to do with this. I shrugged; this was all news to me, but I felt a rush of something that felt very much like relief.

"Oh, for pity's sake it's not *the* Palestine; it's Palestine, Texas," Miss Emily said. "And we're going by bus. Which reminds me," she said, wheeling around to face me. "The moment we get on that bus, *your* services will no longer be required either."

And why did that bother me? Because I wanted to care for Miss Lurleen or because that bus would be leaving Camden?

"Well then I'm not going," Miss Lurleen fussed. "Not without Nettie, and I mean it, Emily."

Before I could say anything, Remmy clipped, "Of course she's going." He closed his eyes and rubbed the bridge of his nose before glancing at me, hard lines drawn across his face, as if it was my idea to get as far away from him as possible and take the sisters with me. But this was not my doing. "Let's back up a minute. First off, Miss Lurleen, a faith healer is not going to cure you."

"Are you blaspheming God?" Emily spat. "Are you saying he can't heal my sister?"

"No. But I've been monitoring Miss Lurleen for more than a year; I know what her condition is, what the natural progression of her disease is. And you're right, it will take an act of God to make her well. But I'm assuming you got hold of the same article I read where they called that tent preacher a hoax."

"Miracle worker," Miss Emily hissed.

After I'd tired of reading the entertainment articles over and over again, I had skimmed that story too. If you were a believer in modern medicine like Remmy, it was clear the reverend was indeed a flimflam man. But with her sister sick, dying, no one could fault Miss Emily for craving a miracle.

He turned his back to Miss Emily and glanced at me before looking at his patient, who was so very frail. "If you leave this bed, Miss Lurleen, to get on a bus." He paused, his voice tight with restraint. "You will more than likely die somewhere between here and Texas, not in your bed. Not in your house surrounded by your things. Not where I know you want to be when you pass."

"You don't know what Lurleen wants," Miss Emily gritted out, but he ignored her.

Miss Lurleen looked Remmy straight in the eye and nodded. She knew this was true; she knew this was ridiculous, but she was doing it for her sister.

Remmy put his things in his battered black bag before turning to me. "The food alone will probably kill her. It'll be full of salt. Call me from the road every day. Collect. Let me know how she's doing.

"You'll need to keep an eye on her for swelling, especially her feet and ankles. Check them several times a day. If they get bad, if she has a lot of trouble breathing, get her to the nearest hospital."

I was no nurse, not even close. "How bad is bad?" I stammered.

He ignored my question, picked up his bag and laid his hand on Miss Lurleen's shoulder. "Wish you wouldn't do this."

"I know." She looked fearful of what was to come. Except for the night she came to the supper table and to use the bathroom, she hadn't been out of the bed for weeks. And, from the remarks Remmy had made, she'd been ill for quite some time.

"Take care." He gave her shoulder a squeeze and looked at me. "Follow me out?"

After avoiding Remmy Wilkes, I couldn't catch up to him fast enough as he headed out the front door and onto the porch. "Remmy, I can't do this. She's so sick, too sick for me to take care of. And on a bus?"

He scratched some instructions and two phone numbers on a prescription pad, ripped off the page, and handed it to me. "Call and check in every day. Let me know how she's doing. If there's a problem, day, night, it doesn't matter; you call me, and I will help you, Nettie, in any way I can."

"No. I'm not leaving; Miss Lurleen said herself that she won't go without me."

"I don't want either of them to go; it's a terrible idea. But with or without you, I can guarantee you, Emily Eldridge is going to drag her sister onto that bus and somebody's going to die, maybe both of them. As horrible as that is, the thing that bothers me most is you're leaving, and I don't want you to go."

"Remmy—"

"No, Nettie, hear me out. A few minutes ago, the look on your face when you saw me at the door? You were dying to run away from me. I'm not sure you wanted to; it was more like you needed to.

"I know that you're hurt, that you're scared. After what your family did to you, I don't blame you. But I learned a long time ago anything worth having is worth working for. Waiting for. So, I'm not going to try to stop you from running because I know that's what you need to do, even if it means getting on a bus with two old ladies who have one foot in the grave. So, you run as fast and as hard as you want, Nettie Gilbert." He pushed a tendril of hair behind my ear and lingered. "But when you're done running, come back to me."

17

EMILY

The late morning sun broke through the billowy clouds in all its glory, and it had never been more beautiful. Emily picked out her best dress, the powder-puff pink linen shift that matched her shoes and hung it on the back of the chifforobe. She sat down at her dressing table, feeling more like the age she felt inside, forty if a day, rather than her actual seventy-one years, and not just because she was quite well preserved.

She used her finger to dab the Pan-Cake Make-Up on, that new Max Factor Hollywood brand she bought at the drugstore the other day. Blending and filling in the lines until she looked almost as ravishing as Evelyn Keyes, that actress on the advertisement that promised to *create flattering new beauty . . . in just a few seconds.* Lord, it was an actual wonder. Emily looked fantastic and she hadn't even applied the new rouge and matching lipstick.

Emily smiled at her reflection, happy digging in her heels and bringing the clock to a screeching halt had actually worked. She might not be able to turn back the clock to when Lurleen was young and working out in her garden like a man, but with her healed, she'd have a few more good years left for sure. After all, barring tragedy, which the Eldridges were only too familiar with, they were long livers. And surely, after the heartache Emily and Lurleen's generation had suffered, the Fates would smile on them. Or maybe good fortune skipped a generation like twins skipped a generation. Regardless, there would be no more Eldridges to carry on, unless Teddy had lived. And Emily had given up on that a long time ago.

The loss still made her well up, and when she dabbed her tears away, she noticed a wrinkle she'd missed; it was on the side she normally slept on. She spackled the thick makeup into the crease and made a note to sleep on her back from here on. Dusting herself with a generous amount of Evening in Paris powder, she stepped into her nylon slip and pulled it up over her brassiere before shimmying into her dress. Looking at herself in the cheval mirror, she realized the outfit cried out for her mother's pearls, which were a bit much just to go to the bus station.

Pocketbook on arm and carrying her shoes, she started down the stairs in her stocking feet, carefully navigating the staircase that normally made her knees weep, her hips ache, but not today. At the bottom of the stairs, she slipped into her shoes just as the girl was coming out of Lurleen's room.

"I'm going to the bus station to buy our tickets for the trip and will be back shortly," Emily announced. The girl nodded. "I'm buying *your* ticket as well; you're lucky I'm not taking it out of your stipend. If I thought Sister wouldn't pitch a fit, I would."

"Thank you," she said evenly.

Emily put her short, white gloves on and started out the door, down the front steps, headed toward DeKalb Street. It was a beautiful walk; Camden was in all her glory, bursting with azaleas and dogwoods. Emily's whole body sang with anticipation for this journey to heal Lurleen. At first, Emily had felt a little selfish when she brought the idea up to Lurleen, but after everything she'd taken from Lurleen, so long ago, surely giving her a few more good years would come closer to setting things right. Though the scales would never be balanced.

By the time she set foot in the Greyhound station, she was almost breathless with exhilaration. She propped her pocketbook up on the counter. On the other side, a young man who looked every bit like a skinny beatnik with his unkempt hair and goatee raised his eyebrows like Emily was some kind of bothersome old woman. "Help you?"

No *ma'am* or *may I*. Emily didn't recognize the boy, but even if he'd changed remarkably since she taught sixth grade, she knew he wasn't one of her students who had good manners ingrained into their beings whether they liked it or not. He was not nor would he ever be handsome, not like some men are, the spindly ones who are scrawny when they are young but age into their bodies much later in life. No potbelly, slim, their awkward faces etched with age, making them handsome.

"Yes, you *may* help me. *May I* have three tickets to Palestine, Texas? *Please*," Emily said, emphasizing the proper words because it was never too late to learn good etiquette. Even for a beatnik.

He pulled three tickets off of a stack, jotted some information on them, stamped each one, and pushed them across the counter. "Eighty-four ninety-seven."

Emily pulled out her checkbook and a pen and started writing the date.

"No checks," the beatnik said.

"Young man, did no one teach you the first speck of manners? It's no checks *ma'am*. And why the *h.* not?"

"Because the sign says so," he said with the most insolent look, pointing to the sign in front of her. Emily wanted to take her shoe off and tan his behind. Even if he was a good bit bigger than she. "Cash only."

Emily looked at the sign, then back at him. "I know you don't know me, but I'm Emily Eldridge. I've lived in this town for—well, since I was born. I bank at South Carolina National Bank; my father banked there and his father before him. I'm sure you can take a personal check from me."

He put the tickets back in the till.

"Young man, I'm a retired schoolteacher and Sunday school teacher at Bethesda Presbyterian Church. There's no need for me to walk three blocks to the bank in these shoes," Emily said, pointing at her pink pumps, but the boy didn't even bother to look.

"No cash. No tickets," he said, tossing his scraggly hair.

Well, if Emily wasn't already burned up, that look did it. She marched herself up Broad Street, feet swelling and throbbing. The girl behind the counter, Emily couldn't recall her name, but she'd taught her in the forties. She'd been quiet and kept to herself, and her name was right on the tip of Emily's tongue when she blushed and pushed the money through the teller window. Even put it in one of those handy cloth bags that were so convenient; Emily used them to launder her undergarments in when she remembered.

By the time Emily paraded back into the Greyhound station she was breathless, and that little nitwit actually had the nerve to roll his eyes. "*May I* have three tickets to Palestine, Texas? *Please*."

"Eighty-four ninety-seven. *Cash*," he said, holding out his hand.

Emily opened the bag and dumped the pennies onto the counter. "What the hell?"

"Don't you dare swear at me young man. *You*. Making me go to the bank, like my check is no good. Be ashamed of yourself," Emily huffed. "Now you count every blasted one of those coins and give me my tickets or I'm going to use that pay phone just outside this place to call your superiors. Perhaps I should do that anyway and suggest that they hire someone with some manners."

He started over twice because he lost count, and it took him the better part of a half hour before he just shoved the money in the till and handed Emily the tickets.

"*Thank you*," Emily said. "Have a *pleasant* day."

LURLEEN

Nettie brought Lurleen's lunch tray in and set it on the bedside table. She hadn't said much since Remmy's visit yesterday. Lurleen had no idea if Nettie wanted to go on this pilgrimage Emily was forcing on them, but she suspected after almost two weeks under the Eldridge roof, Nettie had learned not to cross Emily.

"Chicken salad," she announced. "Oh, and I minced up some apples and put it in to make it a little sweet. My mother does that. When apples aren't in season, she'll use white raisins if she has them.

Oranges too. They're my favorite." She whispered the last word like it was painful.

"Do you miss home?" Lurleen asked.

"Some things I miss," she paused. "Yes."

"I never asked you much about, where was it? Mobile, Alabama?"

"Near there. Satsuma."

"I got the feeling that the less questions I asked, the better."

Her whole body went stiff and she blushed hard. "You didn't think I was—expecting, did you?"

"Well, yes." Lurleen hoped her smile was reassuring. "But I could tell when I met you that you're a good girl, Nettie. And that certainly wouldn't have made you bad. Not in my eyes anyway."

"Thank you," she said awkwardly.

Lurleen propped herself up on the pillows, pulled the tray onto her lap, and tasted the chicken. No wonder Emily was jealous of Nettie; she really had a way with food.

"May I ask you a question?" Nettie said. Lurleen nodded and dabbed at her mouth with the napkin. "Why is the piano off-limits?"

"Did Emily tell you it is?"

"Without words, yes," Nettie said.

"It was our mother's piano, a wedding gift from our father. But after our little brother Teddy came along, he took it over. Oh my, how he could play. For hours, never reading a note of music, yet every note was perfect. Then there was a tragedy and he never touched the piano again; neither did our mother."

"I'm sorry. Your brother must have been a natural," Nettie said, straightening up around the bed; then she glanced at Lurleen. "Oh, I'm sorry. I didn't mean to upset you."

"Yes, Teddy played by ear." Lurleen swiped at her tears. "He was remarkable; he made simple Chopsticks sound as beautiful as Strauss's finest waltz. That was always the song he tried to lure Emily and me to the piano with. Both of us were hopeless, but it kind of became our song. It's hard to hear a piano and not think about Brother. Chopsticks."

"It's really hard to walk by it so many times a day and not sit and play," she said hesitantly. "I've touched it once; the keys didn't work, and then Miss Emily looked at me."

Lurleen smiled. "Don't let her intimidate you, Nettie. While you're living under my roof, this is your house too." But did she really want Nettie to make the spinet sing again? She had no doubt that she was an accomplished musician; just the same, there was something about the piano remaining silent that was as comforting as it was disturbing.

"Thank you. I don't think Miss Emily was trying to be mean." That was a kind assessment. "She seemed more pained than anything, and I would never hurt either of you by playing."

Lurleen finished the chicken salad, scraping the bowl to get every bit. "I know you won't, my dear." Still, Lurleen couldn't help wondering what it would be like to hear Brother's old piano again. Lurleen and Sister had braced themselves for so long, as if the sound might break the both of them in two. And who knows? Maybe it would.

"And may I ask you another question, Nettie?"

"Yes, of course." She sat down beside the bed. "If it's about the piano, I can tell you almost anything you want to know."

"It's not about the piano," Lurleen said. "It's about you."

"All right." She swallowed hard.

"What are you afraid of, Nettie?"

"Lots of things." Her laugh was nervous. "Snakes. Failure. Heights."

"No, I mean with Remmy."

"There's nothing going on with him." She blushed hard. "He did visit a few nights. We just sat on the porch and talked. But that's all. He's really not for me," she said like she was trying to convince herself.

"That's what I told myself when I first met John. I was so afraid to open myself up to the possibility of love; it was much easier to keep my nose stuck in a book. But he was persistent as I suspect Remmy is, and I know him to be a good man. Someone you can trust."

"It doesn't matter how good or persistent Remmy is, I'll never leave my heart unguarded again. And when I'm around Remmy—" She stopped and hung her head.

"You feel open. Exposed." Nettie looked at Lurleen and nodded. "More vulnerable than you've ever felt in your life, which feels horrible and wonderful all at the same time."

"Yes, how did you know?"

"Because I stood on the edge of my fears once, and I let myself fall," Lurleen said, her fingers drawing little circles on the bedspread.

"And he broke your heart?"

"Not intentionally, but yes."

That day John had come into to the library, she'd just come back from lunch. She'd walked all the way back from the lunch counter, her nose in a book. She was reading the new copy of *The Importance of Being Earnest* that had just come in. The only other copy the library had had disappeared a year earlier when one of the Rosemont girls fell in love with reading. The girl was also a bit of a kleptomaniac then, although she thankfully grew out of it later on in life.

But that afternoon when Lurleen left the lunch counter, she had been vaguely aware someone was walking behind her, almost beside her. It was easy to tune people out, especially with the help of Oscar Wilde. She glanced up to see the library just ahead, then read the next sentence and threw her head back laughing. When she reached the door, from out of nowhere, a hand opened it and she stepped inside and took her place behind the counter. Shoving her pocketbook in a cubbyhole along with her book to finish later. When she looked up, the most beautiful man she'd ever seen was standing there, looking at Lurleen the way Emily's suitors looked at her.

"Can I help you?" she'd stammered, which was odd. She'd never had any trouble talking to a man; she did it all the time when she attended church socials, hunted with her father's buddies. It made her nervous when the beautiful man didn't answer, and Lurleen didn't get nervous; she was a librarian for God's sake. "Can I help you find a book?" she said firmly.

"That must be a good one," he said, eyes smiling as he pointed at the cubby. "I followed you for eight blocks and you didn't look up once, not even to cross the street. That's not safe."

That just didn't happen to Lurleen, some Adonis tracking her down, unless of course they were trying to elicit her help to get Emily to notice them. "I have excellent peripheral vision," she'd huffed, but inside her heart was flipping over.

"I heard, and I hear you're quite the huntress as well," he said. He gabbed on and Lurleen didn't hear a word he said, just nodded blankly. "I'm John Young, by the way. I was hoping you'd do me the honor of having dinner with me."

And that was all it took; his crooked smile sealed the deal and Lurleen fell over the edge before she spent one moment with him and listened to his hearty laugh, to his voice that rumbled low and did things to her body she didn't quite understand and would never have believed were possible. She was shocked to learn how wonderful he thought it was that she loved guns and hunting. A direct departure from the rest of the world, who thought she was an odd duck to begin with because she surrounded herself with books. Add the fact she was a crack shot, and, well, it just didn't make any sense that this Adonis was asking her for anything, much less a date. But she said yes that day to John Young, and she never stopped saying yes.

"I'm sorry," Nettie said softly. "I couldn't survive being hurt again, not like Brooks hurt me."

"That's understandable." Lurleen never had the time or the inclination to fall for anyone in her twenty-two years prior to meeting John. Besides, even when the sisters were in college, most of Lurleen's potential suitors were Emily's throwaways, which right off the bat was three strikes. No, Lurleen had read enough romance novels to know that one day her prince would come. And he did.

When Nettie took the tray away and closed the door, Lurleen glanced at the small suitcase Emily had drug out of the carriage house. She sat up with her legs dangling over the side of the bed, taking care to let her head settle before she stood and inched her way over to her chifforobe. She'd wanted to lose some weight for some time. In her old age her body had become quite boxy. Not that Lurleen ever thought she'd look willowy and beautiful like Emily always had; she still did.

She tried on her best housedress, knowing if she put on anything less tomorrow, Emily would fuss a blue streak. It hung on her like a sack, making her feel even sicker. Older. Well, she wasn't going to walk all the way to Karesh's Fashion Shop for a new dress; she couldn't, and Emily would never mention the ill-fitting garment. It would be a confirmation that Lurleen was too sick to make this blasted trip in the first place; a confirmation that she really was dying, and Emily herself would die before she admitted that.

Lurleen packed some undergarments and two more housedresses, a nightgown. She hated to haul her good gray linen suit hither thither and yon. It would be a wrinkled mess when the time came to wear it, but it couldn't be helped. Of course, Kornegay's here in Camden would handle the arrangements when she passed, but Lurleen wasn't sure if they would be able to change her into her funeral suit after her body was shipped home. As much as she didn't care about so many of the frivolous things Emily cared about, she really didn't want to ride across the country underdressed. Even if it was in the back of a hearse, Emily would never let her hear the end of it.

18

NETTIE

Almost four weeks ago, I was standing in a receiving line in the dining room at Columbia College for the alumnae dinner celebrating 119 years of sisterhood. All of the senior sisters were side by side their sophomore little sisters. Several girls, including me, were stag as there was a rash of girls who received diamonds over the Christmas holiday who didn't bother to finish out the school year.

While I'd taken offense to Remmy's insinuation that dear old C-Square was a glorified finishing school for girls who wanted an engagement ring more than they wanted their degree, there was a fair amount of that. Even without a ring, I was relieved when Brooks had officially proposed at Christmastime and excited about the prospects of being chosen, validated. Married. After I returned to school, I went through the motions, not fully appreciating those last moments of being Nettie Gilbert, completely focused on being little more than Brooks Carver's wife.

That night at the reception, I was glowing in my sapphire blue gown, shaking hands, greeting fellow sisters and faculty. Inwardly, I was a mess, tangled up in worry, sure someone I knew and loved back home was dead, most likely Brooks. As horrible as receiving Mother's note complete with an invitation to Brooks and Sissy's wedding was, at least I didn't have to wrestle with the unknown anymore. Pretend I was fine when I definitely wasn't.

Our bus rumbled into the terminal, interrupting my thoughts, its destination in huge white letters on a black sign. Mobile. Thirty-seven miles from Satsuma. I glanced down at the schedule. We'd change buses in Montgomery. Stay overnight, then get up early the next morning and get on bus number seven, bound for Dallas. I was reasonably sure we'd have to stop somewhere along the way between Montgomery and Palestine, but there were no concrete plans other than to just go as far as we could each day.

When I'd helped Miss Lurleen dress this morning, she seemed better than she had lately, and I thought maybe the trip would be good for her; maybe it would be good for both of us. Although the idea of being so close to home was disconcerting, I felt oddly excited, almost naughty, like I was getting away with something, which made no sense. Was the trip a dare I was taking to show I was unaffected by Alabama, by my family's betrayal, that I *could* go home, or in the general vicinity of home, unscathed? Or was Remmy right and I was running from him?

My introspection evaporated with the early morning fog when the driver called that it was time to board the bus. Miss Emily eased up the steps of the bus, pocketbook in the crook of her arm, white gloves on; she looked back over her shoulder for her sister. I was behind Miss Lurleen, my hand on the small of her back as she barely pulled herself up the stairs, holding on to both rails while I prayed hard that she didn't lose her balance and fall on top of me.

The longest half dozen or so steps of my life, and probably Miss Lurleen's too, finally ended and we looked up to see Miss Emily waving to us about five rows from the back of the crowded bus. By now Miss Lurleen was breathing really hard.

"She sick?" the driver asked warily.

"No," I lied, although I had no idea why.

"I'm just old," Miss Lurleen snapped, then straightened and moved as well as I'd seen her walk in the short time I'd known her. She was nearly out of breath by the time she plopped down beside her sister. I put the knapsack we'd brought under the seat and sat down beside Miss Lurleen.

"Isn't this fun?" Miss Emily said. "And did you see the bus is going to Mobile?"

"If," Miss Lurleen said, "by some miracle I live through this, Emily, you should know this is the last time I'm giving in to your whining."

LURLEEN

If Lurleen made it over the Alabama line, it would be the second miracle of the day; the first being when she'd hoisted herself up the bus steps. Even before Pastor Gray had picked them up to take the three of them and their baggage to the bus station, her heart was beating twice as fast as a hummingbird's. Climbing those blame steps, it had screamed at her, and if she hadn't been afraid of squashing poor Nettie, she would have saved herself the effort and fallen dead away before she reached the top step.

But here she was, sandwiched between Emily in all her optimistic folly and poor Nettie, who was noticeably troubled every time Lurleen blew out an exhausted breath, which she did often. If she didn't hate the sympathetic looks she got from Emily or the worried ones from Nettie, she would gulp air like a fish out of water. Which is exactly what she felt like on this bus headed toward certain death.

"Tell me about your family," Emily said out of the clear blue sky, and Nettie's eyes went wide.

Lurleen crossed her arms; even she knew home was a sore subject for Nettie.

"Emily, it's going to be a very long trip, and it will be even longer if you're gong to yammer all the way to Palestine."

"Nonsense," Emily said. "The trip will fly by in no time if we tell our stories."

"You don't even like Nettie, and, right now, I'm barely tolerating you, so no amount of *story* is going to salve that truth."

"Of course I don't like her," Emily huffed.

"I'm right here." Nettie leaned across Lurleen and gave Emily a look.

"And do you want to spill the beans?" Lurleen asked.

"Not particularly. No," Nettie said.

"Oh, you two are just being ridiculous. Of course we're all better off when we tell our stories. I'll go first."

"Dear, God," Lurleen huffed, but Emily wasn't deterred.

L urleen and Nettie were quiet and certainly were not better off after listing to Emily blather nonstop. Almost to Augusta, the bus mercifully stopped in a no-name place, which amounted to a gas station with a reprehensible bathroom and a Co-Cola machine. Three more people, suitcases in hand, waited to get on. It had taken so much effort for Lurleen to hoist herself into the bus, she didn't want to get off when they'd stopped in Columbia, but she'd had no idea when the next stop would be.

There were only ten women on the bus, a couple of unruly kids, the rest men, maybe three dozen or so. Of course being old and sickly looking landed Lurleen near the front of the line for the bathroom. Emily was ahead of her, anxious to check her look in the mirror because the small compact she pulled out of her purse every five minutes just wasn't big enough. But then even the full-length cheval mirror back home wasn't big enough to capture Emily in all her glory.

"Isn't this fun?" Emily asked, as a woman came out of the bathroom and the next person in line towed her little boy inside. She snapped open her compact again and fluffed up her silver curls. "We haven't taken a trip in a long time, Lurleen. This is good for the soul."

This was good for nothing and Lurleen was about to wet her pants.

"Miss Emily?" Nettie was beside Lurleen, her hand cupping Lurleen's elbow. "Would it be okay if your sister went ahead of you?"

Emily gave Nettie a hard look and shut her compact. "I was just going to suggest that," she snapped as the woman and her son came out.

Nettie walked Lurleen to the bathroom door. Lurleen braced herself on the doorframe that was beyond filthy. "Do you need some help?" Nettie whispered.

"No thank you, dear." She took a step inside and closed the door.

The windowless room was barely big enough to turn around in; the smell was abysmal. But Lurleen would kiss the toilet seat before she succumbed to death in a wayside gas station. The water pills Remmy prescribed made her pee all the time; the digitalis made her sleepy and weak. He'd said it might kill her appetite, but no such luck.

Lately, her ankles had looked like overstuffed sausages in her compression stockings, but today they looked good. Better than Lurleen felt, which much to her surprise was fair to middling. After she did her business, she got to her feet, readjusted her clothing, and bathed her hands in the sink that had a giant palmetto bug legs up in it. Hard to believe that four women had been in ahead of her and had left the corpse for the next person. Lurleen got a wad of toilet paper and tossed the thing into the trash out of courtesy for the rest of the travelers and because Emily hated bugs of any sort and would have the vapors.

Nettie looked relieved when she finally opened the door. "I'll get us a Co-Cola," Lurleen said, "while you and Emily use the facility." She nodded toward the rusted, junky-looking machine.

"Orange Nehi for me," Emily sang until she opened the bathroom door. She made a gagging noise and closed the door behind her.

"And for you, Nettie?"

"I'll get a Coke when I get out of the restroom," she said, smiling at Emily's running commentary of horrors that could easily be heard all the way back in Camden. Good thing Lurleen tossed that bug.

Soda pop. It was the first thing Lurleen had bought in weeks; she hadn't even been to the grocery store for pity's sake. The women in line, with the exception of Nettie, started fussing after a while because Emily was taking so long, but she'd never met a mirror she didn't fall in love with, even in a smelly old bathroom. Finally the door opened and Nettie went in just after Emily strutted out to the laughter of the others in line. She gave them a hard look, chin held high, continuing on to the drink machine.

Lurleen handed her an orange drink and couldn't help but notice the two heavy-set women at the back of the line cutting their eye around at Emily. Lurleen craned her neck around to see Emily's backside. "Good Lord, Emily, I can't believe you wore a girdle."

Emily took a swig of the orange drink with a cocky smile, "Why, thank you, Sister. I'll take that as a compliment because I'm not wearing one."

"Yes, you are. I can see it plain as day," Lurleen snapped. "And the back of your dress is tucked into it." Emily blushed hard and righted her dress. "Why would you do that? The last time you wore that thing, you passed out at the church supper and ended up in the hospital."

"Shhh." She fluffed her hair and looked about to see if anyone was watching her. While Lurleen was fully aware that she was old, Emily was under the delusion that she was still the queen of Sheba, even if today her kingdom was a Greyhound bus. "Here I am trying to keep you out of the hospital and this is the thanks I get. You, browbeating me for dressing like a lady."

"Emily, if God had intended women to wear sausage casings, he would have poured us into them at birth. Besides, there is nothing ladylike about a girdle."

"Keep your voice down," Emily hissed, smoothing her hand over the back of her dress to make sure she was indeed fully covered. "And here I thought this would be a lovely trip. I believe I'm going to take my orange drink and sit at the picnic table until we leave."

Nettie walked up just as Emily stalked off. "Here's a dime, honey," Lurleen said.

"That's okay," Nettie said, fishing in her change purse. She pulled out two nickels, put them into the slot, and selected a Co-Cola. She popped off the top and turned it up like she was indeed thirsty. "Miss Emily all right?" Nettie nodded toward the picnic tables where the men were smoking and Emily was sitting, hoping to catch their eye.

"As all right as she's ever going to be," Lurleen said. "How are you doing? Regretting coming on this jaunt with two old ladies yet?"

NETTIE

I turned up the last of my Coke, pulled a banana out of the knapsack, peeled it, and offered Miss Lurleen half. "I'm fine and with no regrets," I said, folding the peel back around the fruit and putting it back in the sack. Poor Miss Lurleen looked at me like I was offering her a dead skunk. "Remmy said you need the potassium, so eat."

Begrudgingly, she obeyed, washing the last of it down with her Coke. I took the empty bottle and put it in the rack beside the machine. "Thank you for not asking me how I'm doing," she said.

"I'm sorry. I—"

"No. Really, thank you. I get so sick of folks asking the same question when they already know the answer."

I couldn't help but smile at Miss Lurleen's candor. Across the way, Miss Emily attempted to flirt; she had crossed and recrossed her legs at least a dozen times, trying to catch the attention of the men sitting on the other picnic table. "She's always been that way?" I nodded toward the men.

"Flirting? Acting younger than her years? Emily has never been one to go gentle into the good night. She'll go to the grave kicking and screaming like an innocent headed for the electric chair."

"She was always beautiful. Wasn't she?" I asked absently, still looking at Miss Emily. When Miss Lurleen didn't answer, I turned my attention to her. Her face was expressionless. "I'm sorry; I didn't mean to imply that you—"

"I wasn't," Miss Lurleen said simply. "Ever. And that's perfectly fine."

"But I've seen the pictures that prove you wrong."

"Do you have a sister, Nettie?" I nodded. "Is she as beautiful as you?"

I was four when Sissy was born. One of my first memories was marveling over the abundance of blond fuzz, and being broken-hearted she wasn't a ginger like me. Those blue eyes that never changed color like Mother promised they would because everyone in our family had green eyes, except Daddy; his were brown. Sissy grew into a gorgeous young woman, petite, with skin that never freckled or burned like mine. That fuzz grew into a radiant blond cape that went all the way down to her tiny waist. She looked nothing like me. She was absolutely stunning.

"Much more so." I almost choked on the words.

Miss Lurleen cocked her head to the side and then nodded. "You and your sister have a falling out?" I nodded. "Over a man?" Her crystal blue eyes peered at me for an answer, but she already saw inside me. I nodded again. "Emily and I had the same. No matter how big the tiff is, and ours was horrific, it won't last."

"You're wrong." I sounded bitter when I really meant to laugh and play off her questions with more of my own about her health, or the weather or the bus ride, anything but this.

"Trust me, it won't."

It had been over three weeks since I received the invitation to Sissy's wedding, almost two months since I'd received a letter or a phone call from her. For as long as I lived, I never wanted to see her bright, shiny face again. Yet, as much as I hated to admit it, I missed her. "And how long did your *tiff* last?" I asked.

"Seven years," Miss Lurleen said. Both of us watched Miss Emily sashay back toward the bus, her long shawl flowing, doing her best to move like Ginger Rogers across the broken red clay. "To the day, I stopped speaking to her."

Seven years? I hadn't even gone seven months without seeing Sissy's loopy scrawl over pages and pages of heartfelt letters or hearing her voice, and it already felt like an eternity. The wiry little bus driver, with the great big western belt buckle and cowboy hat instead of the baseball type the other drivers wore, came out of the men's room and nodded toward us. "Ladies. Time to load up," he drawled. "Leaving in five minutes."

19

NETTIE

Sandwiched between Miss Emily and me, Miss Lurleen was soon asleep, her head bouncing from my shoulder to Miss Emily's as she sporadically made the gentle *puff puff puff* sound that must run in the Eldridge family.

I dug around in the knapsack, pulled out a bag of penny candy I bought at Zemp's Drug Store yesterday, and tilted the bag toward Miss Emily. While she always fussed about Miss Lurleen's sweet tooth, she was the real sugar addict out of the two. She fished around in the sack and pulled out three pieces, the only Hershey's Kisses in the bag, and handed it back to me.

"Thank you," she said, popping one in her mouth. "Next time we stop, I hope there's a diner so we can get some sweet tea in Lurleen."

"Do you think that's a good idea? She drank a Coke just now, and I know she hates having to go to the bathroom all the time."

Before Miss Emily could answer, the little boy a few seats ahead of us spilled an entire cigar box full of crayons and began to wail. But Miss Lurleen didn't stir. His mother chased the colors down the aisle as they rolled everywhere. I waited until Miss Lurleen's head shifted back to Miss Emily's shoulder, picked up the handful that landed at my feet, but couldn't reach the ones by Miss Emily. I handed them to the woman, who was apologizing all over the place to everyone.

Miss Emily didn't budge and gave the woman a cross look that sent her scurrying back to her seat. "All this sitting is going to set off Lurleen's leg cramps," she fussed. "The tea and the bananas should help with that."

"Oh," I said. "Remmy didn't mention tea. Just bananas." Although he probably figured there was no need since there'd be enough sweet tea between Camden and Palestine to float a boat, especially with the sisters' penchant for the stuff.

"That's because he's a nitwit. My beautician, Shari Bartholomew, knows everything about everything. I told her Lurleen was suffering with leg cramps and she said, 'Why, give her her fill of sweet tea and bananas.' Works like a charm."

"Good to know," I said.

"You and Sister have become awfully cozy," Miss Emily said. As if on cue, Miss Lurleen shifted to my shoulder, head reared back, mouth gaped open.

"We hit it off if that's what you mean. She likes for me to read to her, and, for the most part, I like her taste in books."

"She was a librarian, you know. Retired the year before me."

"I should have guessed." I smiled at the idea of Miss Lurleen in the stacks, lost in some great classic; although she did love a good romance every now and then. But who doesn't?

"Oh, she wasn't just any librarian with her nose always stuck in a book; she was a crack shot too. Loved to hunt as much as she loved to read; I grant you there wasn't another gun-toting librarian in the state back then. Probably hasn't been one since."

"My father's a great marksman; he's won a lot of contests, even a couple of statewide competitions. I think he was so disappointed he ended up with girls instead of a son to pass on his love for firearms; not sure it ever occurred to him to teach my sister or me. But I doubt that either of us would have been interested," I said. "I'm surprised I didn't see any guns around your house, though; back home, they hang in cases like fine portraits all over the place."

Miss Emily had the same red-faced expression that she wore when she looked everywhere for her reading glasses. I'd kindly pointed they were on top of her head, but only once because she blessed me out and accused me of insinuating that she was old and doddering. She drew her lips into a thin line; her chin trembled. "Yes, well. She got rid of the guns after the accident."

"Accident?" Miss Lurleen woke with a start.

"It's all right, Sister. Go back to sleep," Miss Emily said.

Miss Lurleen looked around like she was confused and then recognition settled in. She winced hard and shifted her feet about. "Are your legs bothering you?" I asked.

She nodded, worry on her face. "We're so hemmed in. I know I need to get up and walk the cramps out, but—" She didn't have to finish the sentence; with the bus pitching from side to side without warning, there was a very good possibility she would fall. "Maybe I should just stand a bit."

"I'll help you," I said. "You can hold on to the seats and walk the aisle. I'll be right behind you."

"Some hired help you are," Miss Emily sniffed. "You should have brought a Thermos of tea."

"Hush, Emily, and be more considerate to Nettie or I swear at the next stop I'll get on the next bus back to Camden."

"Don't worry about me," I said. "Let's get you moving." Miss Lurleen nodded and faltered a bit, almost growling at the pain. She took baby steps into the aisle and then walked toward the front of the bus, three maybe four steps, holding on to the seats for support. She came to a stop and stood, swaying with the motion of the bus; the little boy who'd dropped his crayons earlier looked up at her and smiled.

"Who are you?" he asked.

"*Darrell Jennings*. That is not nice. You say *hello* to someone, you tell them *your* name, then they will politely tell you theirs," his mother fussed. "I'm sorry. He just turned six."

Miss Lurleen nodded. "My name is Miss Eldridge, Darrell, and this is my friend, Nettie." I waved at the boy and he smiled a dallying smile.

"Nettie and Mrs. Eldridge," he repeated.

"No, it's *Miss* Eldridge," Miss Lurleen said. "And you're a very fine boy, Darrell."

"*Miss* Eldridge? But you're so old."

"I'm so very sorry." His mother's face was beet red; she reached over and pinched his chubby little thigh. "*Darrell*, that was rude."

"Owww," the boy wailed, rubbing the red mark. "But she *is* old."

"He's fine," Miss Lurleen told the boy's mother. "Yes, Darrell, I am very old, and I'm Miss Eldridge because I never married."

He looked like his curiosity was killing him. "But why?" he asked and then quickly tried to cover his legs with his hands in case his mother pinched him again.

I'd never seen Miss Lurleen interact with anyone other than her sister and Remmy, but it was plain that Miss Lurleen had been very good with children all those years she had her nose in a book. I couldn't see her face, but I could feel her tense up at the child's innocent question.

"I just never did," she said. "But if I'd known someone as smart and as handsome as you, I'm sure I would have."

The boy nodded, satisfied with the answer, and opened his cigar box again. His mother shifted the box to her lap for safekeeping and gave Miss Lurleen a tentative smile. "Thank you for being so nice to him," she said. "He's full of questions; sometimes too full. I'm sorry if he offended you."

"Nonsense. He just has a curious mind. Is he reading yet?"

"No. Should he be?" The look on her face said she was flying by the seat of her pants at this mother thing.

"He's bright, inquisitive; there's no reason you couldn't start teaching him. And there's no better place for a child to fall in love with reading than a good book," Miss Lurleen said.

"Thanks," his mother said. "I'll think about it."

"My friend is going to help me back to my seat now, Darrell, but it was very nice meeting you." She glanced over her shoulder at me, turned to face the back of the bus, and I took my place behind her. A few labored steps later, she plopped down out of breath but with a satisfied look on her face.

"I hope you told that mother to control her child. Squealing. Crayons rolling around underfoot. What a nuisance," Miss Emily snapped.

Still out of breath, Miss Lurleen shut her mouth, but only for a moment. "What do you expect, Emily? He's a child. Honestly, how they let you teach impressionable young minds all those years is beyond me," Miss Lurleen huffed. "She was a holy terror, Nettie, the teacher who when the poor children learned they were assigned to her either wet their pants or cried themselves sick. And these weren't little ones like that boy, they were sixth graders. Even the older ones that had been held back and were terrors themselves were scared to death of her."

"Bite your tongue, Sister," Miss Emily spat. "Why, I'll have you to know I taught half of Camden. The half who grew up to be respectable, decent adults, and if they had not had me to jerk a knot in their rear ends, who knows what kind of degenerates they might have become."

"I stand by my assessment, Emily. And another thing; you'd better stop looking at the world like it's some poor child you need to browbeat into submission, because that's what the world will remember you for. And for being petty and divisive."

Miss Emily opened her mouth to respond but clamped it shut, rolling her lips under her teeth. She didn't speak; no one did. About an hour passed and the bus pulled into a large terminal in Columbus. The driver announced the bus would leave in half an hour, that there was hot food available at the diner, but to hurry; the bus wouldn't wait. Everyone filed off ahead of the three of us. I helped Miss Lurleen off the bus and she made a beeline without any help to the nearby ladies' room.

I'd seen Miss Emily the protector, Miss Emily the know-it-all and the bitch full of sass and vinegar, but looking at her now, she was wounded over the last exchange with her sister. "She didn't mean it," I lied, because I was sure Miss Lurleen meant every word she said.

"I'm her sister. I'm impervious to her accusations and pompous rants. Besides, I'm glad she said it. The crankier she is, the better," Miss Emily snapped. I was so thunderstruck, I barely heard her last words before she joined the line for the restroom. "Means she's not going to die."

20

EMILY

Nettie watched Emily, as closely as she watched Lurleen, maybe more so. While it used to annoy the hell out of Emily, she had grown accustomed to it, and, though she would never admit it to Nettie, it was somewhat comforting. Perhaps it was the kinship she and Nettie shared. Emily knew a fellow belle of the ball when she saw one, and Nettie was definitely that and then some in the life she'd escaped to come to work for Sister. And Emily.

Nettie had watched the exchange on the bus like Lurleen and Emily were two thoroughbreds going neck and neck for the finish line at the Carolina Cup. But the truth was, no matter how right Emily was, she'd never win the argument because after John died, Lurleen was elevated to near martyr status. Of course everyone had always loved her, but never loving another man, never marrying, romanced Lurleen's life's story, gave her certain license Emily never had. And Emily wasn't about to marry, not after her part in John's death.

Maybe it was Emily's imagination, but it felt like Nettie somehow understood her. Was it their uncommon beauty that bound them together or was it the secret Nettie carried? No, it couldn't be that; Emily couldn't keep a secret if the remnants of her life depended on it. If she could, she never would have told the police what really happened that day. The memory still made her chest squeeze tight, almost suffocating her. But she'd atoned for so many years, surely the scales weren't so very lopsided anymore.

Lurleen opened the bathroom door and stood in the threshold, her color looked good, better than it had in weeks, but she was breathing so very hard. Maybe this trip would indeed kill her, and then Emily would have more blood on her hands. And for that, there would be no atonement.

Lurleen smiled at the women in line. "Ladies, would you all mind making way for my sister?" she asked. "It's hard for us old gals to go so long, and she'll just be a jiffy. *Won't you,* Emily." Lurleen looked at her to let her know she'd better not dawdle, but the warmth had returned to her beautiful blue eyes. The women stepped aside, and when Emily reached the bathroom door, her sister put her hand on Emily's arm. Yes, Lurleen was making her way back from the dead. And Emily was making her way toward forgiveness.

LURLEEN

Nettie had a long line of people behind her grumbling because she seemed to be haggling with the order taker at the window of the tiny food stand.

"I told you," the dark-haired, hard-looking woman huffed. "We ain't got nothing without salt, lady. Now I got a line of customers here; are you going to order something or what?"

"Please, it's for someone who's ill. Do you have eggs?" Nettie asked.

"Yeah. We got egg salad; I 'spect we got eggs."

"An egg sandwich, just the egg and the bread, please."

"Fried or scrambled?" She raised her eyebrows.

"One chicken salad and two egg sandwiches, please. Scrambled would be good," Lurleen said, sliding two dollars across the counter, "with two teas and a Co-Cola for my friend here."

"I'm sorry. I didn't mean to take so long," Nettie said to the folks in line as she and Lurleen made their way to one of the benches to wait for their food.

"Getting old definitely has its fringe benefits, but they're mostly for the bathroom or the food line. Getting a seat in a crowded room, that sort of thing," Lurleen said. "Besides, we'll be fine. The driver is at the back of the line, and we're not gong anywhere without him."

Nettie nodded and smiled like she had a secret. Lurleen suspected she had many. "I know you love books, but you never told me you were a librarian."

"You never asked," Lurleen said, implying Nettie could ask her anything and she'd return an honest answer. She liked Nettie, a lot, but that wasn't quite the case.

"I didn't bring any books." She blushed, pulling the other half of the banana out of her knapsack. "As much as I've read to you, you'd think I'd have packed at least one."

"Maybe you thought I wouldn't make it this far," Lurleen joked. "I know I didn't."

"Two eggs, two teas, a chicken and a Coke," the woman who took their order shouted. Nettie waded through the customers waiting for their food and came back holding the three drinks in her hands and the bag clamped between her teeth.

Lurleen took the tea when she'd really rather have had the Coke, but Emily would fuss, and it did seem to help her leg cramps. Sister joined them; they ate their lunch in companionable silence, and Lurleen was right, the driver didn't get his food until almost dead last, and their stop in Macon was closer to an hour than thirty minutes. Surprisingly, Lurleen wasn't nearly as tired as she was sure she would be from being drug up one side and down the other. Not that she had any illusions of being healed or even making it to Texas, but if this was an adventure, her last one, she hoped it would be a good one.

"Saddle up," the driver called, shoving the last of his sandwich in his mouth. Who knew what the next stop would be? Of course they'd have to change buses in Montgomery. If Lurleen made it that far.

Many of the travelers got on other buses in Macon, so there was room enough for each of the women to take a bench seat, put their feet up. Nettie and Lurleen on one side of the bus, Emily on the other. Even with her water pills and avoiding salt, Lurleen's ankles were huge, but overall she felt pretty good. Just tired.

The gentle rocking of the bus lulled her to sleep, and twice she almost fell off the seat. Completely addled, she felt Nettie's sure hands on her shoulders gently holding her in place while Emily tied her shawl and Nettie's pretty blue sweater together and handed it to Nettie. With one end over Lurleen's shoulder and the middle of the contraption across her chest, Nettie threaded the other end through the crease where the seat back met the bench and tied it behind the seat like a sling. Nettie gave it a good yank, most likely ruining her sweater; Emily's shawl was almost as old as she was and completely indestructible. The two of them looked so proud. Lurleen looked ridiculous belted into her seat, but she was able to get some rest without falling on her behind.

21

NETTIE

Satisfied Miss Lurleen was belted to her seat, I gave in to the rocking of the bus, hoping to high heaven that I could sleep straight through Alabama. Of course that wasn't possible when we stopped so often. And it didn't help that I could feel 'Bama's sultry pull, drawing me home like a siren's song.

A few short weeks ago, I was sure, after Sue's wedding, my next trip from South Carolina to my home state would be my last. I would claim Satsuma as both my heart and my home, marry Brooks and live there forever. Now, the closer the bus got to the Chatta-hoochee River that separated Alabama and Georgia, the more I felt like my skin was three sizes too small for my body.

Given the time constraints and the fact that Miss Lurleen was on death's door, it wasn't possible to bypass the Yellowhammer State. I gripped the edge of the seat and braced myself. As the bus neared the Chattahoochee, my heart kicked hard against my chest as if Alabama herself had wronged me.

Was it a siren singing me home? Or was it the song of my sister, a duet that had bound us together since birth? For a moment, I allowed myself to feel the ache I felt for Sissy. When her own pain echoed back, my eyes flew open, and somehow, I just knew. She needed me.

The calculations were automatic, instinctual. Almost frantic. I could leave the Eldridges to fend for themselves in Montgomery, catch the next bus bound for Mobile. It would stop in Satsuma, just long enough for me to get off. I wouldn't be home in time for supper, but would arrive during the most perfect part of the day, when the people I loved best sat on four small porches hunched together in the clearing between the groves.

Everyone would be elated to see me, and Sissy would throw her arms around my neck. We'd all settle in and laugh and tell the same stories I never tired of hearing. Then, when it was bedtime, Sissy and I would go to the room we shared, lie across her twin bed or mine, and she would tell me what was so terribly wrong that I could feel it in my bones.

Was intuition the true siren, tricking me into feeling fiercely protective of Sissy like I always did? Feel sorry for her? It had to be because Sissy had everything. Mama and Daddy. Brooks and his baby. I wanted to cry, but I couldn't.

The sign for the great Chattahoochee was a blur. Seconds later, I was in the bosom of my home state, and I thought I would die if I didn't get out.

Unfortunately, 'Bama is about as wide as she is long. We'd gone over four hundred miles since Camden, and it was wearing on the sisters. So when the bus stopped in Montgomery, we took a taxi to the Jefferson Davis Hotel. Outside of taking the bus to and from Columbia, I'd never traveled much at all. The hotel was the first I'd ever stayed in and was as marvelous as anything I'd ever seen.

The bellman took our bags from the cab and ushered us to the front desk.

Miss Emily propped her huge pocketbook on the counter, fluffed her silver curls, and made sure she had the attendant's full attention. "We'd like one room, please."

"Two rooms," Miss Lurleen corrected.

"We don't need two rooms, Sister," Miss Emily snapped.

"I'm tired, Emily. We all are. I want a bed to myself, and I won't have Nettie sleeping on some pallet on the floor. It's bad enough you're dragging us across all creation like this; the least you can do is give us a good night's sleep." The irritation in Miss Lurleen's voice was thicker than apple butter as she slid three tens across the counter. "Two rooms. Please," she said to the attendant. Pushing the register forward for her to sign, he made change and produced two keys.

"And will you be dining with us tonight?" he asked.

"Not if you have salt on the menu, because it will kill this one if she doesn't die of meanness first." Miss Emily snatched one of the keys off of the counter and headed toward the elevator.

Miss Lurleen handed the other key to me and took off after her at a surprisingly good clip. We all made it to the elevator with a bewildered-looking bellman, who most likely didn't cotton to confrontation. He pushed the call button and kept his head down.

"I'm giving Nettie the room to herself," Miss Lurleen said.

"Really?" Miss Emily interrupted. "I thought you all would want to have dinner together, order the same foods, and then have a rollicking good hen party until it's time to get back on the g.d. bus with me to save your life."

"Ladies," I said. "We're all tired. Let's just be nice, and—"

"I would if Emily would stop being so touchy about everything. And bossy," Miss Lurleen fussed.

"I'm not the bossy one," Miss Emily huffed. "You claimed that prize the day you were born."

"Well, I'm the eldest in this family, and until I'm not, I'll act like it. Now take that bow out of your back this instant."

The elevator doors opened and the sisters entered. Neither the bellman nor I wanted to step into the catfight box. He was the braver one, or, more likely, he wasn't worn to a frazzle because he'd traveled over four hundred miles in one day on a Greyhound bus with the Eldridge sisters.

"Are you coming?" Miss Emily snapped.

I pointed to the phone booth in the lobby. "I'll be right up; I have to make a call."

"I'll put your things in your room, ma'am," the bellman said with a nod. I offered my key, but he shook his head. "Keep it. I have a passkey."

It was well after six when I opened the door to the booth and sat down on the bench. I knew Remmy's office number by heart and dialed zero, praying Katie wasn't still at her post. The operator put the collect call through and Remmy picked up on the first ring and accepted the charges.

"Hey," he breathed into the phone, sending shivers down my

thighs and scattering my mind into a million pieces. "I'm glad you called. How's it going?"

"Surprisingly well," I said, struggling to regain my composure. I was calling Remmy because he was Miss Lurleen's doctor, not because I missed him, missed hearing his voice. "For the majority of the trip, the bus wasn't very crowded and Miss Lurleen was able to prop her feet up; that helped with the swelling. When she was awake, I had her up and walking every half hour or so."

"That's good, Nettie."

"I'm trying to steer her clear of salt, but you're right; it's difficult. We've stopped over in Montgomery for the night at a very nice hotel. I'm hoping their restaurant will have some healthier choices." There. That sounded professional. Almost businesslike.

"Good, and how are you holding up?" he asked.

"I'm fine," I clipped.

"You don't sound fine. You don't sound like you. Is Miss Emily being a pill?" he asked, but before I could answer, he added, "Or is it that you're so close to home?"

"*No.*" All right, so Remmy Wilkes was good at diagnosing things, at diagnosing me. "Yes. I just want to get out of here, but the sisters would be dead if I'd pushed us on to Mississippi."

"Well, if the trip didn't kill either of them so far, you've had a very good day. Hope tomorrow is just as good." There was a long silence. "I miss you, Nettie."

I missed him too, his easy way, his handsome face, the way he took time to untangle the jumbled mess I'd become since Sissy and Brooks's betrayal, separate the strands and know me, the real me that didn't live on a pedestal. At that moment, I felt as homesick for him as I had ever felt for anyone or anyplace. But it couldn't be real, could it? Did I want to be in Remmy's arms because I had feelings for him or because that would put me over five hundred miles from my troubles? Was I such a runner that I couldn't pass through the offending state of Alabama without wrestling with the urge to bolt?

"I have to go now, Remmy." The words almost stuck in my throat. "Get ready for dinner."

"Call me again tomorrow?"

"If I can."

"Far as I know, Bell Telephone didn't stop putting out phone booths once they got west of Montgomery, so I'll take that as a yes." His voice was playful, and I found myself almost smiling, twirling the phone cord around my finger and then back again. "Anything changes, you call me," he added.

"If anything changes with Miss Lurleen, I definitely will," I said.

"If anything changes with *you* either, Nettie," he said.

I blushed hard and switched the subject. "I'm so terrible; I didn't even ask how your day was."

"Better, now that I've heard your voice."

"I really do have to go, Remmy." I hung up the phone and hurried to the elevator, pretending I was completely unaffected by Remmy Wilkes. The doors opened and swallowed me up; unfortunately they spit me out on the fourth floor just as the sisters were coming out of their room to go to dinner.

In my room, the bellman had placed my suitcase on the luggage rack to the right of one of the twin beds. Though it was nowhere near the coast, the room had a loud tropical décor with turquoise accent chairs and floral draperies that matched the bedspreads. There was no time to change clothes, just run a brush through my hair and put on some lipstick. Hurrying out of the room, the sisters were still waiting in the hallway. Trammeled between Miss Emily and me, each of us with a hand cupped under Miss Lurleen's elbow, we guided her down the hall and into the elevator.

"When was the last time we went out to dinner, Sister? To a really nice place?" Miss Lurleen asked as we stepped into the grand hotel lobby. She was walking a little better, not completely out of breath and struggling like the next step would be her last. Maybe Remmy was wrong about this trip killing her.

"We've never been anyplace quite like this. Not that I recall," Emily said, pulling on her gloves that ended just below her elbows.

A tall man with ebony skin, dressed in a black tie, a crisp white shirt, and white suit, approached and nodded. "Good evening, ladies, and welcome to the Urban, the finest restaurant in the great state of Alabama. May I seat you?"

"Yes, please," Miss Lurleen said. "A table for three."

"Very well," he said. "This way." He led us to a table in the center of the crowded dining room that wasn't quite as fancy as the lobby, but the prints on the wall and the turquoise linens carried over the same tropical theme as was in my room upstairs. He held Miss Lurleen's chair, and she sat down with a plop.

Miss Emily waited until he pulled out her chair and then eased into it as he passed out the menus. She crossed her legs and fiddled with the long strand of pearls around her neck. While I was still in my traveling clothes, she had definitely dressed for dinner in a some-what fitted floral dress that was mostly pink. Her lipstick matched the darker fuchsia shade in her dress; she'd put on a pair of teardrop pearl earrings and had a little silver clip in her hair.

One table over, an extremely handsome man maybe in his midfifties sat nursing his cocktail, perhaps waiting for someone. Miss Emily had what could only be described as a sultry look on her face when she spied him. Our table was just a couple of feet away from his, and when Miss Emily *accidentally* dropped her napkin, he didn't pick it up. One of the many waiters keeping watch over the crowded room rushed over and picked up the napkin. Miss Emily cleared her throat and dropped it again. The man either didn't notice her or her napkin or he was born without manners, because he didn't pick it up. Or fall madly in love with Miss Emily like the men of her day must have when she played that trick.

The same waiter obviously had no idea he was watching a professional coquette; he rushed over, scooped the napkin off of the floor, and put it in her lap. "Ma'am," he said, voice hushed, "ain't no shame in tucking your napkin in the top of your dress like a bib." Miss Emily gave him a look that would have put fear in God himself, and the waiter scurried back to his station.

"Oh, for pity's sake, Emily, are you playing dropsy?" Miss Lurleen scanned the dining room and immediately pegged Miss Emily's target. "My Lord, that man is at least twenty years your junior, maybe more."

"Hush your mouth, Lurleen. I simply dropped my napkin, that's all." Red-faced, Miss Emily turned her attention to her menu. A different waiter than the one Miss Emily sent scurrying greeted our table, filled the water glasses, and asked for our orders.

"I believe I'll have the Virginia ham," Miss Lurleen said. "And candied yams. I haven't had those in ages."

"She absolutely will not," Miss Emily snapped. She put her reading glasses on and perused the menu.

"Emily, I'm quite capable of ordering for myself."

"Well, I'm not going to let you kill yourself just to spite me and cut this trip short." She lowered her glasses and addressed the waiter. "What do you have without salt?"

"No salt?" He scratched his head and looked over the menu in his hand. "None in the applesauce. Bread's real good, and it don't have much. Cole slaw's got some sweet to it; don't think it has much of any either. I believe the yams would be okay; they're awful good. But that's all sweet stuff. I'll ask the cook, but I believe the meatloaf don't have much salt." He gave Miss Lurleen a sheepish look. "I sure wish you could have that ham, ma'am, it's awful good."

"Thank you," Miss Lurleen huffed. "Just give me a dab of all of that except the meatloaf, but I do want to see the dessert tray."

I ordered the special because it was cheap and I knew Miss Emily would fuss about having to pay for the meal, but Miss Lurleen would insist on it. Miss Emily ordered the Virginia ham as well as every side dish her sister probably adored. We ate our meals with little small talk, and Miss Emily kept her napkin to herself.

After dinner, with the coffee poured, the waiter served the mile-high chocolate cake Miss Lurleen ordered, and she asked for two extra forks so that Miss Emily and I could have a taste. I savored a forkful of the gooey rich dessert and moaned.

"Are we far from your home, Nettie?" Miss Lurleen asked.

The next bite of cake went down the wrong way, and I choked on her words. Gulping down some water, I tried to regain my composure and produce a confederate smile.

"Good Lord, child. Did you murder someone?" Miss Emily asked, patting me on the back hard enough to dislodge a major organ. "Is that why you're so jittery?"

Still coughing, I shook my head. "No, ma'am," I croaked.

"I'm sorry, Nettie. I didn't mean to upset you," Miss Lurleen said.

I shook my head and gulped down some more water. "No, it's fine," I wheezed. "Satsuma's about—a hundred miles from here—maybe a little more."

"Well, if you and Lurleen insist on making this a hen party, even your darkest tale will go down better with more chocolate." Miss Emily forked another piece of cake. "Do tell, Nettie Gilbert, what is it that has you nearly asphyxiating?"

"Yes, Nettie, tell us your story," Miss Lurleen said, motioning to the waiter to bring another piece of chocolate cake.

"It must be racy," Miss Emily said, scraping the plate for the last of the frosting. "I love a good scintillating tale."

"That's not what interests me, and it's rather cruel of you, Emily, to relish in Nettie's predicament, whatever that may be," Miss Lurleen snipped before she turned her attention to me. "You wear your burden so well, dear, it's almost invisible. But the closer we got to your home state today, the more I felt it too."

"I'm sorry, I didn't mean to—"

"And I didn't mean to imply *you* were burdensome," Miss Lurleen added. "I just hate to see you carrying your troubles alone. It's not good for you."

The waiter put the second piece of cake in the center of the table. "Well, we know you're not expecting. So, it can't be that," Emily said.

"*Emily*," Miss Lurleen barked.

"Did you rob a bank? Join the Communist Party?"

"*Hush*, Emily, you know she's done nothing of the sort. Have some more cake, Nettie." Miss Lurleen speared an especially large piece and closed her eyes, luxuriating in the rich flavor. I didn't want any more, but I obeyed and learned that chocolate could loosen the tongue far better than any truth serum.

"My sister betrayed me," I began.

Emily looked rather startled and motioned to the waiter. "Check please."

"Yes," Miss Lurleen said firmly when the man arrived at our table. "You may bring the check, but I'd love a cup of coffee with this last bite of cake please." I declined coffee because I knew I wouldn't sleep, and even without it I probably wouldn't anyway.

"Of course, ma'am. 'Nother piece of cake for the table?" the waiter asked.

"Oh, why not," Miss Lurleen said.

And then their eyes were on me. Miss Lurleen's soft and blue and understanding. Miss Emily's look was hard to peg, the jealousy that was always there seemed to be tinged with something else that looked a lot like guilt.

"Dessert for the ladies," the waiter said, taking the empty cake plate and replacing it with an even bigger slice than the one before.

"I had a fiancé back home." I stabbed a big chunk, closed my eyes and let the chocolate goodness loosen my tongue. "In Satsuma; his name was Brooks. A few weeks ago, my mother sent me an invitation to my baby sister's wedding; she has to get married. Her and Brooks—" I shoved another piece into my mouth to keep the tears at bay, and surprisingly enough it worked. "Are expecting."

"Oh, Nettie." Miss Lurleen placed her withered hand on mine and gave it a gentle squeeze. "I'm so sorry."

Miss Emily said nothing, no verbal jabs, no disparaging remarks. Silence. She wouldn't even look at me, and while her silence should have felt like some small victory, all it did was make me want to hear her story. What had she done that had made Miss Lurleen so angry, she'd lived under the same roof with Miss Emily for seven years and didn't speak to her?

I continued, my voice barely above a whisper. "As you can imagine, it's hard for me, being so close to home."

Miss Lurleen pushed the partially eaten third piece of cake away, signed the check, and drained her coffee cup like it was a good stiff drink. "I'm not sure what the best medicine is for your predicament, Nettie. Any ideas, Emily?" Miss Lurleen asked, her imperfectly arched eyebrows raised high.

"Yes." She nodded and raised her azure blue eyes to mine, her face expressionless. "I suggest we get the hell out of Alabama." And, for once, I agreed wholeheartedly with Emily Eldridge.

22

EMILY

What Nettie's sister did to her was terrible, but it didn't even come close to Emily's transgression, and no amount of chocolate cake could make Emily share that story with the girl. As mean as she had been to Nettie, it would kill Emily to see the girl gloat over her sin. Even if Nettie didn't seem to be the gloating kind.

Emily lay awake all night, while Lurleen slept like the dead. The blameless. And all she could think about was Teddy. She hadn't allowed herself that luxury, that torture, in a very long time. Oh, her brother came to mind often, but she'd always hand-picked the sweet memories until there was only the boneless truth; and she wasn't strong enough to ruminate on that any longer.

Her strength had always been her curse, something no one saw below her pretty exterior. It made her do things she didn't want to do, persevere when she wanted to do nothing but throw her hands up, maybe even turn her toes up on the underside of the grass. Emily certainly looked like a delicate flower. She wanted to be delicate, but she was twice as sturdy as Lurleen. Her backbone endured, carrying her forward day by day, a perpetual punishment.

Lurleen never said, but Emily knew she believed wholeheartedly Teddy was dead. Sometimes Emily wished he really were dead. At least she would know he was at peace. Those four years after the accident when he lost his mind were evidence enough that would be the only way he would ever know peace. But Emily suspected his guilt was like hers, propelling him forward whether he liked it or not. And what had happened wasn't even his fault. He was just a child. Emily was the grownup, although barely, and, judging from her rash and immature decision, she hadn't been much of one at all.

A car backfired on the street. Emily's body stiffened. Her heart beat out of her chest and she could barely breathe. "Sister," she called out. But all she heard was the *puff puff puff* of Lurleen's breath. The rapid-fire sound pierced the quiet three more times before the engine roared away. Long after it was gone, Emily's heart was still racing, her body as rigid as a single, unbreakable bone. "Sister," she whispered again. Still no answer. "Teddy," she mouthed the word and touched her heart.

The morning of the accident, Emily had gotten up extra early and primped for John's arrival. While Lurleen looked like a man in her hunting clothes, Emily had on her best blue dress that made her eyes sparkle. The day before when Emily had met him at the garden gate, John didn't even look at her, or at least not like she wanted him to.

John Young was every bit as beautiful as Emily, the only man she'd deemed truly worthy of herself. Tall, well over six feet. Broad shoulders, a tapered waist. Rugged features that with those fathomless brown eyes ignited Emily's body and her heart. Being just a year apart, there had always been a perpetual friendly competition between her and Lurleen, one that Emily always won. Although most of the time, she suspected that was the case because the competition was one-sided.

In John's case, it didn't matter. He never looked twice at Emily and hadn't even been in town a month when he'd fallen madly in love with Lurleen. And there they were going hunting together again. Of course Emily knew, even though they came back with a few quail or ducks there was *some* hunting going on, but there had to be something else to it for John to all but ignore Emily.

And Teddy idolized John, especially after John gave Teddy one of his old guns and promised to teach him how to hunt deer, something Teddy had never had an interest in before. But Teddy couldn't spend enough time with John, couldn't get enough of the stories of John's travels, growing up out west, and if Papa had been alive, he would have loved John too.

The last hunting story John had told around the supper table the night before had everyone except Emily enthralled; all she could think about was how she was going to get that man to notice her when he only had eyes for Sister. Well eyes for Lurleen and an elusive and most likely legendary twelve-point buck local hunters claimed to have seen and had dubbed Goliath. John held the record in his home state of Iowa, having slain a Goliath-sized deer, and Teddy wanted to be just like him. He'd told Emily so every time Lurleen went off hunting with John, and Teddy had been over the moon when John took him out to the rifle range to try out the hand-me-down gun.

It was a Saturday morning; Mama had left for work at the DuPont plant like always, well before seven. She'd been on shift work since Daddy had died, because it paid more and because Emily was sure it pained her to be in their home with her three children with her sweet husband noticeably absent. It wasn't that Mama didn't love her children, but between work and the loss of her husband, Mama had been going through the motions for years. Which was where Emily and Lurleen came in.

Now that Emily was fresh out of college with her first teaching job and Lurleen had been working at the Kershaw County Library in Camden for a little over a year, the girls were expected to keep house, work, and look after their brother when the need arose. As long as everyone could stay busy, their minds occupied, no one—especially Mama—could dwell on the huge hole Daddy had left when he passed away. And Brother, sweet Teddy, was the very best child in the whole world. Charming, always funny, always entertaining whether he was tearing up the piano or sitting at the dinner table regaling everyone with tall tales about whatever had happened at school that day.

But Emily didn't like living in a house where nobody acknowledged the hole that could never be filled; it made her feel inadequate, so much less than the rest of the world saw her. And she liked that view of herself, the ravishing young schoolteacher, on the list for every party, every important dinner, on display for only the handsomest, most promising eligible men in town to fawn over, fight over.

Her plan had been to pick one of her many suitors and get out of Mama's rule and out from under the pall that had hung over the house. She'd narrowed it down to a half dozen men over the summer and had planned to choose one before school started next September, but then John Young moved to town and took a big job at the plant Mama worked at.

He was a good bit older than Emily and a challenge. He did not fawn. He did not fight. He didn't even notice Emily. And God, she'd never wanted anyone or anything like she'd wanted that man. Even after he'd fallen for Lurleen, Emily believed she had a chance. He was beautiful, Lurleen was not; sooner or later he'd see Emily the way the rest of the world did.

She was daydreaming on schemes to catch his attention that day when she went out back to feed the cat and happened upon John and Lurleen by the carriage house. John had Sister pushed up against the wall, kissing her, one hand in Lurleen's bonny brown hair, the other sliding into the front of those horrid hunting khakis she insisted on wearing that made her look like a man. When Emily made her presence known, Lurleen jerked away from him and looked both relieved Mama hadn't caught her and horrified that Emily had.

Much to Emily's surprise, Lurleen's hair was down and she'd actually put on rouge *to go hunting.* John didn't so much as look at Emily. Right then and there, she decided she'd fix both John and Lurleen good.

It was Lurleen's turn to watch Teddy; Mama was working at the mill and her daughters were certainly old enough to look after their fourteen-year-old brother. Lurleen had begged Emily to trade with her so she could go hunting with John the opening day of deer season, and Emily had agreed at first, until she'd seen them by the carriage house. John didn't even apologize, just gave Lurleen a crooked smile that said he would finish what he started later. Worse yet, Lurleen blushed and returned the sentiment with another kiss, right on his lips.

Emily couldn't breathe, couldn't speak, until the two of them separated and started for John's truck with their arms around each other. Teddy ran out of the house and said hey to John, who kept walking and just waved over his shoulder like he didn't have time for the boy. Nor the inclination for Emily.

"It's *your* day to watch Brother, Lurleen." Emily's voice came out harsh and dripping with envy.

"Emily, no. You said—" Lurleen pulled away from John, but he grabbed her hand and didn't let go.

"It's your day, *Sister*."

"Can I go with John and Lurleen?" Teddy begged. "Please, Emily. I wanna bring home a big buck like him. A state record."

Lurleen shook her head. "No, Teddy, you can't go. Opening day is too dangerous for a novice."

"But I'm good, aren't I, John? You said so yourself."

Lurleen was a regular at the shooting range; sometimes she drug Brother along. When John learned of her penchant for guns, he became a regular too and started to teach Teddy how to shoot, something Mama had forbidden. When Teddy blurted out the secret at dinner one night, Emily was sure Mama would ban Lurleen from the shooting range and from John, but Mama thought it was wonderful that John was spending time with Teddy. Apparently because he was a man it was okay for John to teach him, but it was also okay because anyone could see Mama's fatherless son adored John.

"Yeah, kid, you're good, but Lurleen's right. There'll be more hunters than deer looking for that big buck. It's not safe, buddy."

"Emily," Brother whined. "I wanna go. Please let me. Lurleen was supposed to watch me; she can watch me just as good in the woods as she can here."

Emily knew what she was doing. A third wheel would take the enchantment right out of Lurleen's little rendezvous. A little brother would definitely kill the romance, even if it was just for a little while. And John deserved at least that for slighting Emily, for not coming under her spell like every other man in Kershaw County. "Of course you can go, Teddy," she said, looking straight at Lurleen.

"Never mind. I'll stay," Lurleen said, looking longingly at John. "It is my turn to keep him."

"I'll stay with you," John said.

"No, I'd hate for you two *deer* aficionados to miss opening day," Emily said. "I insist you go and take Brother with you."

"Great," Brother yelled, and tore into the house. He came out with the rifle John had given him and joined the happy couple.

"This isn't a good idea, Emily," Lurleen said.

"It'll be all right, sweetheart. We'll do our best, keep him close," John said to Lurleen. Which was exactly Emily's plan; Brother would stay so close, there would be no breathless kisses for Lurleen, and John certainly wouldn't try to get into her pants with Teddy around.

Emily was so proud of herself, after they left, she celebrated with a long bubble bath and then fixed her hair for her date that night. She didn't even hear the police car when it pulled up out front, but when she floated from her room to the kitchen to get a glass of sweet tea, she saw a policeman ushering Lurleen into the house; she was covered in blood.

"Lurleen." Emily flew to sister; her face was blank and ghostly pale. "Lurleen."

"She's okay," the policeman said.

"My brother. Teddy. Where's my brother?" Emily screamed. She ran to the screen door but didn't see anybody in the squad car. "Oh, my God. Please. Where's my brother?" Emily flung herself at the officer, pummeling his chest. "Where's Teddy?"

"He's at the hospital," the policeman said. "Someone at the station called your mama; she's on her way there from work."

"Has he been shot?" Emily sobbed. "Dear God, is he dead? Please, no."

"He's in shock." Lurleen's voice was flat; she looked like she was in shock too.

Grateful, Emily threw her arms around Lurleen, but she peeled Emily off and backed away from her. "You took him from me," she gritted out through tears. "Don't touch me."

"But Lurleen, Brother's fine." Sobbing uncontrollably, Emily reached for her, but Lurleen let out an inhuman yowl. She slapped Emily hard across the face, snatched a handful of her hair out, and went back for more. The policeman grabbed her but not before Lurleen got Emily in a headlock and started pummeling her face. Emily screamed, the taste of her own blood filling her mouth.

The policeman pulled Lurleen off of Emily. "That's enough. It was horrible what happened," he shouted, "but she's your sister; you're going to need her."

"I hate her." Lurleen glared at Emily, spittle flying like a rabid dog. "She's dead to me," she screamed. She pulled away from the policeman, went to her room, and did not emerge until three days later, just before John's body was taken to the train station in Columbia to be shipped home to Iowa. Mama took Lurleen to the funeral home and she sat alone with his closed casket for hours until they loaded it in the hearse.

By that time, Brother had felt the full weight of what he'd done. Somehow he'd managed to slip away from John and Lurleen to try to shoot that g.d. deer that was folklore. Alarmed, John and Lurleen split up to look for him. Lurleen heard a shot and then Brother screamed. The policeman said it was a wonder when she threw her gun down and ran in the direction of the scream that she didn't get shot. When she got there, Brother's body was draped over John's torso, his face covering John's or what was left of it. It was an accident. That's what the game warden and the police had said, nobody's fault, but that wasn't true. It was Emily's fault.

Emily told the police her part in John's death, but she never told Mama or anyone else for that matter, and neither had Lurleen or Brother. Emily's part in ruining Teddy, in John's death, was both her cross and her secret to bear. A secret that drove Brother mad, a secret that turned out to be Lurleen's revenge because she knew Emily could never tell Mama what had happened. Years passed, Emily's guilt gnawed at her from the inside out, and by time Lurleen did speak to her again, Mama had passed away and Teddy had been gone for four years.

Was he alive? Was he dead? Would she ever know one way or the other?

"Emily?" Lurleen's voice pierced the nightmare Emily had lived and relived for so much of her life, sometimes it seemed it was her life. "Are you crying?"

Emily didn't answer. Just concentrated on breathing, which was next to impossible. She squeezed her eyes shut for one last covetous moment and wished to God she'd been able to outrun her secret like Nettie Gilbert had outrun hers. But it was so deep, so potent, even in the bosom of her sister's forgiveness, it was still there.

23

LURLEEN

Much to Lurleen's shock, she was up early, just before six. Emily was snoring away, like she usually did when she first went to sleep, which made Lurleen wonder if Emily had gotten any sleep at all last night. While Lurleen hadn't really wanted to come on this trip, she had to admit, aside from the physical trials, their little jaunt had been, well, fun so far.

She felt relatively good and wondered if she could get one of the waiters to sneak her a ham biscuit for the road at breakfast, but maybe that was pushing things a bit. Grudgingly she washed down her digitalis and her water pill with a swig of water Emily must have put beside the bed last night.

She dressed, slipped out of the room quietly, and knocked softly on Nettie's door. A few seconds later, the door opened. Nettie was gathering her hair into a long ponytail. She was dressed in the lovely yellow skirt she'd worn her first day of work and a frilly white blouse. "I'm going to let Emily sleep a bit; I was headed down to the dining room to get some breakfast and wondered if you were up and wanted to join me."

The sweet girl blushed. "I don't think Miss Emily would like that, and I really don't want to get off on the wrong foot today."

"All right then. I'll get a bite to eat, and you all join me when you're ready. What time do we have to be at the bus station?"

"The bus for Shreveport leaves around ten," Nettie said.

"That'll give me plenty of time to drink coffee and have a fine breakfast."

"But," Nettie said hesitantly.

"I know, no ham."

She nodded, lips pursed. "I should walk you down."

Lurleen started to protest, but she didn't for Nettie's sake. Nettie ushered her to the elevator; even with the prospect of being on a bus all day, Lurleen felt a little better today. Not that she was better, but she'd figured out a thing or two since they left Camden yesterday. Staying in bed all the time was not good for her, and not just because of her heart. Every minute of every day was about waiting to die when she should have been focused on making the most of the time she had left.

Over a year ago, after she got sick, if you'd asked Lurleen where her last outing would have been, she would have said the library. Just to walk in and smell the books, walk along the shelves running her fingers across the spines of classics that stole her heart, a good mystery or a romance that took her breath away. To take a young child who swears they hate to read to the stacks and find that one book that unlocks their heart and makes them fall in love with reading.

Never in a million years would she have opted to be held captive on a bus with Emily and a young woman she didn't know well, headed to Texas to see a faith healer who probably was a hoax. But lo and behold if she wasn't excited, even hopeful that there really was a miracle at the end of this snipe hunt.

She passed over the ham again but did have a bowl of grits that hardly had any salt at all in them, some scrambled eggs. Toast. She was on her third cup of coffee when Nettie and Emily joined her in the dining room. Sister looked a wreck, although for Emily, that meant slightly less than perfect. While breakfast was lovely, Nettie still seemed on edge, much like she was yesterday. But they were soon off to the bus station.

Lurleen was dying for a book to read and bought a paperback romance she'd read recently at the newsstand. Pickings were slim and it was either that or a western, which she had no interest in. Emily was almost subdued, quiet. Lurleen tried to poke fun at her a few times, but she barely responded, and when they got on the crowded bus, Emily went right to sleep with her head leaned against the window.

"Is your book good?" Nettie asked.

"Yes. I'm not sure if this woman is a very good writer or if it's just good to read again. Of course I could have read to myself back home, but it was nice having you do it. There's just something about hearing the written word aloud."

"I agree." With her long red hair scraped back, her features looked even more tense than when Emily was on the prowl. Lurleen suspected it had everything to do with Nettie's proximity to her homeplace. Of course, Thomas Wolfe was posthumously credited with suggesting you can't go home again, and although Nettie seemed to be living proof of that, Lurleen disagreed. While the protagonist in Wolfe's story had in his hometown's view besmirched them, Nettie was the one who had been wronged. She should be able to do whatever she pleased after what she'd been through.

Lurleen knew absolutely nothing about Satsuma or Alabamians as a whole, but it seemed to her someone owed that sweet girl a heartfelt apology. Not that it would change what had happened, but Lurleen suspected it would help Nettie heal. Of course Remmy would be only too happy to help mend her heart, and why not? He was good and handsome and caring. If Lurleen thought hard on every boy she'd known over her years living in Camden, she couldn't pick a better one for Nettie.

"As a nosy old woman I'm entitled to ask, was it Remmy you called yesterday?" She blushed and nodded. "And how is he?"

"He's fine. Concerned about you."

"And you as well, I suspect."

"Yes."

"Of course I've known Remmy since before he was born, Katie too. Knew his parents well. It was a shame what happened to them."

"He mentioned the accident, but never really said much other than it put Katie in the wheelchair."

"It was quite tragic; one minute Remmy was driving his family to a restaurant to celebrate his graduation, and the next a truck crossed the yellow line. Remmy swerved but couldn't avoid the truck and ended up being plowed into the concrete pylon of the bridge, crushed the passenger side of the car into a perfect triangle. His parents died instantly. Katie was on their side of the car; her legs were ruined. Remmy and Katie's beau were barely hurt. Physically.

"The accident changed their lives; after Katie was confined to a wheelchair for the rest of her life, her fiancé promptly jilted her.

Remmy was supposed to take a big job in Charleston, but he ended up moving back home to Camden to take over his father's practice."

Emily snored softly as Lurleen changed the subject to a happier time. She shared stories about Remmy growing up, his mother pulling him into the library by his ear to return the books he had stolen. *The Sword in the Stone* and *The Boy's Book of Adventure*, a collection of stories that was quite popular back then, mostly because there weren't a lot of books written specifically for boys.

Lurleen watched the road signs fly past and finished telling the reptile stories Emily still held against Remmy. She was tired, but her work was done; she let out a tired, satisfied sigh and smiled.

Nettie's brow furrowed. "What?" she said tentatively.

"You can relax now, dear. We're in Mississippi."

NETTIE

After talking me out of Alabama, Miss Lurleen fell sound asleep between Miss Emily and me. The sisters snored softly while I studied the map I'd bought at the bus station in Camden. It was worse for wear from being unfolded and refolded often, like somehow that could make the thousand or so miles pass quicker. The sisters had traveled so well yesterday, I'd hoped we could make it all the way to Shreveport, leaving just a short ride to Palestine the following day, but no such luck.

Even with healthy doses of sweet tea and bananas along with her daily medications, Miss Lurleen's legs were swollen so tight, when I poked my finger against her ankles, the skin didn't give at all. And she was pained; it was evident in her face. Miss Emily must have been worn out too, because she barely said two words the whole day.

When the bus pulled into Monroe, Louisiana, I spoke to the woman in the ticket office and about nearby hotels.

"There ain't much in the way of hotels. Hotel Frances used to be a real nice place, but not since the motels out on Highway 80 opened up. I hear them motels are real swanky. Hear they got all kind of modern conveniences, though I ain't quite sure what those would be."

There were either no cabs in town or none available. We paid the woman's sister to shuttle us back out to the highway to the Magnolia Motel. She thanked us all over the place for the two dollars we gave her and promised she'd be around to collect us in the morning and get us to the bus station on time.

The sisters went on about the motel's diner being crowded; they couldn't wait for suppertime. I was still full from when Miss Emily and I had gotten hotdogs in Meridian. It was hard eating mine since Miss Lurleen was still relegated to bananas and sweets, but Miss Emily gobbled hers down in surprisingly unladylike fashion. I wasn't sure if it had something to do with the sisters being old, but one thing I noticed about them was their world seemed to revolve around their next meal.

Miss Lurleen asked for two rooms again, and the desk clerk said he had a room with two twins and a Murphy bed. "One room is just fine," I said.

Three shiny new phone booths stood across from the office. The man carried the sisters' luggage to our room; I set my suitcase by the space on the wall, claiming the Murphy bed, and went back out to use the phone. The operator put the call through. Katie's voice on the other end made the bottom drop out of my stomach.

"Well hello, friend." I wasn't sure if she was being catty or genuine. "Haven't heard from you in a while. I suppose I should reissue that invitation I purposefully forgot after Remmy fell head over heels for you."

"Oh, I don't think he's—"

"Oh, but he is. And, after considering the alternatives here in Camden, no offense, Nettie, the idea of Remmy with a fellow C-Square sister is thrilling. So, will you come to dinner?"

"Didn't he tell you? The sisters and I are on a—" What? A wild-goose chase? A pilgrimage? "Trip."

"My brother doesn't tell me much of anything these days, but you're on a trip with the Eldridge sisters? I can't imagine the fun you must be having."

It wasn't all bad; as a matter of fact, yesterday wasn't nearly as horrible as I'd feared it would be. And today, even though both the sisters were tired, Miss Lurleen seemed much better off than she was when she was back in Camden, lying in her bed all day, waiting to die.

"I wouldn't call it fun, but parts of the trip have been very nice."

"So, you must be calling to speak with Remmy."

"Yes, if it's a good time."

"He's been so grumpy all day, it's a perfect time. Hang on a second."

Remmy picked up the phone and told Katie to hang up on her end.

"Bye, Nettie," Katie chirped. "Hope you haven't pulled all your pretty red hair out by the time you get back to Camden."

"Katie. Hang up," Remmy said firmly. "Hey," he breathed, "so they do have phone booths west of Montgomery. How's it going?"

"Good. We traveled about three hundred miles today, less than yesterday. Miss Lurleen had a good bit of swelling, and it didn't seem wise to continue. I wasn't with her at breakfast; she may have broken down and eaten something she shouldn't have."

"Maybe or it could just be the natural progression of the disease," Remmy said. And then he was quiet for so long, I thought the connection had been lost.

"Remmy?"

"Right here."

"Oh, I thought I'd lost you."

"I just wanted to hear you talk. How are you feeling?"

About him or in general? "I'm tired too, but good. The idea of another full day of travel is daunting for me; I can't imagine what it must seem like for the sisters. When we get to Palestine, I told them we should take a few days to regroup."

When we began this trip, I would have said *if* we get to Palestine, but, barring a catastrophe or the bus breaking down, we would be there tomorrow. And then what? Would we be there in time to see the healer? Would Miss Lurleen be crushed, disappointed? Or would she be healed?

The magazine had said the tent meetings were held almost every night at the local fairgrounds. The crowds were so big it would be difficult to get close enough to see the preacher much less be healed by him. One of the photographs in the magazine showed thousands of people around the tent, many huddled by loudspeakers, listening to the message. I'm sure after reading the article, Miss Emily envisioned bullying her way to the front of the altar with Miss Lurleen in tow. And to be honest, after coming all this way, I would be right there with her to make sure Miss Lurleen got her miracle if there was one to be had.

"You never answered my question, Nettie. Are you doing all right?"

"Yes, but Miss Emily has hardly said a word all day, and it's bothersome."

He laughed. "Never thought I'd ever hear anyone complain about that."

"Remmy, I'm serious."

"I never presume to read a woman's mind, but, knowing a little about human psychology, with the sisters in such close quarters morning, noon, and night, it's bound to stir some stuff up, or, at the very least wear on them. They do have quite a history."

"I know some of it. Last night at dinner, I told them my whole sordid story. I was sure Miss Emily would be gloating, but she barely said anything then and hasn't said hardly anything since. I didn't mention my concern to Miss Lurleen because I didn't want to worry her, but I am worried."

"I know you are, honey, but I'd look at her silence as a gift from God."

"That's not funny, Remmy."

"I'm sorry I'm making light of your predicament; truth is Miss Lurleen's probably going to die; that's a lot to put on you, Nettie. As for Miss Emily, watch her for the same symptoms as you do for Miss Lurleen."

"Oh my God, you're not saying both of them could be sick, are you?"

"They have a family history of heart disease, so it's possible. I'll be honest with you, I don't like the idea of this trip one little bit, not for my patient and not for you."

"I'm fine, Remmy, really; and you're right, Miss Emily would have drug Miss Lurleen out here whether I'd come or not." I paused. "You didn't expect us to make it this far, did you?" *You didn't expect me to make it this far.*

"To be honest, I didn't think y'all would get past Georgia. I was wrong, but I'm not wrong about this. Even though Miss Lurleen says she doesn't believe in this guy, she's only human and a part of her does. She gets herself worked up enough at that tent meeting, she might very well go into cardiac arrest right in front of you, and there won't be anything you can do."

I knew Miss Lurleen was going to die from the start, and somehow taking care of her in her quaint old home back in Camden made that easier to handle. Now when she died she would be in a strange place, surrounded by strange people, with the exception of me and Miss Emily. We needed a miracle.

"Nettie?"

But what if we couldn't get her near the preacher? What if we did and they pulled her onto that stage and didn't let us anywhere near her? What if she died without Miss Emily or me holding her hand? The thought made my heart beat out of control. Hadn't we set out on this journey for healing? Had Miss Lurleen really agreed to the trip to appease her sister? Or was she just tired of waiting to die?

"I'm sorry. What?"

"Whatever happens, I'm here for you," Remmy said.

24

EMILY

They were just thirty-five miles out from Palestine, according to the last sign. Emily should have been relieved. Jubilant. But after having fussed until she'd gotten her way so that Lurleen could get herself healed, it seemed the closer they got to the city, the more vexed Emily became.

Last night, she hadn't been able to get comfortable at all, and she'd laid the blame squarely on Monroe, Louisiana. The place was definitely nothing to write home about, and while everyone and their brother raved about these *motels* that were springing up all over creation, the Magnolia Motel left much to be desired. The diner food was greasy and didn't sit well at all, although Sister looked as happy as an opossum in a corncrib with her meal. Lurleen had garnered the sympathy of the cook when he heard she couldn't have salt, and he'd smothered her fried liver in slimy grilled onions with an extra layer of grease to make up for her dietary restriction.

The motel bed was fairly decent, but Emily still tossed all night. While she usually had Teddy to blame for her insomnia, last night was her own doing. What if this preacher really was a hoax? What if Emily had used up the little bit of time Lurleen had left on some kind of snipe hunt? What if Remmy was right and Lurleen was going to die in Palestine or some other podunk town between here and Camden?

Papa had died happy, fishing on the bank of the Wateree River. But Mama had died a little every day, watching Teddy destroy himself until there was nothing left of her. Convinced he'd killed her too, and in some ways he had, Teddy disappeared. When it was clear there wasn't enough money in the world to find him, Emily hoped he was dead too. At least he wouldn't live in torment anymore, not like Emily did wondering if he was alive. If his life would have been different if she hadn't been brimming with petty jealousy so long ago. If Emily had just done the right thing.

Seven years after the accident, when Lurleen finally broke her silence, she never said a word about Teddy. He was another unmentionable casualty in the wake of Emily's green monster. At first Emily was relieved Lurleen didn't speak to her; she couldn't bear to hear the scathing rant she could feel on the other side of her sister's tongue. Later, she yearned to hear Lurleen say their brother's name; even if she was hateful, at least it would have been the beginning of a conversation that needed to happen. But it never took place.

The bus pulled into Palestine. There were no throngs of people milling about like Emily was sure there would be. That was a good sign; maybe the preacher had already healed everyone and he'd be able to get to Lurleen right away. Not that she had the time to waste, no, but it had always peeved the old girl to sit and wait. And if Emily got Lurleen healed, maybe Emily could finally get herself redeemed.

The Texas sky was cloudless and went on forever. She'd expected everything to be bigger in Texas and was surprised at the scrawny trees, compared to the mile-high pines and big, showy oaks back home. The town looked no different than any of the others they'd passed through; Emily didn't quite know what she was expecting. Certainly more than this.

While Nettie and Lurleen waited on the luggage, Emily spied what looked like a lovely hotel, towering over the other buildings. Hopefully, they'd have a room available and they wouldn't be relegated to some awful new motel on the outskirts of town. Glancing at her watch, it was just after three. They'd have plenty of time to freshen up, maybe take a nap before the tent meeting. Even though Emily was as spry as a new sparrow, it wouldn't be wise to walk to the hotel carrying her heavy bag, and that certainly would put Lurleen in the grave.

She hailed a cab. A colored boy who couldn't have been much older than twelve, thirteen at the most, greeted Emily then asked to help with their bags. She nodded, and he barked at his much younger friend to get the others and follow him to the waiting cab, while Lurleen plodded slowly toward the car with Nettie on her arm.

"Y'all going to the Redlands Hotel?" the older boy asked Emily as he handed the bags to the driver.

The boy looked rather unkempt but was mannerly. It was a wonder he could walk in the pair of brogans he wore with the tops cut out, his long toes hanging over the fronts of his shoes. The other child was barefooted, just as raggedy, but looking to the older one every five seconds or so to make sure he was doing everything right.

"Yes. We are, and then we're going to see the Reverend Jimmy Coe," Emily said.

The boys exchanged looks but waited until the cabbie finished putting the bags in the trunk of the cab and Emily gave them each a quarter. "He ain't round here no more, ma'am," the younger boy said the second Emily greased their palms.

"Hush up." The older one shoved the quarter in his pocket and elbowed his friend in the ribs.

"He's *not around* here *anymore*," Emily corrected. "And of course he is. We saw for ourselves in *LIFE* magazine."

"No ma'am," the younger boy said before he was punched again. "*Ow.* Thurnell. Stop it. She gave us a whole quarter; she ought to know that man killed that boy and the policeman put him in jail."

"What's that?" Lurleen said, completely winded from walking from the bus to the cab.

"Nothing," Emily cut the boy off.

This couldn't be. Panic zinged around her body like something feral, desperate to escape. She plastered on a smile and told herself the boy was just being stupid or cruel. Of course the healer was in Palestine. Where else would he be? And if it wasn't a joke, he was just flat wrong. Had to be.

Didn't Jesus heal that paralyzed man in Palestine? No, that was Capernaum. Those biblical names are so easy to confuse, but Jesus was holding his own sort of tent meetings, wasn't he? Not that this reverend was Jesus or anything, but he had to have some kind of pull with God to heal all those people the article had mentioned. But wasn't it sin that had paralyzed that man in the Bible? Emily knew a thing or two about that. There had to be healing and redemption here in Palestine. There just had to be.

The cab took them to the hotel. Hardly anyone was in the lobby. Emily's heart sank when the clerk said he had plenty of rooms. Why wasn't this place bursting at the seams with the infirmed, the healed spreading the good news? Even Jesus knew healing the sick was his best advertisement. And hadn't the article said as many as ten thousand gathered nightly to hear Coe? The town wasn't that large; folks would have to stay somewhere.

"Two rooms," Emily said. She was sure if the boy was right, Lurleen and Nettie would never speak with her again much less want to sleep in the same room with her.

LURLEEN

L urleen's body had fooled her into thinking she was better, but she felt each infirmity today and then some. Her legs were swollen and were killing her, and she hadn't even had the first speck of salt. She could hardly catch her breath just walking the few steps up and down the aisle of the bus, and there were times her chest ached. Not like it did for Mama or Papa or Teddy or John. Muscle and sinew stretched tight across bones screamed at her to stop this foolishness. Go home. To Camden. To heaven. And if Emily and Nettie weren't standing right there, Lurleen would have screamed right back. *Take me, Jesus. Take me now.*

Long before this crazy jaunt, Lurleen was ready to die. She'd had her baggage packed for most of her life, having chosen the secrets she would take with her like she would have chosen pieces for her trousseau if John hadn't died.

He'd known her thirty-seven days when he'd proposed that morning by the carriage house. To say he'd swept her off her feet was an understatement. Lurleen. The gun-toting librarian who'd always been immune to romance? But she was so in love with him, she would have done anything for him, with him.

She'd said yes and didn't want to take the ring off, but John didn't want Mama to feel slighted and said he'd ask her for Lurleen's hand good and proper when she got home from work that night. Lurleen had just put the ring in his hunting jacket when he pinned her against the wall with his body, his mouth, his hands touching her in ways that no one ever had or ever would again.

John had said, after they went hunting, he'd go home and wash up before coming to supper to talk with Mama. Of course she would give her blessing. Teddy would be over the moon to have John for a brother. However, Emily in all her jealous glory was a different tale.

When she'd caught John kissing her, Lurleen had wanted to wipe that awful look off of her face. Show her the ring. Yes, to rub her nose in it, but also to show her Lurleen and John were forever so she could stop throwing herself at him. But, as it turned out, forever wasn't nearly as long as Lurleen thought it would be.

Lately, she'd been praying for what Remmy promised was certain death. She had no desire to be healed and only gave in to Emily's crazy whim just to shut her up. In her weakened state, Lurleen never thought she'd make it to see the Mississippi River, much less Palestine. And she hoped Remmy was right and the healer really was a hoax so that she could die with her baggage intact, because she didn't think she could keep what happened to Teddy a secret much longer.

At first she didn't tell Emily for spite; her constant pining for Brother was Emily's punishment for ending John's life, wrecking Lurleen's. Mama's. Teddy's. But telling Emily now would only destroy her, and what good would that do?

Nettie helped Lurleen to the registration desk where Emily was talking to the attendant, probably flirting. "I'm so sorry, ma'am," he said to Emily.

"Are they all booked up?" Lurleen said, gasping for breath.

"Oh, no ma'am. Got plenty of rooms. I was just telling your friend here Reverend Coe was arrested."

"Arrested?" Nettie repeated.

Emily's chin was on her chest, her eyes closed. She shook her head violently, her voice growing louder with every word. "No. No. No. My sister came here to be healed. Where is Coe now?"

"The county jail, ma'am. Right after that article came out in *LIFE* magazine, the crowds got way worse. You couldn't get anywhere near the place, but more and more people came to be healed. A couple of weeks ago, a star football player come clean across the state to go to the tent meeting. He was just a high school boy, was gonna play for Texas come September, but he broke his leg working on his daddy's farm.

"The preacher pulled him out of the audience and asked him did he want to be healed. Of course, with him going to college soon, he said yes. Preacher took the cast off right then and there and commanded the boy to stand and walk. When he did, the leg crumbled and part of the bone went clean through his artery," he stated, looking through a stack of newspapers on the counter. "Turned out, the preacher had ringers in the audience, brought the wrong boy onto the stage. He bled out right there in front of everybody. I've got the article somewhere around here; show you the picture if you want."

"I'm so sorry for the boy, but no, thank you," Lurleen said. She picked the room keys up and handed Nettie hers. "Get some rest, Nettie. Emily and I will do the same and we'll all have a late dinner."

"Lurleen." Emily raised her eyes and whispered, "I'm so sorry. I thought—"

"There's no need to be sorry, Emily; this has been a lovely trip. We'll rest up for a few days and then take the long way home to Camden." Lurleen smiled. "I'd like to finally see that ocean you've bragged about for years."

NETTIE

I can't say where hope resides or even why it does. I knew the moment I saw the article on the faith healer that he was a fraud, and should have argued with Remmy against this trip. Not that it would have made a difference with Miss Emily wielding guilt and coercion like a double-edged sword. Yet I'd grown to love Miss Lurleen. I'd wanted her to be healed and had hoped that I was wrong about the reverend.

With the exception of sympathy for the young boy who'd died, Miss Lurleen seemed completely unaffected by the news when the desk clerk said the reverend had been jailed. I suppose she'd expected as much. But Miss Emily had believed with her whole heart, or had hoped with all her heart, because hope was all she had left. And now she didn't even have that.

"Can I get you anything?" I asked as the bellman deposited the sisters' bags on the luggage stands. Miss Emily didn't answer, just sat down on the bed, still in total disbelief.

"No, dear. It's been a very long trip. Get some rest. We'll see you around eight?" Miss Lurleen asked.

"Yes. Of course." I closed the door and entered my room. It would be after four back home, too early to call Remmy. He'd still be working, and Miss Lurleen was right; we could all use a good rest.

I slept hard but not for long. When I woke up around six thirty, I was groggy and even more tired than when I'd closed my eyes. I thought about rolling over until it was time for dinner, but it was more likely that I'd sleep straight through to morning. I got up, drew a bath, and soaked the traveling dust off. I'd piled my hair on top of my head before I got into the tub and left it like that. I slipped into a white pair of pedal pushers and a blue top. Miss Emily would probably frown on my casual dinner attire, but we'd come over a thousand miles, by bus no less, and from here on out, I was dead set on being comfortable.

I took the stairs down to the lobby and asked for the nearest phone booth. The attendant pointed to the bar. The Happy Hour crowd was in full swing, but when I closed the door on the booth, it shut out most of the noise.

When Remmy picked up on the first ring, I felt every muscle of my earsplitting grin as he accepted the charges. "Hey," I said.

"Hey, Nettie. Y'all still in one piece?"

"We're staying at the Redlands Hotel; it's very nice here in Palestine, which I learned very quickly is pronounced Pali*steen*. They get really touchy here if you use the biblical pronunciation."

"Well, if they want folks to say it that way, they ought to spell it different," he said. No laughing, no lazy drawl.

Talking to Remmy at the end of the day had become my reward for looking after the sisters. No matter how fearful or tired or exasperated I was, hearing his voice made me feel better. Gave me hope that I could change because even now the idea of returning to Camden, returning to him, was terrifying. But with Georgia, Alabama, Mississippi, and Louisiana between us, I could relax, enjoy the easy conversation, how safe he made me feel.

But there was a tightness in his voice; the way he said my name said something was wrong. "Remmy, are you okay?"

"Mr. Buck died today."

"Oh, Remmy, I'm so sorry."

"Stubborn old coot had pneumonia and was complaining his chest hurt; wouldn't let me admit him to the hospital when I checked on him last night. I went by his house this morning and found him on the floor. Pretty sure it was a heart attack."

"Remmy, it's not your fault."

"It is my fault. I should have called his son Cletus, who acts like he doesn't give a rat's ass about the old man. They fought all the time, but at least Cletus would have made Buck go to the hospital. Shoot, I all but forced him in my car to take him myself, but he still wouldn't budge. After that, I came back to the office, hoping you'd call."

"Oh, God, Remmy, I'm—"

"Stop right there. I'm not blaming you, Nettie. I just wanted to tell you what happened." He hadn't mentioned a thing about Mr.

Buck last night. I suspected that Remmy was accustomed to every-one relying on him, and it wasn't easy for him to rely on someone else. Another thing we had in common. "I canceled my patients the rest of the day and sat by this phone, waiting for you to call because I needed to hear your voice."

I felt every mile, every inch between us. I wanted to be with him, comfort him, help him the way he'd helped me. "If Buck didn't want to go to the hospital, Remmy, you couldn't have made him."

"You're right." His voice was so thick with regret, it was breaking my heart. "Folks come to me and expect me to fix them. Makes me feel a little bit like God until God reminds me I can't fix anyone, especially someone I really care about. Then I feel like shit."

"But you do help people, Remmy." It was one of the things I loved most about him. "You helped me."

"Not sure that counts, Nettie. You're not nearly as broken as you think you are."

25

EMILY

"Did you see the train station?" Lurleen smeared orange marmalade over her toast, took a bite, and closed her eyes for the sugar rush.

Emily had seen the station on their walk about the city yesterday. It was surprisingly large for a town the size of Palestine, and if she hadn't seen it, she would be more than aware of its presence with trains coming and going at all hours. "Yes, Sister," Emily said. "Would you like to take the train back instead of the bus?"

"I believe I would. We could get a sleeper car, break up the trip into two days instead of three."

"But the train doesn't go all the way to Camden," Emily said.

"True enough," Lurleen said. "We could always call Pastor Gray to fetch us from Columbia or I'm sure a certain young doctor would be more than happy to pick us up and take us home to Camden."

With the exception of her class trip to Folly Beach, neither Emily nor Lurleen had ever been more than a hundred miles or so from Camden. Lurleen had always talked about traveling, perusing books at the library about faraway places and daydreaming about visiting. Emily had wanted to too, but never did. There was always the notion that someday, Teddy would come home, and she wanted to be there to welcome him. Throw her arms around him and never let go.

The only reason she'd suggested this trip was for Lurleen. Even then it was hard to leave, because an inkling of hope that Brother was alive and well would always live as long as Emily did. The back door would remain unlocked. She'd even left his favorite banana pudding in the refrigerator, just in case. Although, she suspected when she got home, it would be brown and ruined and untouched.

"I can ask Remmy when I call him tonight," Nettie said.

"In my day, a woman didn't telephone a man. It was indecent," Emily said.

"And why didn't we?" Miss Lurleen asked. "What difference does it make who calls whom?"

"It's simply a rule, the very definition of decency," Emily snapped before turning her attention to Nettie. "There is a fine art to courtship and flirtation, Nettie, and—"

"And if Emily actually knew what that art was, she might well be married instead of being an old maid like me." Lurleen winked at Nettie.

"Bite your tongue, Sister," Emily snapped. "We are *not* old maids."

"I think we are the very definition," Lurleen said.

It was good to see Lurleen rested, laughing, poking fun, even if it was at Emily's expense. After a day and a half of lazing around Palestine, Emily was still exhausted and disappointed, although

Lurleen's nonchalance over this pointless trip served to quell the latter.

It was good to get out and see the town that ended up being the prize at the end of their journey. It was a charming place with a lot of things a young person like Nettie would have probably enjoyed if she wasn't saddled with Emily and Lurleen. On her walk about town, Emily noticed a horde of cute boys hanging out at Heck's Drive In. If Nettie had any sense, she'd catch the eye of the most handsome one and get him to take her to dinner or maybe to see *Monkey Business* playing at the Texas Theatre near the bus station.

As long as she lived, if Emily never saw a bus again, it would be too soon, although she'd never tell Sister that. But if she absolutely had to, she would grit her teeth and ride that Greyhound all the way back to Camden. The only difference, this time, she would forgo the motel experience, because she'd had quite enough of those as well.

Emily was more than happy to give Nettie her and Lurleen's bus tickets to trade in along with enough cash to pay the difference for the train fare. Nettie returned with the tickets and a train schedule, and they planned their route home over dinner.

"The beaches of *Biloxi*. Sounds exotic, doesn't it? Have you ever been there, Nettie?" Lurleen asked.

"No ma'am. Sometimes my family would go to the beach in Mobile. It's about a half hour from Satsuma; we just went for the day."

"Oh, and let's remember to find the bookstore the gentleman at the front desk told us about," Lurleen said. "I believe it was Swift & Holmes. I want to get a book for the trip."

"Yes ma'am," Nettie said. "Would you like for me to pick one out for you?"

"We'll both go; I'd love to see the inside of a bookstore once more before I—" Lurleen looked at Emily and glossed over her certain death with a smile. "Of course you're welcome to come too, Sister."

Oh, let them have their fun; Emily didn't want or need the invitation to their little club. Looking over the brochure-like map, her finger landed squarely on Alabama. "Mobile sounds especially lovely, compared to *Biloxi*. Perhaps we should go there instead," she said, trying to get a rise out of Nettie. Usually Emily's verbal jabs felt wicked and good, but the words only left her feeling a bit guilty.

Anyone with eyes was well aware of the girl's aversion to Alabama. Nettie had been nothing but nice to Emily, fulfilling her promise to be both nurse and caretaker. And friend. As hard as Emily had been, Nettie had never returned her unkindness. Not once.

"You're right, Sister," Emily said. "Biloxi does sound exotic. I'm sure the ocean is especially beautiful there. We can stay at a hotel on the beach and have our toes in the sand by suppertime tomorrow."

NETTIE

I scurried around, pulling myself together along with my things, wishing I had packed the night before. I hadn't fallen asleep until almost morning. Maybe it was the naps I'd taken to catch up on my rest from what had seemed like a never-ending bus ride. Or maybe it was Remmy's words that he needed me rolling around in my head. I'd never had that with Brooks. We just were. Always together because that's the way it was. We were a handsome couple who were bound together for so long, our friends expected us to be that way forever. I had accepted the natural progression and never questioned it. Not once.

Did that mean I never loved Brooks? Did that mean I'd never been in love before? Of course I'd been in love or what he'd done wouldn't have hurt so bad. But it wasn't the wound that he'd caused that kept me from healing; it was Sissy's part that stung hard. Throbbed, competing with the love I had for her.

The shrill ring of the bedside phone startled me, but I should have grown accustomed to it. After Miss Emily figured out she could order me around by the house phone as easily as in person, she'd used it often over the course of our trip.

"Good morning," I said, steeling myself for one of her jabs.

"Hey."

"Remmy?"

"Did I get you at a bad time?"

"I'm getting ready to catch the train back to South Carolina. How did you know to call here?"

"You said you were staying at the Redlands, and there's only one of those in Palestine. Only one Nettie Gilbert for sure."

"They'd almost hang you if they heard you saying it that way. The looks we get when one of us lets it slip. I think Miss Emily does it on purpose just so she can glare right back." When he laughed my heart fluttered, the same sensation traveling down to my belly. "Feel better today?"

"So now you're playing doctor," he laughed. "Why, yes, Doctor Gilbert; I do feel better just hearing your voice. But I still miss you; still want you home."

"You say that like you belong in Camden now," I teased.

"Long as you're here, it sure feels that way," he said. "I turned down the job in Columbia."

"Remmy. You said that job was everything you ever wanted."

"I thought so, but when I thought about leaving patients like Miss Lurleen in someone else's hands, I just couldn't do it."

"As long as you're happy with your decision."

"I am and I'm happy with you. When are you coming back?"

"Unless the sisters extend their beach trip in Biloxi, we should be back in Columbia Sunday evening. I'm supposed to ask if you'd mind picking us up."

"You're asking an awful lot, Nettie."

"I'm sorry. I—"

"It'll be impossible not to kiss you hello in front of the sisters. I'm not making any promises about being decent in their eyes, but you can bet I'll be there."

"Miss Lurleen's disappointed we'll be coming in in the evening. She wanted to ride in your car with the top down."

"Convertible works just as well at night as it does during the day." He laughed. "I'm looking forward to showing you, alone."

"I'd like that."

There was a long silence and he blew out a breath. "That's good to know, Nettie Gilbert. Does that mean you're done running?"

I'd only known Remmy a few weeks, and already he knew me better than anyone ever did, and sometimes better than I knew myself. He'd pegged me as a runner from the beginning. The question was, did I want to run back to him? No, I was done running. I would get on that train, glide through Alabama without her raising the first hackle. And when I saw Remmy, I would dash purposefully into his open arms.

"Yes," I said.

"Then come home to me."

The cabbie picked us up at the hotel and deposited us at the train station. The sisters were as giddy as schoolgirls, excited about traveling in the comfort of the train with our own roomette. The tall, lanky porter showed us to our berth, pointing out the luxuries along the way. The sisters settled in and gabbed nonstop after we pulled out of the station.

I watched the scenery go by. Squatty Texas trees changing to slightly taller, scant-looking, bald cypresses as the train crossed into Louisiana. The train stopped in New Orleans, and a horde of people filed onto the platform.

Aunt Madge, Uncle Doak's wife, was from New Orleans and had always talked about how much better it was than Satsuma, better than the entire state of Alabama, she claimed. Nobody much liked her thinly veiled complaints, but then no one uttered a word in defense, including me, for fear that she'd get angry and stop making the Creole jambalaya from her mother's side of the family and handmade boudin sausages and other Cajun dishes from her daddy's side that made every last one of us beg for more.

From the rail yard, New Orleans didn't look any different from any other town we'd passed through, but the best thing about the Big Easy was we would be in Biloxi in a couple of hours. Train travel suited all of us. It was my first time, and I liked having room to ourselves as well as a dining car with excellent meals. Miss Emily looked completely rested, so much better than she did back in Palestine, and Miss Lurleen wasn't as short of breath as she'd been since we'd begun our trip.

Wouldn't Remmy be surprised if the trip that was supposed to kill her had actually made her better? But then he'd made very sure I knew that wasn't possible.

Miss Emily gasped and threw her hand over her chest. "Oh, my, Sister! We don't have proper bathing attire."

"If you think I'm getting in some kind of beach getup at my age, Sister, you've got another thing coming," Miss Lurleen snorted. "The very idea." Her laughter turned into a cackle, and Miss Emily and I joined in loud and hearty enough to be heard in the dining car three cars over.

"I'm having the best time," Miss Emily said when she came down from her laughing fit. "I feel like we're throwing ourselves a party."

"And why the hell not?" Miss Lurleen said, setting them off again.

26

EMILY

Emily kept a close watch on Lurleen and kept her entertained; she didn't want to nod off and miss sister's seeing the ocean for the first time. Of course they'd seen plenty of water along the way, the mighty Mississippi, Lake Pontchartrain, but she knew nothing would compare with the endless expanse of the Gulf of Mexico. Except maybe the Atlantic. Yes, if Emily could give Lurleen anything, it would be the Atlantic Ocean tied up in a colorful bow. But after this trip, dragging Lurleen east of Camden just to see the ocean would be pressing her luck, and now, Emily only wanted for Sister what she wanted for herself. To die at peace surrounded by her precious things at home.

Yes, the gulf would have to do. And when the train reached the tip of Mississippi and it came into view, it did not disappoint. She shimmered in all her magnificence like a Mississippi belle who couldn't decide whether to wear her most beautiful blue gown or her very stunning green one, so she'd worn both. As the scant few clouds moved over the expanse, pockets of water took on a striking cobalt color, some a gunmetal gray. And the sand was like someone had spilled millions of bags of sugar, and looked so different from the grayish-colored sand on beaches back home in South Carolina.

"Holy Lord," Sister whispered, grabbing Emily's hand. Lurleen absolutely glowed with wonder and Emily couldn't wait for Sister to feel the water swirling around her ankles, the sugar-white sand between her toes.

"It's beautiful, isn't it?" Emily gave Sister's hand a squeeze as the gulf showed off like the prettiest girl at the dance. Glittering. Beautiful.

"Thank you, Sister," Lurleen said. And Emily felt like her own heart might burst right then and there over Lurleen's delight.

"It is beautiful," Nettie affirmed.

"Thank you." Emily's words tumbled out, almost startling the poor girl. Emily offered an apologetic smile. "We could never have done this without you. And I'm not completely sure we could have found another fool for our folly."

Lurleen threaded her hand in Nettie's and raised their clasped hands up. "These are the only fools I care to folly with."

The train pulled into the station, and Emily had the cab take them to the best beachfront hotel in Biloxi, which turned out to be the Savoy. Emily asked for a single room with two beds and a rollaway, her way of including Nettie in the slumber party. And Nettie had certainly earned that privilege.

The bellman took their bags to their rooms, and they'd taken turns changing out of their traveling clothes. Nettie was in those dreadful pedal pushers again, but so be it. Lurleen wore the blue dress that matched her eyes, the one Emily had picked out for Lurleen to be buried in. Although she hadn't shared that with Lurleen, and Sister was never as particular about what she wore as Emily was. Of course Lurleen had drug that horrible gray suit along, but Emily was only too happy to save her sister from yet another fashion faux pas.

Each armed with a towel, they marched down to the lobby and out onto the huge veranda that overlooked the beach. Of course it was the gulf, and the waves were making a pitiful effort to be heard. Yes, if Emily could change one thing, which was always a caveat because she could *never* just change *one* thing, she would make the waves a little bigger. The ocean a little louder. The sky a little bluer. But just for Lurleen so that when she got to heaven and looked down on Emily, maybe she would remember only the good things. How very much Emily loved her.

Sister was trembling when her feet touched the sand and even faltered a little, almost pulling Emily down, making her heart beat so fast, she felt light-headed, but to be honest, Emily wasn't sure who was pulling down whom. Nettie steadied Lurleen, who did the same for Emily, and the three of them continued their march down to the surf, which for the love of God could have had a little more oomph to it.

When they got to the edge of the water, Lurleen didn't stop. Laughing, squealing, she walked right in until the water swirled around the tops of their thighs. By now, Emily's hand was numb, Sister was holding on so tight. Emily couldn't speak; there were no words for this moment. Every puny wave that pushed against them swayed Lurleen.

Emily's vision began to blur. She blinked hard and it cleared just long enough to see Lurleen's jubilant face. Emily's heart literally burst with joy, and the last thing she saw before she left the earth was the love in her sister's eyes.

LURLEEN

Lurleen couldn't stop laughing until she saw Emily's face droop. She knew what was happening. She screamed at Nettie to help her get Emily back to the shore, but it was too late. The lifeguard on the beach pulled Emily out of the water; he turned her on her side and beat her back to try to get her to cough up the water, but Lurleen knew she hadn't drowned. She was already gone before she collapsed into the surf.

Lurleen crumpled by Emily's side, and Nettie did the same for Lurleen until the ambulance arrived and took Emily away. She and Nettie sat on the beach for what must have been hours before Nettie got up and wordlessly extended her hand to Lurleen. They went into the hotel, where the staff hovered over them until they reached their room. Lurleen couldn't open the door, just pressed her forehead against it and started to cry again. Nettie was sobbing for an old woman who until today had never been nice to her, and she was crying for Lurleen because she'd lost her sister again. Forever.

Just last night, Lurleen had lain awake on the train, planning on telling Emily the secret she'd intended to take to her grave. She was going to wait until after they checked into the beach hotel and saw the ocean together. Ask Nettie to give them some privacy, and then she was going to tell Emily one of those detectives they'd doled out all that money to had actually found Teddy. In prison in West Virginia.

But the closer they got to Biloxi, the harder it was to even think about speaking the truth. And why do it now? To unburden Lurleen's own soul? Why, she had never seen Emily so happy as she'd been since they got on the train, so absolutely flush with excitement, gasping for breath as they laughed over the silliest things. That was the way she wanted to remember her sister. Not brokenhearted. Not broken like she surely would have been if she'd known what had happened to Teddy.

Of course it was none of Emily's doing. Brother had set his course for destruction long before he left home. He started getting into trouble before he turned fifteen, vandalism, stealing. He hung out with a rough crowd, a bunch of hoodlums, mostly older than him, who drank, gambled, and pulled sick pranks. Alcohol and Teddy became good friends by the time he was sixteen, but they never agreed with each other. It made Brother mean and destructive to anyone who got anywhere near him.

Word around town said that same rough crowd, part young men, part juveniles, had gotten drunk and then turned four dogs loose in Albert Jessup's turkey farm. They watched as the dogs went on a killing spree, leaving hundreds of birds dead in a matter of minutes. Up until then, Brother's antics hadn't harmed anyone but himself and Mother, who grieved his descent into madness to her deathbed and beyond, but Jessup wanted retribution. Rather than go to jail, Teddy left the morning of his birthday without so much as a word.

Lurleen had gotten up that morning to find his bed made, his rucksack missing. He'd roamed as far as West Virginia and had taken a job in the coalmines in Mucklow. Believing he was a murderer because of John's death and Mama's, one by accident, the other slow and painful. He'd proven himself right in a bar fight and had barely made it to nineteen before he killed a man.

He went quietly to prison, and waited to be executed. Two years' worth of letters from Lurleen were never returned to her, but she doubted he'd ever read any them. She'd even called the prison and spoken to the warden, explained everything about John, about Teddy's alcoholism, his feeling responsible for Mama's death. The warden liked Teddy and agreed to let Lurleen speak to him by phone, but Teddy had refused.

And in case Lurleen had any ideas about coming up to see him, Teddy had told the warden he'd exercise the only right he had left and refuse to see her.

"I'm sure he loves you; he just doesn't want you to see him like this," the warden had said. Although, Lurleen doubted Teddy had said so. "He says he's ready to die, ma'am."

Of course he was. He'd been ready to die since he was fourteen and errantly pulled the trigger, killing John Young. It'd taken him seven years to fulfill his own destiny, and, as much as Lurleen hated it, on his birthday, February 16, Lurleen had honored his last wish and let him go home to Mama and Daddy alone.

The warden called the house when the execution was over. Lurleen had been waiting by the phone. He expressed his condolences, said there were folks who belonged in prison, but even with what Brother had done, he didn't believe Teddy was one of them. Lurleen hung up the phone and went upstairs to Teddy's room. She threw herself on his bed and sobbed into his pillow until she collected herself. She went downstairs to break the ridiculous silence she'd kept for seven years to constantly remind Emily everything horrible that had happened was her fault. Even though years ago, Lurleen had admitted to herself that what had happened was nobody's fault.

Emily was standing in front of the refrigerator, in stocking feet, all dolled up from one of her many dates that she never allowed to go beyond a free meal and gay conversation. There was a tune on the radio, Lurleen couldn't remember what it was, but Sister was shuffling her feet and singing. Happy. Until she looked up and saw Lurleen standing there.

Her face went as blank as Lurleen's had every time Emily had looked at her throughout seven years of silence. During that time, Mama had passed. Lurleen had handled all of the arrangements because Emily was crushed. But Lurleen never uttered a consoling word, never laid a hand on her sister. The silence had continued so long, Lurleen didn't know how to stop it because it had become as much a part of her and Emily as their sisterhood.

And God knows, Emily had long since given up on ever hearing Lurleen speak to her again. She had accepted her punishment without protest because she felt she deserved it. And if she didn't believe that from the beginning, Lurleen's refusal to acknowledge her existence reinforced the point.

"There's some banana pudding on the top shelf," Lurleen said. It was a stupid thing to say. Of course there was pudding. Always on Brother's birthday, courtesy of Emily, who believed with all her heart Teddy was alive and well and would come bursting through the door and devour the whole bowl before tearing up the piano that remained silent long after Lurleen's armistice.

"Are you speaking to me again, Sister?" Emily whispered.

"Yes, I believe I am," Lurleen had said like they'd just had the longest conversation and she was tired, so very tired.

From that moment forward, Emily never once mentioned Lurleen's silence, she just accepted that things would go back to being the way they'd always been, and she was so happy, there was no point in telling her what had happened to Brother. Besides, Lurleen was so ashamed that she'd kept his whereabouts and his death a secret because she had robbed Emily of Teddy as surely as Lurleen had been robbed of John.

Even as anguished as Teddy had become, he loved Emily best. She always found a way to comfort him when he tormented himself. They had a special bond he and Lurleen didn't share. Emily was his favorite, and he would have done anything for her if he could have. He would never have deliberately taken another man's life. He would never have left home. He would have sobered up. But he was so very sick and could do none of those things.

In the beginning, Lurleen never intended to protect Emily from any of this. She wanted her to feel the blame, the hatred Lurleen had for her. Keeping Brother from her for spite had been a much more potent payback.

But paybacks are indeed hell, and Lurleen could almost see the ends of the tethers of her life. It wouldn't be long now. She knew it was selfish to let Emily leave this world without knowing Teddy was finally at peace. Spineless. And Emily had deserved to know the truth. Still, Lurleen couldn't come right out and tell her face-to-face, for Lurleen was indeed a coward of the worst kind.

She was going to wait. Wait until the time was right. Wait until Lurleen was settled in her bed back home. Wait for that quiet moment, just after Emily had turned out the lights and said good night. The pregnant pause just before the door closed. Lurleen was going to tell her. All of it. But she couldn't. Emily was gone.

27

NETTIE

My hands were shaking. After the first few words, I couldn't speak.

"She's crying sir, just gave the number and broke right down," the operator said, "so I'm guessing this is a collect call."

"Nettie? Nettie?"

"Sir, do you accept the charges."

"Yes," Remmy barked. "Nettie, honey, talk to me."

Miss Lurleen had cried herself to sleep by the time I left the room and ran to the nearest pay phone. I'm not sure how long he listened to me cry, consoling me. Swearing because he couldn't hold me.

"Nettie, honey, I'll get there as quick as I can. Where are you?"

"Bi—loxi." I hiccupped.

"Goddamn it. I can't hang up the phone, not with you like this, but I want to be there with you." I could hear desk drawers opening and closing and then pages rustling. "I'm looking at the atlas. I can drive there, be there in maybe fourteen hours. Hell, that's too long. I can drive to Augusta and fly to Mobile for sure. Maybe they have a flight to Biloxi; if they don't, I can rent a car or take a taxi. Soon as I get to you, honey, we'll all fly home together. You and me. Miss Lurleen. God, Nettie, please don't cry."

I'm not sure if it was sheer exhaustion or the insanity of watching someone I'd grown to love die right in front of me, but I laughed at the thought of getting Miss Lurleen on an airplane. "That's such a sweet sound, honey," Remmy said. "God, I've never felt so helpless in my life. I should be with you, but for the life of me, I can't hang up this damn phone and leave you alone."

"I'm okay," I lied. "But I'd better go. Miss Lurleen might wake up, and I don't want her to be alone."

"Miss Emily died?" Remmy asked incredulously.

"They said she had a stroke."

"How's Miss Lurleen?"

"They took her blood pressure and gave her something to help her sleep, but she fought it; I really need to go in case she wakes up."

"Go be with her, and I'll be there as soon as I can get there."

I nodded my head, but the three of us began this journey together; it was only fitting that Miss Lurleen, Miss Emily, and I come home together. Besides, Remmy riding in on a white horse was all well and good, but I knew I needed to find my own happiness before I fell into his arms.

"Don't come."

"Nettie—"

"I'm going to be fine, Remmy. Miss Lurleen and I have each other."

"Honey, I just want to be with you."

"And I want that too. I do. Just not now. I'll see you when we get to Columbia."

"Are you sure you don't want me to come?"

Snippets of the last few days with the sisters raced through my mind, blurring with images of my own sister. "Right now, I'm not sure of many things, but I know I need to finish what I started, and I'm sure of you, Remmy. I'm sure of you."

"You really know how to make a guy fall for you, Nettie Gilbert." He sounded happy. Relieved. I swiped my tears away and laughed too because I was already gone.

I awoke with a start at three a.m. when Miss Lurleen sat up wailing, sobbing, gasping for breath. The loss was so deep and so fresh, if the pain had been constant, it would have taken her life. But it came in waves of laughing and crying and stories. Pieces of her and her sister's life she shared with me.

"You're a good friend to me, Nettie. To Sister," she sighed after she rode the last wave of grief down.

"I loved her," I laughed, swiping at my tears. "She didn't want me to, but I did."

"I love you, sweet girl, and because I'm very old, I have a certain license to say any old thing I want. And, whether you want to or not, you're obligated to hear me out."

"Of course. You can say anything to me."

"You might not like this very much, but again, I'm old and I'm right most all the time," she chuckled and took my hand. "First of all, you may call me Lurleen. All my friends do, and you can drop the *yes ma'am* and *no ma'am* as well. Secondly, I told you I didn't speak to Emily for seven years."

"Yes, Mis—" She raised her eyebrows. "Of course, Lurleen," I said. My mother would have washed my mouth out for such a breach of etiquette.

"I have few regrets in my life, but that is the sorest one. I tried to make it up to Emily over the years, but nothing could ever truly repair the ugly scar my silence left. I have unsaid things I will take to my grave, things that Emily should have been told, and now she's gone." Lurleen's voice trailed off. I put my arms around her and pressed her head into the curve of my neck. Not once since I'd met her had she ever worn any dusting powder or perfume, but she was wearing a hint of the Evening in Paris her sister had worn unsparingly.

She pulled away and swiped at her eyes. "I don't want that for you, Nettie. I'll go home with you if you like, or if you want to go home alone, I'll take Emily on to Camden. But you must go to your sister, if not for yourself, for me."

"She needs me," I whispered. "I could feel it when we passed through Alabama; the feeling isn't as strong, but it's still there. She needs me."

"Then go to her." Lurleen held both of my hands in hers. "Forgive her."

"I'm not sure I can." It was easy to hold on to all of the sordid details. Forgiveness was complicated. The hardest work.

"No one's asking you to agree with her, Nettie; you don't even have to like her. But you must forgive her." Lurleen smiled. "She's your sister."

We'd fallen asleep around seven or eight in the morning and slept until noon when we dressed to go make arrangements for Miss Emily's body to be embalmed and shipped back to Camden. On the way to the funeral home, the cab went about four blocks down Main Street. "We'll get out here," Lurleen said.

"But the O'Keefe Funeral Home is over on Howard Avenue," I said, following her out of the cab. She waited for me to take my place at her side, cupping her elbow, and nodded toward Learners' Dress Shop. "Emily would want you in a stunning new dress when you see that bastard, and I believe I'll get one too."

"No, Lurleen—"

"No arguments, Nettie. We're doing this for Emily, and that's final."

Almost an hour later, we emerged with two shopping bags with a dress for each of us, and a new pair of pumps for me. I hailed another cab, and the driver gave us a look when I told him where we were going. Still, the car rolled forward about fifty feet. He turned left and went maybe a hundred more feet and there we were in front of the funeral home, where Lurleen singlehandedly changed the casket industry in the interest of women everywhere, but particularly for her sister.

"Well, why can't you get one in blue?" Miss Lurleen snapped.

"Madam, a Cannon casket is the best money can buy, which of course is what you asked for. Unfortunately, it doesn't come in any color except hand-burnished mahogany."

"Obviously an attempt to appeal to men. You ought to know that women prefer color, something that matches their favorite dress or their eyes. Sister's eyes were blue," she huffed. "Can you at least paint the thing blue?"

"We don't—I'm not sure we could—," he stammered.

Lurleen took a pen and her checkbook out of her pocketbook and raised her eyebrows. "Well?" she snapped.

He looked at the checkbook and then at Lurleen. "I suppose we could, but it will cost extra."

The hotel staff was very kind in light of Miss Emily's untimely death. The manager sent a doctor to check on Lurleen. The staff stopped by our room several times bringing snacks, Cokes, sweet tea. When Lurleen asked the manager if he knew of a place we could rent a car to go to Satsuma overnight for a family matter, he didn't ask any questions, just loaned us his.

It was definitely the quickest seventy-five miles I'd ever driven, although I wasn't speeding. The small sign for my barely there town came into sight too soon. I was grateful to have Miss Lurleen riding shotgun. The terrors I'd felt passing through Alabama on the bus were nothing compared to what I felt now. Teeth chattering, I was pouring sweat, heart beating out of my chest.

When Lurleen put her hand on mine, I slowed, then stomped on the brake, making the truck behind me nearly rear-end us. He sat on his horn and zoomed past our car. "Breathe," she said softly, but I couldn't. What if Sissy had decided she was done with me like I had said I was done with her? What if my sister didn't need me anymore? Didn't love me anymore?

"We'll sit here till you're ready," Lurleen said. "And you will be ready. You're made of strong stuff, my dear."

Much like the hills had melted into piedmonts and their gentle slopes into lowlands, the days had blurred since we left Camden. It was Thursday, just after six o'clock; Sissy would be home from work by now.

She'd gone to work right out of high school at the Alabama Farmers Cooperative office in Mobile as their lone secretary. She usually rode with the Blakeney girl who worked at a bank in Mobile. Sissy had been saving for a car for almost a year now; Papa wouldn't let her buy one on time, though she could have if he'd signed the papers.

Now, her money would be pooled into her new life with Brooks. Her baby. That wouldn't sit well at all given Sissy's pride in her own paycheck, and why shouldn't she be proud? She worked hard, did a good job, and yet the moment she told her boss she was expecting, he would likely fire her on the spot. Or maybe she hadn't told her boss yet. Maybe she was ruminating, making herself sick over the whole fiasco.

I had always known everything that went on with Sissy, or I used to. Sissy loved her job, loved getting dressed up to go to work, to type memorandums, and answer phone calls. She'd been so proud when she'd landed the position on her own, without any help from Daddy or his friends. She'd gushed about how grown up she felt, how she didn't see any reason why women couldn't work as long as they wanted whether they had children or not. But if she wasn't fired, she would have to quit her job long before the baby came. Brooks would see to it.

Whenever Brooks and I had talked about having a family, he'd been adamant that I would stay home from the minute the bun was in the oven until the kids weren't school age anymore. I'd hoped he might change his mind since teaching was such a wonderful profession for a mother, what with the summers off. Of course teaching piano out of the house was fine by him. Sometimes he'd even hinted he might give on the subject of my teaching, as long as it was at our children's school.

But would Sissy be happy without her job? And why was Brooks so quick to make iron-fisted decisions that weren't solely his to make?

"I'm ready." I swallowed hard and nodded.

"I'm sure you are, dear. Let's get a move on; I want to meet this sister of yours." Her last words had a little bite to them.

When this whole mess started, I'd wanted nothing less than the people I loved, who also loved Sissy, to rise up and shame her, persecute her until her every thought was sorrowful for having betrayed me. But after having seen the Eldridge ire up close and personally, I didn't want it directed at my baby sister.

I shifted in my seat to face Lurleen. Angry drivers honked and zipped past me. "I don't know much about driving, dear, but I'm pretty sure it's against the rules to sit in the middle of the highway like this with your blinker thingy on."

I cocked my head to the side. "Sissy's young," I stammered.

"But old enough to know better," Lurleen said, pulling on Miss Emily's short white gloves like they were for boxing. Heaven help Sissy.

The flatlands of my homeplace had never been more beautiful. Miles of new satsumas dangling from the trees. Cotton fields and newly planted corn in between orchards. Tall stately pecan trees that seemed bigger and better on Alabama soil than anyplace in the South.

I turned onto the dirt road that split two satsuma groves. Four tiny houses came into view. A half dozen vehicles, mostly pickup trucks, were parked near the shared barn behind the houses. Daddy's old truck that ran when it wanted to was under the shed alongside Uncle Doak's new truck he bought every year, just to get a rise out of Daddy. My cousin Griffin's hand-me-down pickup from his father was there; a friendly dig from Doak that an eighteen-year-old was driving a better vehicle than my father. The big truck that took oranges and pecans, cotton and corn to market sat next to Mother's car. Everyone was home.

We pulled up into the bare dirt space in the center of the four clapboard homes that looked like neat squares in the middle of the groves. Between Nana's house and mine, the plates were set on the table Daddy had honed out of a massive oak tree that had blown over after a storm when I was six. There was a vase of sky blue hydrangeas in the center of the table, and Mother's gardenia and rose bushes were showing off with their intoxicating fragrances. Twelve place settings were laid out perfectly, a stark contrast to the rustic table that could seat as many as thirty people and had.

I loved that table, always felt so special around it, with everyone I loved gathered there. I used to picture my own children added to the brood, listening to my father tell how God had provided the tree to make the table as surely as he'd provided the lamb for Abraham to sacrifice instead of sacrificing his own son, Isaac.

The screen door pushed open. Not recognizing the strange car, my mother had a cross look on her face as she wiped her glasses on a small towel. She slung the dishcloth over her shoulder and squinted hard. She could never see two feet in front of herself, but then she put her thick black horn-rimmed glasses on. "Nettie?" The word ended in a squeal as she ran to the car. "You came. Thank God, you came."

She smacked her hands against my window like it wasn't there, grinning like nothing had changed between us. But I couldn't move. She opened the car door and pulled me out, hugging me, calling everyone to come see me. The prodigal had returned home.

Screen doors opened. People called my name and flew to my side. Daddy ruffled my hair with an earsplitting grin. Nana Gilbert wedged her shoulders into the crowd, fussing for a turn to hug my neck. I was jubilant. Back on my pedestal. Until the screen door to my house opened once more.

Always beautiful, Sissy looked more fragile that I remembered, frail. Her long blond hair was unbound, hanging close to her waist. Her heart-shaped face was serious, lips drawn in a tight line as she watched the celebration from afar.

"I'm Lurleen Eldridge." With all the hullabaloo, I hadn't even heard Lurleen get out of the car. "Nettie's friend," she said firmly, like she was choosing which side of the church to sit on at a wedding.

"Oh, I knew you'd come, Nettie," Mama gushed. "But you didn't tell me you were bringing a guest. So glad you could come for the festivities. The whole town will turn out and then some; we're really putting on the dog for this wedding."

"What?" I mumbled, but I don't think anyone heard me over the merrymaking. I hadn't come for the wedding, at least I didn't think I had. I'd come to see Sissy because she needed me. Because I needed her. I looked at the screen door where Sissy had been, but she was gone.

"Nettie Jean Gilbert! Where are your manners? Introduce Mrs. Eldridge to everyone this instant."

Funny how Mother fell back into her commanding tone as if she still held sway over my life. But I did want Lurleen to know everyone. "Lurleen, this is my Aunt Opal, my—"

"Young lady, respect your elders," Mother clucked. "It's *Mrs. Eldridge*, and we are so pleased to have you as our guest. I'm Dorothy, but you can call me Dot; everyone does."

"It's *Miss* Eldridge," Lurleen replied, giving my mother's hand a firm shake. "And Nettie is my very dear friend, so she can call me anything she wants."

I continued on with the introductions, ending with Aunt Madge and Uncle Doak's youngest son, Charlie, who was twelve. "Lovely to meet all of you," Lurleen said, just as a red truck rumbled down the lane with *Carver Feed and Seed* emblazoned on the side.

My heart did not leap the way it always had, nor did it sink like it had every time I'd thought about receiving an invite to Brooks's wedding. Mother was quick to my side. "He's family now, Nettie. Comes for dinner most every night, just like he always has. I'm not asking you to be nice to him, but I do expect you to maintain some measure of decorum."

He didn't notice me until he got out of the truck. He stopped dead in his tracks, and the sea of family that had engulfed me parted. Miss Lurleen was still by my side. She didn't say a word. She didn't have to; I could feel her quiet strength, her solidarity as the rest of the people I loved leapt onto the fence and straddled it for all they were worth.

This wasn't how I wanted it to go. I didn't want to see Brooks at all. I wanted to say what I had to say to Sissy and leave. Take Miss Emily and Lurleen home to Camden where they belonged, where I was reasonably sure I belonged. But things never go the way they're supposed to. Somehow the very universe knows the one thing you're avoiding and throws it right in your face.

Brooks nodded my way. Lurleen linked her arm though mine; her other hand cupped my fist, giving it a gentle squeeze. Love. Solidarity. Sisterhood.

"Nettie, dear. I'd like to wash up before supper. Would you mind showing me to my room, please," she said like she knew I wanted no part of Brooks Carver.

I nodded. Before I could move a muscle, Griffin and Charlie grabbed our bags. Griffin started to take mine to Mother's house. "Griffin? I'll be staying with Lurleen at Nana's," I announced, watching Mother flinch. Then she nodded like it was only fair, considering.

I cupped Lurleen's elbow and guided her across the uneven ground toward Nana's front porch. "Nettie." Brooks's voice made me freeze. Tremble. Although not with want and need like it had in the past.

"Dinner's almost ready, son," Mama said to Brooks. "Sissy's in the house. You go on inside and get washed up now."

We continued up the steps to the porch. Miss Lurleen looked back over her shoulder as I opened the door, and mumbled something under her breath that made me smile. Tears stung my eyes, and my chest went tight. Lurleen huffed and said it again, adding the swear words to complete the tribute. "G.d. *pissant*."

28

LURLEEN

Honestly, it was all Lurleen could do not to pinch that boy's head off right in front of God and everybody, and how mightily he deserved it. Driving up to the house for supper, like the sisters were as interchangeable as he'd assumed they were. And now the whole family was going to sit around the supper table together? Good Lord, had any of those people ever had one shred of concern for Nettie? One ounce of understanding of what that would be like for her?

Lurleen slipped her shoes off to go across the hall and check on Nettie. Before she could, Helen, the grandmother, knocked at the same time she opened Lurleen's door and then stepped inside. "Hello." Lurleen stopped in her tracks. Right off the bat, she'd pegged Nettie's mother as the flighty woman she was; this one she wasn't so sure of. "I was just going to look in on Nettie." Lurleen pointed as Helen closed door.

"Before you do, I want you to know that I don't approve of what Brooks did to Nettie," she said, her voice hushed. "What they all did to her," Helen said tightly and jerked her head in the direction of Nettie's childhood home.

"I don't believe you," Lurleen whispered back, making the woman who looked to be a good bit older than Lurleen gasp.

"Who are you to make that determination? Why, it would behoove you to remember you're a guest in this house. Besides, my own son, Nettie's father, said it was for the best to let things lie so I did. It tore my heart out not to reach out to that poor girl, comfort her," she huffed. "And you're dead wrong, I care very much about my granddaughter."

Before Lurleen knew it, Emily's words hissed out of her mouth. "The blond pregnant one?"

But it was wonderful to feel them inside her, fighting for Nettie, wonderful to feel Sister's sass and vinegar from the other side of the grave. Yes, indeed, what would Emily Lorene Eldridge have to say if she were here? Plenty.

"Have you always let a man do your thinking for you? And just where were you when that child's world went to hell? What did you say to her to console her when that sorry excuse for a man rutted her own sister and made a baby?"

"You will not speak to me that way in my own house. I'll have you to know I raised two fine boys by myself after their father died. We kept this grove, this family going. We always keep the family going. Why, be ashamed of yourself. And such talk," she hissed right back. "What kind of lady are you?"

"The pissed-off kind." Helen sucked in a breath, but Lurleen continued, voice low. The last thing she wanted was to alarm Nettie, but the thing she wanted most was to give this spineless woman a piece of her mind. "And I am *not* ashamed, although you should be."

"You have no right to come in here and speak to me like this," she gasped, plopping down on the bed like someone had cut her legs out from under her.

"I'm claiming that right. Now. I love that girl, and I'm so lucky she loves me back because when Nettie Gilbert loves, it's not just with her heart but with everything she's got," Lurleen snapped. "I would do anything for her. *Anything.* But what I would first and most assuredly do, had I been privileged to know her at the time her entire family *betrayed* her, is what I'm doing now. Standing up for her."

"Do *you* have children?" Helen knew the barb would catch before she cast it. "Yes, well, I didn't think so. You wouldn't understand what it's like. Nobody wanted to choose sides. I didn't. I couldn't."

"The irony is that Nettie doesn't even realize how strong she is, or maybe she does," Lurleen snapped. "She didn't *need* your love divided into two equal portions. She didn't *need* your sympathy, but she deserved it, far more than any of the likes of you ever deserved her." Lurleen shook her head slowly, eyes still narrowed. "And no, I do not have children. But if I did, I would die before I hurt them the way you people gutted that dear girl. And you can take that to the g.d. bank."

Just then Nettie's door opened. From the hallway, she called for her grandmother, then Lurleen, then her footsteps moved away from the door. "Now, you and I are going to walk out of this room in a civil manner," Lurleen said, her voice still hushed. "And if Nettie asks what this was all about, I'm going to tell her we had a nice conversation, which is the truth, Helen, because you needed to hear the truth. And while you all have an obligation to love *both* of those girls *equally*, make no mistake as to just whose side I am on.

"Right here, Nettie, dear," Lurleen called.

Nettie opened the door, and her smile faded for a moment. She was dressed in the stunning jade-colored dress Emily would have wholeheartedly approved of, but instead of the cute little pumps they'd bought to go with it, she was wearing a pair of whitish lace-up shoes she called Keds. Nettie looked at her grandmother, then back to Lurleen, and swallowed hard. "Everything okay?"

"Just peachy," Lurleen said, pushing past Helen. "Shall we see if we can help your mother with dinner?"

NETTIE

Daddy and Uncle Doak had Brooks out by one of the trucks, with the hood up. Good. They could keep him busy for all I cared. As I was giving Lurleen the nickel tour, he'd looked up from what he was doing, directly at me. I quickly turned my and Lurleen's attentions to Mother's impressive rose garden that was in full bloom.

At Christmastime, after Brooks had proposed, I'd slipped into Mother's bedroom and woke her up without waking Daddy. We went into the kitchen and drank hot cocoa, just her and me, giggling, talking about my wedding day, how beautiful it would be. "Of course, it should be in June or even May," Mama had said. "The roses will be at their peak, and we'll have them everywhere. I can even make one of those corsages for your hair out of my little white tea roses. Oh, Nettie, they'll be gorgeous against your red hair. You're going to be a ravishing bride."

Miss Lurleen's long sigh brought me back to the present. "You're tired," I said. "This is all too much for you, I just knew it."

"I'm not at all tired. As a matter of fact, I haven't felt this spry in a long time," Lurleen said. "I'm just trying to figure out how I'm going to get through dinner with *Brooks* sitting at the table and not strangle him."

My eyes stung as I blinked back tears and kissed her on the cheek. "I love you."

"I know you do," Lurleen huffed, "which explains why I'm here and makes me wish Emily was too."

A pang of grief sliced through my belly. We probably wouldn't even be in Satsuma if Miss Emily hadn't died. The feeling came as suddenly as it went; I stood ramrod straight, feeling the loss of her, but feeling something else. Her strength. Miss Emily knew the true value of sisterhood and what it felt like to suddenly be cut off from it. Yes. Somehow, someway, if Emily Eldridge were still alive, she would be here standing with me. Maybe she was.

I helped Lurleen up the steps and opened the door to my home. My eyes went straight to my piano. It was like seeing a long-lost friend. I went to it immediately, ran my fingers over the keys, but not enough to make them sing. "Will you play for me later?" Lurleen asked, smiling. I nodded. "And when we get home, I want to have someone come out to the house and tune Teddy's piano. I suspect the person my mother used is long since dead. We might have to have someone come from Columbia."

"I'd like that very much," I said, "and of course I will play for you after dinner."

I never realized how small our house was, but after living in the Eldridges' rambling home, it felt tiny. Mother loved the ornate, which explains why my father never liked to sit in the living room. There was a mishmash of fancy, spindly secondhand furniture and an inordinate number of lace doilies Nana had crocheted. Too many family pictures were jammed about the mantel, the telephone table. My life in black and white, from birth until this past Christmas. The picture of Brooks and me opening presents was missing.

"Is that you?" Lurleen pointed to a skinny girl with pigtails sitting in the crook of a pecan tree.

While the bulk of our family income came from oranges, Daddy also grew pecans, corn, sometimes cotton. He'd tried his hand at cattle, but didn't have the knack for them. I nodded and showed her another photograph just like the other one, only it was me and Sissy in that same tree. Daddy had fussed at us because pecan trees are not the best climbing trees, and he'd had to climb up after us to get us down on more than one occasion.

There were three times as many pictures of Sissy as there were of me. Brooks was in a couple of them with her, stoic smile or no smile at all. "I'm really having a problem with this." Lurleen gestured at my family history.

"There were plenty of pictures of me before—" It suddenly occurred to me that Sissy must be every bit as confused as I was. Of course it wasn't easy for her to see years and years of pictures with me and Brooks, maybe even painful. "It really doesn't matter anymore," I said, and it didn't. I would have a new history going forward, one without Brooks Carver. I would have a niece or a nephew to love, and I would have Lurleen and Katie, Dean Kerrigan and Sue, a horde of C-Square sisters. And I would have Remmy. "It's fine, Lurleen." I gave her shoulder a squeeze. "*I'm* fine."

Lurleen sat at the kitchen table while Sissy, Mother, and I bustled around the kitchen like old times. At least the bustling part was. Sissy still wouldn't look me in the eyes. Didn't breathe a word.

She'd pulled her hair back and changed out of her work clothes and into a pair of denim pedal pushers and a pink top that made her eyes a beautiful cornflower blue. My eyes went immediately to her belly. It was as flat as ever, but she was four months at the most and wouldn't start showing for a while.

What would it be like to see her swollen, huge with Brooks's child? He was so tall and she wasn't even five feet. Would her belly grow so big that she'd fall over if she wasn't careful? Brooks was a big guy, and he had a big albeit beautiful head, which was likely hereditary. Poor Sissy would have to push that out of her—

Hands on her hips, Sissy cleared her throat, jerking my attention to her face. I gave her a wan smile and shrugged before getting back to the business of dinner. Soon all of the bowls and platters were assembled on the outdoor table. Mama had brought out her best china in honor of Miss Lurleen. Or maybe she had it out for the impending wedding.

Everyone had always had a specific place at this table, even Brooks, only Sissy was sitting in my place. There were always two places set at one end of the massive table where Daddy and Uncle Doak sat side by side. Doak's wife, Madge, was to his left; Mother sat to the right of Daddy, of course; Nana was beside her. I helped Lurleen onto the bench seat and sat down sandwiched between her and Charlie.

While Daddy said grace, I could feel Brooks's eyes on me, but I refused to look at him.

"Amen," Daddy said, helping his plate to the gracious spread. "Hungry."

Bowls of vegetables Sissy and I had put up last summer were passed around, black-eyed peas, butter beans, okra. Mama had sectioned the meatloaf into portions before Lurleen and I arrived, then cut one of the pieces into two very small servings. I helped my plate to the smaller one, and Lurleen took the other before passing the plate to Charlie, who looked awfully grateful that someone had taken the smallest piece besides him.

Stone-faced, Brooks whispered something to Sissy. She hadn't touched her plate. She shook her head, keeping her eyes on the table. I could feel her anguish in my bones, but before I could say anything, Mother piped up. "Eat, Sissy. You have to take care of yourself." No mention of the baby, just a glance in my direction to show she was being considerate.

Brooks nodded. I'd seen that frustrated look on his face before. When he didn't want me to go away to college. After Christmas break when he put me on the bus to go back to Columbia. Sissy chewed in slow motion, barely eating anything. Probably wishing for our normal dinner banter over who would wash and who would dry, instead of what was to come.

After dinner, the men went back out to the truck. Brooks gave me a hard look and then joined them. There was a flurry of activity taking plates and bowls, platters and glasses to our kitchen to be washed. While Mother, Sissy, and I cleaned up, Lurleen sat at the kitchen table with my aunts. Aunt Madge was always a stitch and could tell a story like nobody's business; she started telling tales about my homeplace, my family. Me.

Still not saying a word, Sissy kept washing dishes, dipping them in the rinse tub and then handing them to me to dry. I leaned over and whispered in her ear and waited. "*Skunk.*"

She said nothing, just handed me another dinner plate.

"Skunk," I whispered again, almost giggling to draw her into the game we'd played for as long as I could remember. When she didn't answer back, I nudged her elbow and answered for her. "Possum."

She hung her head as the world we knew carried on about us, in spite of us. Her shoulders shook. "Don't cry," I whispered. "Please don't cry, Sissy."

"Could you"—she swallowed hard, still not looking at me—"please take the scraps out to the animals?"

She plunged her hand into the water, hissed, and jerked it out. A tiny angry line dripped blood, making me want to cry. While absolutely nothing about this scenario was like it had always been before, and nothing between Sissy and me might ever be the same ever again, the fact that she always forgot and put the butcher knife in the soapy water made my heart soar.

"Please." She didn't look at me, just fished around and pulled out the offending knife before shoving her hands back in the water. "Just go."

I nodded and excused myself with the scrap bucket. "Will you be long?" Lurleen asked. "I'm really looking forward to hearing you play, but I'm very tired."

"I'll just be a moment," I said and hurried out to the barn.

The barnyard glowed in the full moonlight. Toby and Mack, Lacy and Pete, Daddy and Uncle Doak's bird dogs were thrilled to see the slop bucket, and me, I'd like to think. The barn cats materialized out of nowhere with their new kittens in tow, politely weaving in and out of my legs to say thank you for their supper. As I scratched one of the tiny ones on the head, I felt a familiar pair of hands on my hips. I wheeled around, accidentally knocking over the empty bucket.

"Shhh," Brooks said, towering over me. Dark eyes looking into mine.

I jerked out of his grip and pushed him away as hard as I could. "Don't you touch me."

"Nettie, honey—" He reached for me and I shoved him away.

"And don't you *honey* me," I bit out. "If I didn't love my sister so much, I would have spit in your eye at the supper table."

"What about me?" he asked. "Don't you still love me because I love—"

The crack of my hand meeting his face was deafening, although no one besides Brooks and me seemed to be aware of it. I could hear Daddy and Uncle Doak laughing about something over by the shed where they'd been working on the truck, the soft clatter of Sissy finishing up the dishes in the kitchen.

"I deserved that, Nettie." He moved toward me, but I stepped back, almost tripping on one of the hounds. "And I'm sorry. I'm so damn sorry, but I don't want this, this *wedding*. I want you. I've always wanted you."

"You should have thought about that before you took Sissy's virtue." His head snapped back like I'd slapped him again. He was either an idiot for thinking I hadn't known she was a virgin, or an imbecile for thinking I didn't know everything about my own sister. "Sissy is young and impressionable and even you remarked at how she'd always followed you around like a puppy since she was little. She may or may not have known what she was doing, but you are almost four years older than her, Brooks. You knew exactly what you were doing."

"Please, Nettie, hear me out. I love you. I've always loved you." He reached for me, but I crossed my arms over my chest. He put his hands up in surrender and looked into my eyes.

"Okay. Okay. Just hear me out," he said. "God, if I could take back that one moment, that one time, I would. But it happened and she got pregnant and everything just spun out of control. I don't want to marry her, I want to marry you. Now."

My head was dizzy with his words. Throbbing. "You have lost your mind."

"No, Nettie, we can run away together. Live anywhere you want." He had closed the distance between us and was towering over me in a way that used to make me feel special. Safe. "I love you so much, Nettie. Please say yes."

A cold chill slithered down my body. He'd said those exact same words the night he'd proposed to me. He mistook my trembling for weakness, but anger was rioting through my body, shaking it to the core.

"*Grow up, Brooks*," I spat.

His brow creased like I was speaking a dead language. "What did you say to me?"

"Grow the hell up. You give my sister your name. You buck up and be the best goddamn husband and father in the world or I swear to God, I will come back to Satsuma and castrate you with a chicken's beak."

"But Nettie, you love me," he choked out. "You don't mean that."

"Try me," I growled, snatching up the bucket and heading back inside.

Sissy glanced up when I opened the screen door and then quickly back down at the dirty dishwater in the sink. I took my place beside her, still trembling, gutted for her but grateful she hadn't heard a word Brooks had said to me.

Plain and simple, he didn't deserve Sissy, but Remmy was right, the world isn't kind to women who have babies out of wedlock. And even though every soul in town knew Sissy, things would be no better for her. She had no choice; she'd have to marry Brooks. Not to mention what Mother would do if Sissy called off the wedding. And if Brooks dumped Sissy, she'd be marked for life as the girl who got knocked up.

"Oh, Sissy," I whispered and plunged my hand into the water to hold hers. Head still down, she looked at our clasped hands and nudged my hip ever so slightly. Her voice was barely above a whisper.

"Possum."

29

LURLEEN

The morning sun streamed through the lace curtains. Lurleen was beyond tired. She felt the full brunt of the trip Remmy had warned would kill her but had taken Emily's life instead. Sister's body was lying, hopefully in a lovely blue casket back in Biloxi, waiting for Lurleen to take her home. While Lurleen still felt the pull that always draws sisters together, even after one or maybe even both have gone to the grave, it felt right to be here with Nettie.

She'd played beautifully last night. The strains of Chopin, Strauss, Bach in the middle of an orange grove, and while Lurleen had wanted to jerk a knot in Sissy's rear end for what she did to Nettie, she couldn't help but feel sorry for the child. As Nettie played the piano for the whole lot of them, her sister sat next to a man who obviously did not love her; his hand clasped hers in obligation. And the girl knew this. Why, even a stranger like Lurleen could see it was eating that poor child from the inside out.

Some rumbling in the kitchen prompted Lurleen to stir. Most likely that Helen, whom Lurleen hoped she'd put the fear of God's ire in or at the very least, the fear of the Eldridge ire. Lurleen eased her rickety old body out of bed and dressed. So many aches and pains. She was looking forward to getting her new body. Seeing her family, and of course Emily, who was probably flirting with all the handsome angels and holding court while she waited on Lurleen to join her.

Her door opened and Nettie's sweet face appeared. "You're up." She smiled.

"And surprisingly hungry," Lurleen said, which made Nettie's smile widen and Lurleen feel a little guilty. She'd gotten so attached to the girl. The same for Nettie, and Lurleen worried if her passing would be hard on her because she hadn't lied to Helen or told her anything she didn't already know. Nettie Gilbert knew how to love, how to make you feel loved. It was a gift that Brooks boy had obviously squandered, and you could see the cost on his face. It was a gift Lurleen would treasure long into eternity.

"It's nice out this morning. Mother will serve breakfast at the outside table. There's a bench between the roses and the gardenias, if you'd like to sit before we eat," Nettie said. "I'm going to help out in the kitchen. Mother said Sissy's taking the day off, I'll talk to her after breakfast, and then we'll be on our way."

"That would be lovely, dear," Lurleen said. She barely got the words out and plopped back down on the bed.

Nettie rushed to her side. "Are you all right?"

"I'm fine. This trip has taken far more from me than I'd thought it would."

"You rest. I'll come get you when breakfast is ready, and we'll leave right after we eat," Nettie said.

"Has your sister spoken to you at all?" Lurleen asked.

"Not really, she said something last night. One word. Our word. But it's a start. Even if she doesn't talk to me now, I know we're going to be okay." A sad smile crossed her lips. "You gave me that, and I'm so grateful."

NETTIE

I hurried over to my house. The kitchen was already a flurry of activity. I jumped into the familiar dance of getting a meal ready for two hungry men, two growing boys, and a handful of women. Everything was almost ready when I asked mother if I could make a phone call.

"Why, Nettie Jean, you've never asked to use that telephone in your life," she said, hauling a tray of big fluffy biscuits out of the oven. "Sissy, stir that gravy. If it sticks it'll be a mess."

"It's long distance." Sissy looked up at me and then back at the pan.

"All right," Mother said, "but don't talk long."

I called Remmy's home and prayed Katie didn't answer. While she'd given me her blessing when I'd called the office the other day, I wasn't sure how she'd feel about my calling their home so early in the morning.

"Hello."

"Hey, Remmy. I'm glad it's you who answered."

"And I'm glad it's you too. Feels like it's been years since we last talked."

"Nope. Just a little over a day."

"How's Miss Lurleen holding up?"

"Surprisingly well. Things might be different when we get back to Biloxi and take the train home, but right now, it's kind of like Miss Emily is still with us."

"She probably is." His laugh was soft and warmed me from the inside out. "She was always stubborn; if she didn't want to go to heaven, not even God himself could make her until she was good and ready."

"Lurleen's really tired; that worries me."

"That's understandable," he said. "So, now you're on a first-name basis? I've known the sisters my whole life and have never had that honor."

"She's insisted. I think she believes I earned the privilege."

"I'm sure you did. How are you doing? Did you see *him?*"

"Brooks? Yes, I saw him last night. He wanted me to run away with him," I whispered into the phone, even though everyone was well out of earshot. "The idiot."

"You aren't calling me from some exotic locale, are you?" he teased.

"If you can call Satsuma exotic, then yes."

"I can't blame the guy for trying, but I feel sorry for your sister. Are the nuptials still on?"

"It seems so. As bad as I feel for Sissy, I can't stay for the wedding. I won't."

There was a long silence. "Because you still have feelings for him?"

"Because I wouldn't be able to stand idly by and watch that idiot marry my sister."

"That's a relief," Remmy said.

"You didn't think that I still—"

"I'm a guy, Nettie. We're not the smartest creatures on the planet when it comes to women."

"Until last night I didn't realize just how stupid you all could be."

"Never thought I'd be defending Brooks, but it's not entirely his fault; there's some kind of veil that goes up between your world and mine; happens when a boy hits puberty. That's why men are clueless about the fairer sex; that's why talking to you every day, I learn something."

"Oh, really?" I teased. "What have you learned from just talking to me on the phone?"

"Nettie, if you don't get off, your father will pitch a fit when the bill comes," Mother hollered from the kitchen.

"You'd better make it snappy," I laughed. "My mother says I have to hang up."

"Give me your number, and I'll call you back on my dime."

"Quick. Tell me everything you know," I teased, expecting one of Remmy's patented smart remarks. "I have to go help with breakfast."

"I know that you're more than just a soft, beautiful creature who takes my breath away. You're smart. So damn smart and strong. And somehow, you make a guy like me who prides himself on knowing everything actually feel good that I don't know anything. Makes every moment with you my next best moment. A gift to open, to discover."

"Nettie!" Mother yelled.

"Oh, my," I breathed into the phone. "You really know how to make a girl fall for you, Remmy Wilkes," I echoed his words.

"I sure hope so."

Daddy and Uncle Doak came in from the fields starved; they came into the kitchen for coffee and to wash up. The minute Daddy walked through the door, Mama gave him a tentative look and jerked her head toward Sissy. I knew that she was as concerned as I was. Sissy looked worse than she did yesterday, like the impending wedding was killing her. The worried lines on Mother's face said she was worried for the baby, and for her own baby.

Daddy's face was impassive. He loved Brooks, always had. They hunted and fished together all the time, especially after Brooks's father died a few years ago. They tinkered with the cars together. Lamented over but loved Auburn football. Daddy had said on more than one occasion, if he could have picked a son out of the nursery at the hospital, it would have been Brooks, and having him as a son-in-law would be the next best thing. I guess it didn't matter to him which daughter brought him into the family.

Mother gave Daddy another cross look for him to say something.

"You all right, Sissy?" his deep voice rumbled.

"Yeah, Daddy, I'm fine." He looked at Mother and shrugged, his job done.

When breakfast was on the table, I went back to Nana's to get Lurleen. She and Nana were sitting at the table, drinking coffee.

"Breakfast is ready," I said.

When Lurleen rose, I cupped her elbow, but she asked for one of the hand-carved canes my late Grandpa Gilbert made that were sitting beside the front door. "I'll go have a seat. You need to speak with your grandmother."

"But you said you weren't feeling well. Sure you don't want me to see you to the table, Lurleen?"

"I'm well enough." She smiled and patted my shoulder.

I saw her out the front door, watched until she reached the table, and then walked back into the kitchen.

"Sit down, Nettie." I took the seat across from Nana, who looked as tormented as Sissy did.

"If you're worried about Brooks and Sissy, Nana, don't. I don't love him. I'm not sure I ever did, and I threatened his—life if he hurt her."

Nana looked down at her hands but not at me. "This isn't about that. Your friend says I owe you an apology."

"You don't owe me anything. I'm fine, really."

"She's right, you know. At the very least, I owe you an apology for not speaking up when this whole mess started and then for letting your mother tell you the way she did. I know it made sense in her etiquette-obsessed mind, but it was cruel and wrong. And I owe Sissy, for letting this go as far as it has. My punishment is seeing that boy who doesn't love her in the least by her side. Unfortunately, it's her punishment too, but I *am* sorry, Nettie, so very sorry."

"Sissy and I come from strong stock, Nana." I took her withered hands in mine. "I hope she'll be strong enough to not walk down that aisle tomorrow, but if she's not, I hope she and Brooks will learn to love each other."

. . .

"That's a fine vehicle you have there, Miss Eldridge." Daddy's attempt at making breakfast conversation.

"Lurleen, please. And goodness knows the car isn't mine."

Daddy gave me a hard look like I'd bought something on time against his wishes. "It's not mine either," I said. "Lurleen and her sister, Emily, and I were traveling together when Miss Emily passed away in Biloxi. Someone loaned us the car; we have to return it after breakfast."

"I'm so sorry for your loss, Miss—" Mother dropped the meat fork, then fumbled to pick it up, the color drained from her face. "Wait. You're leaving? Nettie, this can't be. You're staying for the wedding. You just have to."

"No, Mother, I don't," I said. "I didn't come for the wedding. I came to speak with Sissy and then I'm leaving to take Lurleen and Miss Emily home to Camden."

"It's all right, Dorothy." Daddy patted her hand. "The wedding will go off just fine. We'll see Nettie in a few weeks at graduation."

"No, you won't." I swallowed hard. "I took a leave of—"

"Your senses if you left school," my father snapped.

"Well, I did take a leave of absence, and I'm glad."

He swiped his mouth with his napkin and threw it in his plate. "You know? You women beat all. One getting knocked up. One completely crazy over some fool wedding. And *you*." He pointed at me. "You're the one who wanted the fancy education. If you'd stayed home and married Brooks right out of high school, none of this would have happened."

Uncle Doak, his sons, everyone including Mother went stock-still and quiet. While we may have very well lived on top of each other between the groves, all four families had made it a point to mind their own business as much as any Gilbert can.

"I have things to say to Sissy that I won't say in front of you all, but you should know that I'm glad I left school. At this very moment, if I had to choose between my degree or learning everything I learned from Lurleen and Miss Emily, I would throw it all away to know them. And for you to say I could have prevented this horrible wedding by marrying Brooks when I was as much of a child as Sissy is reprehensible."

"Don't you sass me, young lady. You're not too old for me to turn across my knee." Daddy jabbed his finger at me.

I stood and slapped my palms down on the ancient oak. "I'm not sassing you. I'm telling you the truth, which is something we don't do enough of around here, but we should. Since Uncle Bill died, Aunt Opal has wanted to sell her house and move back to her family in Birmingham, but she was afraid to tell you all, afraid she'd lose you. And Griffin—"

"Hey, don't bring me into this." He held up both hands. "I'm fine."

"How many times have you told me you wanted to go to college? How many times have you said you didn't want to spend your whole life on this farm?"

"Stop it, Nettie," Mother snapped.

"And you, Mother. How long are you going to pretend you're happy when you're too afraid to try to figure out what makes you happy? Because it sure as hell isn't a bunch of rules and impeccable etiquette."

"Sit down, Nettie, now," Nana huffed. When I did, Lurleen gave my hand a squeeze.

"Thank you, Nana." Mother swiped at her own tears.

"Well, she's right, Dorothy," Nana bit out. "And every single one of us, including me, should be ashamed of the way we treated Nettie. We're lucky to have her, and I will be sad to see her go, but she wants her own life. How that happened, I don't know; we didn't raise her that way. But at the very least, she deserves to live her life the way she sees fit."

"But your degree, Nettie." Mother gave me a sorrowful look.

"When the time is right, Mother, I swear I'll go back to school and finish."

Everyone looked dumbfounded when Sissy spoke. "Will you ever come back home?"

"Of course I will."

The rest of the breakfast went on record as being the most silent Gilbert family gathering ever. When the dishes were done, I excused myself from the kitchen and tugged Sissy out the door. We walked hand in hand in silence down into the pecan orchard to our tree, the one Daddy rescued us from when we were little, the one I'd rescued my baby sister from.

"I hope you didn't bring me here to climb that tree, because I've forgotten how. And I probably shouldn't," she added softly.

"You haven't forgotten anything. You know how to rescue yourself, Sissy. You always have."

"Not out of this mess." Her face contorted with pain, shame, anger. Instinctively, she touched her belly, then looked at me and shoved her hands by her sides. "I'm so scared, Nettie."

I took her in my arms and held her while she cried, whispering how very much I loved her and nothing would ever change that.

"I thought if I—I thought he'd love me. But he doesn't, and it took—" She pointed to her belly. "This for me to figure out I don't love him, not like I thought I did."

"Sissy, you don't have to marry Brooks because Mother or Daddy say so. Tell them you don't want to go through with this. If you want, you can go back to Camden with Lurleen and me."

Sissy's eyes were downcast. Brow furrowed in pain. "I wanted to stop the wedding. A couple of days ago, I told them I lost the baby. Daddy said nothing. Mother said the invitations had already been sent out. She said not to tell Brooks until after the wedding. She told me there would be other babies."

"But you didn't lose it," I whispered. She shook her head and convulsed into tears.

After a while, she swiped at her eyes with the backs of her hands. "I felt it move yesterday."

"What does it feel like?" I whispered, smiling, my hand going to her tummy. "Can I feel it too?"

"I'm not sure; it's so slight." She moved my hand to her lower abdomen. "Aunt Opal told me it would feel like butterfly wings. I guess it does feel kind of fluttery." I looked into her eyes and smiled. I loved her so much. It tore at me to see her so unhappy.

"Come away with us, Sissy. Come back to Camden with Lurleen and me. We'll raise the baby together. Lurleen would adore having a little one around." But even Camden would treat Sissy no different than any other place would treat an unwed mother. "If you don't want to do that, you don't have to marry Brooks. There are homes you can go to—"

"I even thought about that, especially after I lied about the baby to Mother and Daddy, but after I have it, I don't think I can give it away." I wrapped my arms around her and held her close. She pulled away just enough to see my face. "Why did you come back for me? I know I wouldn't have."

"I have a very dear friend who lost her sister, got her back again, and then lost her forever. At first I thought I'd come home for her, to finally mend her biggest regret, but that wasn't it. I didn't want to lose you forever, Sissy. I couldn't. I love you, Sissy. I forgive you."

"But I don't deserve your love or your forgiveness."

"Hush now; I love you. I'll always love you."

"I don't know why," she said against my chest. "Not after what I did, I don't know how you can still love me."

"Because we are sisters."

30

LURLEEN

Lurleen worried herself sick waiting for Nettie to come back. She sat on that little bench between the rose and gardenia gardens. It was a peaceful place surrounded by satsuma trees full of tiny oranges as far as she could see on one side and a smaller grove that backed up to a pecan orchard on the other. And while it was a lovely, even intoxicating place to sit between such fragrant flowers, she still kept her eyes on the woods.

Nettie had given Emily and Lurleen so much and she didn't even know it. Then Lurleen had meddled perhaps where she shouldn't have. She'd put this idea of an indestructible sisterhood in Nettie's head, and Nettie had bought it hook, line, sinker, and half the pole because she wanted to. Needed to. Right now, Lurleen wasn't even sure there was such a thing. All she had to go by was her and Emily, who would roll over in her beautiful blue casket if someone called her and Lurleen's sisterhood ordinary.

But then the girls came out of the woods, not hand in hand like Lurleen had hoped they might but walking lockstep with their arms around each other. Her heart stretched tight across her chest and she'd never been so grateful to be right in her whole life.

Nettie spied her and the pair neared the bench, stopping in front of Lurleen with smiles on their tear-streaked faces.

"Everything all right, dear?" Lurleen asked, already knowing the answer.

Nettie gave her baby sister a squeeze and kissed the top of her head. The girl looked so longingly back at Nettie, it broke Lurleen's heart in two, but the girl loved Nettie too much to ask her to stay.

"I'm so sorry you lost your sister." Sissy kissed Lurleen on the cheek. "Thank you for giving me back mine."

"No need to thank me, my dear." Lurleen reached for her hand and gave it a gentle squeeze. "You never really lost her to begin with."

What a piss-poor job," Lurleen hissed. Even from the back of the viewing parlor, the casket didn't look at all like Lurleen had hoped it would, not like the color of Sister's eyes or the sky on a cloudless day; it was an institutional, washed-out blue, bordering on dull gray and not at all shiny like it was before it was painted. No. It was the exact color of a pair of eyes, blind from birth, cloudy gray ones g. *damn it.*

Lurleen had pictured something gleaming and blue, something Emily would be proud to be buried in. Why, it was a wonder Sister wasn't kicking and screaming to get out of the thing. Nettie cupped Lurleen's elbow as they neared the hideous box, and Lurleen stopped just as a slice of Sister's face came into view, her delicate nose, her forehead, silver curls. Just as Lurleen's knees began to buckle, the pissant director hurried into the parlor, putting on his jacket like he'd just gotten out of bed.

"What is this?" Lurleen snapped, waving at the monstrosity.

"We did the best we could, ma'am," he said in that undertaker tone that gave Lurleen the creeps. "I told you we're not painters."

The thick uneven brush marks were evidence of that. Whoever the imbecile painter was, hadn't even taken care to put masking tape on the hardware. Jagged, painted lines competed with fat splatters on the fine brass. "A five-year-old could have done a better job. And I told you I wanted the paint the color of her eyes or her dress. No one would wear a dress made out of this abominable hue." She took a step closer and prayed her anger would get her through the next few moments because honest to God, it was impossible that Emily was gone from this world. That she was in a *g.d.* box.

"I want," she gritted out, utterly heartbroken and furious at God for taking Emily before her. Grateful Emily didn't have to feel the loss Lurleen felt now. Sister was never coming back and the void she'd left, the void Lurleen had evaded, slammed into her, nearly knocking her to the ground.

She wanted to collapse on her sister in a puddle of tears. Seep into the fabric of Emily's pretty blue dress, and lie in state with her. Instead, she swallowed hard and straightened her backbone; the only thing she could do, a way to honor her other half. "I want my money back. For the hideous paint job. And a generous discount for ruining Sister's coffin."

The undertaker didn't say a word, just nodded and left the room. "I'm sorry," Nettie said with her hand on Lurleen's shoulder.

Lurleen nodded and edged forward. Emily had too much makeup on for Lurleen's taste; she would have loved the way she looked, as vibrant as a made-up corpse can. What the undertaker lacked in painting skills, he'd made up for with the way Emily looked, like she was napping during *Backstage Wife* except her lips were a thin line, not pursed together making the gentle puffing sound. Her favorite earbobs didn't make her lobes angry and red like they normally did, and when Lurleen kissed her forehead she was so very cold.

Lurleen braced herself on the paint-spattered brass railing. Nettie pulled the items out of Lurleen's purse that Emily never left the house without, her favorite shade of pink lipstick, her gloves, her mirrored compact, and presented them to Lurleen. Nettie froze and her eyes went wide when Lurleen turned her own pocketbook upside down, emptying the contents onto the floor. She held it open for Nettie to drop Emily's things into and snapped it shut, slipping it into the casket beside Emily, who would die if she got to heaven without her pocketbook.

Lurleen didn't know how long she stood there. Too long for sure. Nettie picked up the items on the floor, put them in her own purse, and, in a hushed voice, asked Lurleen if she was ready to go. Lurleen shook her head and sat down on a chair in the front row, Nettie by her side. Lurleen let the memories and the grief wash over her. The good and the bad rolling in like the tide, the former far eclipsing the latter. She didn't think she had any more tears left to cry, but she was wrong. Nettie cried with her, for Lurleen, and perhaps for her own sister.

The man finally walked back into the viewing room, check in hand, and apologized all over the place for the paint. Lurleen nodded at Nettie; she helped Lurleen out of the chair and they left the parlor.

Their last night in Biloxi was a stark contrast to their triumphant arrival. Lurleen did have Nettie walk her down to the ocean one last time, for Emily. The next morning they boarded the train. Someone must have told the porter about Lurleen's loss. He put her and Nettie in their finest roomette and had a server check on them, bringing them meals so that they could grieve in private. Or maybe it was to make up for Emily, who was surely outraged for riding in cargo.

After a million times, Nettie finally stopped asking if Lurleen was okay. It wouldn't change anything.

31

NETTIE

I was so busy scanning the crowd at the train station in Columbia, I didn't realize I had my hand pressed against the window until Remmy raised his and grinned at me. He was standing next to a man I didn't recognize on the platform. Lurleen stirred beside me. She had slept on and off for most of the way home, but still seemed very tired. Feeble.

Hands on both railings, Lurleen trembled as Remmy supported her under one arm from the front and I supported her under the other from behind. My heart leapt every time Remmy glanced at me, smiling before he went back to concentrating on getting Lurleen safely on the ground. When we were finally on the platform, the man nodded at me and then Lurleen and expressed his condolences as other passengers got off and the workers unloaded and reloaded the train.

"Thank you, Jennings," Lurleen said warmly to the man who

appeared to be much older than her. He was wearing a crisp black suit, white shirt, and skinny black tie and was melting a bit in the afternoon heat. "Nettie Gilbert, this is Jennings Boykin; he works at the Kornegay Funeral Home."

"You're welcome, Miss Lurleen." The man nodded at her and then at me. "Miss Gilbert."

"And how are things in Red Hill, Jennings?" Lurleen asked.

"Better than I expect they are for you. Grace says to tell you hello and she was awfully sorry to hear about Miss Emily."

"While it doesn't bother me one bit, Emily would be chagrined to hear you call her Miss. Coming from you, it would make her feel old, and we both know how she felt about that." Lurleen smiled and then turned her attention to me. "Jennings sold my father his first brand-new car."

"Worked at a lot of things," Jennings chuckled.

"But you found your calling at Kornegay's," Lurleen said firmly.

"Ninety-two and still going strong," he said proudly.

Now, if I'd been Lurleen I would have worried about a ninety-two-year-old driver taking Miss Emily to the funeral home back in Camden, but the man didn't look anywhere near that old. I suspect it was his work that kept him young. And his attention to detail. He winced as the ugly blue casket was carried down the loading ramp by four men. Jennings whistled to the workers and motioned for them to bring it his way.

"What in the world?" he said as it neared.

"Don't start, Jennings. I was trying to do something nice for Emily It's not like I can't see with my own eyes it went awry," Lurleen snapped. "I'm going to get that boy who painted my dining room last summer over to Kornegay's first thing tomorrow. We'll wait until next Sunday for the service and the burial. That should give him enough time to get it right."

Remmy was looking at me like he could eat me up, but he kept a gentlemanly distance, most likely out of respect for Lurleen and Mr. Boykin. His intense stare made my heart flutter, a hard blush traveled from my top to my toes, and I had to tear my eyes away from him to keep my composure.

The men filed past and Lurleen ran her hand along the side of the casket. "How're you feeling, Miss Lurleen?" Remmy drawled.

"One minute I'm as fine as I can be, the next minute, horrible," she whispered, watching the men load the casket into the hearse and shaking her head. "Simply horrible."

"Let's get you home," he said, and we guided her to Remmy's car with the ragtop down.

She stopped short like she wasn't too sure about the convertible. "We've got a ways to go to get back to Camden; I'll put the top up," Remmy said. She swiped at her eyes, shook her head, and took Miss Emily's scarf out of her pocketbook. It was as turquoise as the gulf had been that first day. Tying it under her chin, she offered me a yellow one that would have looked lovely on a blond Miss Emily when she was in her prime.

"As much as Emily pretended she didn't like you, Remmy, she did, and by the way she said she despised your car, I'm sure she adored it. So, if you don't mind, I think I'd like to ride with the top down. See what all the fuss is about."

Remmy grinned at her, melting my heart into a little puddle, and then at me, completely shredding what was left. "Miss Gilbert," he said opening my door. I slid into the seat, stopping on the passenger side, dying to slide on over and plaster myself to him. Eyes full of wanting, he looked at me, took my hand in his, and kissed my palm. The soft brush of his lips traveled up my arm, my whole body ratcheted up tight, in the very best way, and I didn't want him to stop.

"Oh, for goodness' sake," Lurleen huffed after Remmy looked longingly at me and then put the car in gear to back out of the parking lot. "Kiss the girl."

Being a Southern gentleman, I expected Remmy to ignore Lurleen or laugh off her remark. Instead, he shoved the car in park, yanked me across the bench seat and gave me a hello kiss the likes I'd never known before. Not even with him. When he pulled away he smiled, eyes on me. "Thanks, Miss Lurleen."

"Well you looked like you were going to burst if you didn't kiss her, so you're welcome. And another thing, you may call me Lurleen." Remmy's head jerked toward the backseat. "I believe you earned it."

Lurleen liked the top down so much that when we arrived at the house on Laurens Street she and Miss Emily shared, she asked Remmy to ride around the block a few more times. When it became apparent she was avoiding her home, she sucked in a breath and told Remmy she was ready. He and I helped her up the front steps; she tried to act like it didn't bother her when she entered the house, but it was obviously as impossible for her to imagine this house without her sister as it was for me to imagine my life without mine.

Remmy entered the bedroom after I got Lurleen dressed and under the covers; he checked her over like he had every day since I'd known him.

"Did you get some supper?" he asked with his fingers on her wrist, looking at the second hand on his watch. She nodded. I didn't want to dispute her word because she'd barely eaten two bites, so I kept quiet. As good as the food on the train was, neither of us had felt much like eating.

"How are you sleeping?" he said, poking at her swollen calves.

"Not at all well," Lurleen said with a guilty look in my direction. While she'd sworn she was sleeping just fine to me, I hadn't slept either and had heard her fitful night of tossing and turning. Crying for her sister.

"Do you want something to help with that?" he asked. She nod-ded and he took a bottle out of his bag and drew up the syringe.

"Knock me out?" Lurleen asked, chin quivering, slight smile.

"If you haven't slept, this'll be plenty," he said and administered the dose. "I'm staying tonight, Miss Lurleen, if that's okay with you and Nettie. If you wake up and need anything—"

"It's more than fine with Nettie," she said with a wry smile, her tongue already a little thick. "And don't worry about me, if I need you I have that infernal cowbell Emily gave me."

"Thank you," Remmy said.

It only took a few minutes before her eyes fluttered shut, then I took his hand and led him out of the room. When he closed the door behind us, I wrapped my arms around him and would have climbed inside of him if I could have. With my face pressed into his neck, he felt like home.

"I never meant to fall like this," I breathed.

"Awful glad you did." He slanted his mouth across mine. I heard the thud of his bag on the floor before he scooped me up and started for the sofa.

"Upstairs," I whispered. He didn't hesitate, just took me to my room and set me down like I was still fragile, but I was so far removed from that damaged girl who didn't know what she wanted.

"I missed you." He took my mouth again, his hands threaded in my hair. I pulled him down onto the bed, laughing. "God, I love you," he said trailing kisses down my neck. "I know it's too soon to say that, but I'll be damned if I can hold it in one more second, Nettie. I love you."

I smiled against his lips.

It wasn't until he left, just before dawn, that the cowbell rang loud and clear. I dressed and hurried downstairs to find Lurleen propped up in her bed reading. When I helped her to the bathroom, she was a little steadier than she had been the night before. Instead of going back to bed, she came into the kitchen with me and drank coffee while I rummaged through the refrigerator to find something for breakfast.

On Miss Emily's command, I'd cleaned out the refrigerator before we left on our trip, so there wasn't much. Some spoiled milk, some condiments, and a big bowl of banana pudding topped with a thick caramel-colored meringue.

I didn't think Miss Emily had believed me when I told her to bathe the banana slices in lemon juice, but she must have because they didn't look too bad to have been a week old. We had the pudding for breakfast with coffee, although there was barely enough to make a decent-sized pot.

"It would be rude of me to ask how your night was," Lurleen said, stirring her coffee while my face turned ten thousand shades of red. "But just so you know, my sleep was deep and dreamless," Lurleen said. "Which brings us to today. What are your plans, Nettie?"

I swallowed hard. What were my plans? After Remmy made love to me last night, my mind was full of wants and needs, none of them having anything to do with my immediate future. Remmy and I hadn't slept at all; when we weren't kissing, touching, I was telling him about the trip. Going home to Satsuma. Sissy.

"I really want to call home and see how the wedding went, whether it was good or bad or happened at all, but I won't." I scraped my bowl to avoid looking at Lurleen. "Sissy told me she'd call or write when things settled down. I don't know how, but I know she's okay; I'm just not sure what that means."

"Yes," Lurleen said, "but what are *your* plans?"

"We're out of those Eskimo Pies you love so well, out of everything really. I thought I'd go to the A&P after breakfast. Stop by the pharmacy; you're almost out of digitalis too."

"That's not what I meant and you know it, Nettie."

"Well, I'm staying. Here. As long as you'll have me, if that's what you mean," I said firmly.

"Fair enough, but only because I'm a selfish old maid who doesn't want to die alone. Now, what do you want to do with yourself besides take care of a fussy old woman with one foot in the grave?"

"Whether you like it or not, Lurleen, both of your feet seem pretty firm on this side of the grass for the time being."

She laughed and closed her eyes as she savored the last spoonful of pudding. "Well, any day above ground is a good one."

"Remmy says he never expected you to make it back from Palestine alive; he thinks you're immortal." She laughed at the very idea. "And I'd really like it if you were," I added softly.

She handed me her bowl and I rinsed it out along with mine. Stirring her cold coffee, she put her spoon down, eyebrows raised. "I'm serious, Nettie. You're far too young not to have plans."

I nodded. "My roommate's wedding is in a few weeks." I loved

Sue, but I hated the idea of leaving Lurleen alone, even for the wedding. "I thought I'd ask Katie Wilkes or one of the women from your church if they could stay with you that weekend. It would be awful to miss Sue's wedding; I'm kind of the maid of honor, and I did promise her I'd be there."

"So you shall. Is Remmy going?" She smirked. "From the way he looks at you, I'd say he's got designs on wedding plans of his own. And June weddings can be quite contagious."

I blushed hard. "I haven't asked Sue yet if it would be okay, but I hope so." Would Remmy think I was trying to drop some big hint? Coerce him? Katie would have a field day with that.

"I haven't been to a wedding in ages." Lurleen smiled. "No one wants to invite a spinster to their wedding; they must think it's bad luck."

"Would you like to be my date, Lurleen?" I asked.

"I would think if you're *kind of the maid of honor*, they would let you bring two guests."

"I'll ask Sue, but I'm sure she won't mind."

"And after the wedding?"

"I want to go back to school when the time is right." I put my fingertips on Lurleen's shoulder; she tipped her head to the side, sandwiching my hand there. "But much more than that, I want to be here for you."

32

NETTIE

It turned out Lurleen was not immortal. Nine weeks after we buried Miss Emily, she passed away in her sleep. I didn't call the ambulance or even Remmy. Just sat with her and felt the loss of loving someone so dear, a friend. A sister.

The phone rang several times around midmorning. I stayed by Lurleen's side, heartbroken she was gone and elated she was with Miss Emily where she belonged. The phone started ringing again and then stopped and continued on and off that way for a few minutes. Not long after that, I heard the screen door bounce in the jamb and footsteps running toward the bedroom. Remmy stopped in the doorway for a moment and then rushed to my side; it was then that I started to cry and didn't stop.

I was a mess when I went to the funeral home to make the arrangements, but wasn't surprised I didn't have to do much, just choose flowers that were in season. Lurleen had taken care of all of the details years ago, right down to the hymns she wanted sung. Of course Miss Emily had nothing planned; when Lurleen had chosen her flowers, she told me Emily was a roses and satin kind of girl. When I'd asked her what kind of girl she was, she'd replied, "The simple kind. Daisies. Lilies. Even carnations feel too frilly for me."

So the church was full of every manner of summer lily; a blanket of snow-white daisies covered the casket that was painted to match her sister's, and the church was packed with Camdenites who'd known and loved their gun-toting librarian. I rode the waves of grief much like Lurleen had with her sister, laughing and crying, and through it all, Remmy never left my side.

The morning of the funeral, it had rained then poured during the church service, but when the azure blue casket reached the burial site, the clouds parted on cue to reveal the loveliest August sky. Remmy squeezed my shoulder and smiled at me when Pastor made a joke that Miss Emily was showing off for her sister; everyone laughed. But that's the kind of sisterhood she and Lurleen had, the kind that loves and forgives and makes a stormy Carolina sky cloudless and beautiful.

The Eldridge home welcomed hundreds of guests who brought more food than they ate, which didn't seem possible. Children ran about the house playing while folks laughed and reminisced about the Eldridge sisters. Most of them I recognized from Miss Emily's service. The same enormous spread was laid out with enough fried chicken to feed nearby Shaw Air Force Base, every manner of casserole, desserts galore. And lots of banana pudding. The ladies of the Kershaw County Library Auxiliary insisted I mingle with the guests while they fussed about, making sure platters and bowls stayed filled. Paper plates and cups stayed picked up.

I'd noticed a chubby little redheaded boy who was maybe nine eyeing the piano, which had a beautiful tone after Lurleen had it tuned. He opened and closed the lid several times before his mother warned him to leave it alone. He watched until she was deep in conversation, opened the lid, and touched a few of the upper keys.

"Do you play?" I asked. He shook his head, unable to take his eyes off the keyboard. It called to him like it had called to me and Lurleen's mother. Her brother, Teddy. I sat down beside him, placed his hands on the right keys. The old piano began to sing. Chopsticks.